MY ROOMMATE'S A JOCK?

Wade Kelly

Dreamspinner Press

Published by
Dreamspinner Press
5032 Capital Circle SW
Ste 2, PMB# 279
Tallahassee, FL 32305-7886
USA
http://www.dreamspinnerpress.com/

My Roommate's a Jock? Well, Crap!

Cover Art by Brian R. Williams
brianrwilliams.com

ISBN: 978-1-62380-254-7

Printed in the United States of America
First Edition
December 2012

eBook edition available
eBook ISBN: 978-1-62380-255-4

Acknowledgments

I WANT to say thank you to my beta reader Laura ☺ for helping make this story awesome. A special thanks to Deeze for helping to choose the title of the book! I am ever grateful for my family who love and support me in my writing pursuits. And for Lena—I hope this book makes you laugh; I know you need a good laugh.

And to my dear friend Matt: "It well may be, that we will never meet again, in this lifetime, so let me say before we part, so much of me is made from what I learned from you, you'll be with me like a handprint on my heart. And now whatever way our stories end, I know you have re-written mine by being my friend... Because I knew you, I have been changed for good." (From the musical Wicked: "For Good".)

Chapter 1
A World in Decay

SOMEONE told me I'm a cynical fatalist, but I prefer the term *realist*. I guess I tend to see things of this world in a slow process of decay, either from a scientific perspective—since I'm a physics major—or from personal experience. The way I see it, that guy Murphy had it right every time. Do you know him? He's the one who wrote Murphy's Law: "If anything can go wrong, it will." It's actually a quote of the fourth law of thermodynamics, and the originator is unknown. (I read that on Wikipedia, but that's beside the point.)

The long and short of it is, things go wrong in my life—always have.

It should not have surprised me when my roommate of the past three years decided to graduate and move to Texas with his girlfriend. The nerve of him! Jonathan was the best roommate ever. He was neat, and quiet, and never had sex on the couch—that I know of. He tolerated my quirks and always made me tea on Sunday mornings.

I miss him.

The summer was boring after he left.

Who was going to play canasta with me? Or build puzzles? Or realize that I needed chocolate as I studied for every test whether I asked for it or not?

I trudged around campus in a state of despair for days after he left.

Okay, I realize that the term "days" doesn't make me sound very hopeless, but being the realist that I am made me see that milling around with my chin resting on my chest was only going to get me run over if I happened to miss the sidewalk and wander into traffic. I moped for an appropriate amount of time and then typed up a flyer for the campus bulletin board: "Roommate Wanted."

I never needed to find a roommate before.

Back when I enrolled at this college, Jonathan Keys practically stumbled over me in the housing line. The college had just acquired three more single-family homes on the edge of campus grounds and opened them for occupancy. First come, first serve. There was a minimal upcharge over regular dorm fees, but the perks were worth it. Guidelines for tenancy were minimal as long as the house was maintained properly—which basically meant that if you trashed it, you got kicked out—but otherwise, those who lived there governed themselves. No RA! (Resident Assistant for those not aware of dorm-speak.)

Awesomenicity!

The house I was "lucky" enough to make it into had six bedrooms, a kitchen, a living room, a dining room, and three baths. Four of the other guys assigned to the same residence were sports fanatics and one was a math major. I loathe jocks! Not that you can lump all sports guys together and assume they know everything about sports, but my point is, I had nothing in common with those guys. Jon was the math major.

We made it through one semester of parties and hooting at the television during football season before a suite in a neighboring house opened up. Jon knew the housing overlord and requested the suite before it was open to the general (college) public. It was so much nicer!

This house was two houses down the street, so moving was a breeze. The layout was also different from most campus housing. Instead of one floor of bedrooms and then living space on the bottom floor, this unit had three floors of two bedrooms and living space combined. I wasn't sure about the efficiency of that design; perhaps it was three rental apartments at one time before the campus purchased it. I didn't know.

Whatever the explanation, Jon and I had it made! The top floor was just ours—two bedrooms, one bath, a kitchen, and a living area to share.

And then my buddy Jonathan graduated in May.

It was the worst day of my life.

I kind of didn't mention to anyone that I was living alone at this point because if I did, the housing department would peruse the list of "standby" students and assign someone to my perfect little corner of the campus. I wanted to avoid that. I thought if I advertised in places that promised interesting prospects—i.e., the physics building and the library—then I would hopefully avoid the types of people I dreaded living with: *jocks!* Ahem. *clears throat*

The plan was going okay, I guess. I had a few guys call me up, but I was looking for someone who reminded me of Jon—someone smart and funny, and who didn't care if I watched History Channel on Friday night. Two guys inquired. I just didn't feel right saying yes.

In retrospect, I should have at least met with them instead of shooting them down over the phone, but my heart just wasn't in it. I was still moping about Jon moving. I was about to put up another flyer in the electronics lab when the housing director stopped me. "Isn't there an opening in your building?"

I looked up, bewildered, blinking as the sun burned into my retinas. "Um…." I hesitated. "Who's asking?"

He gave me a look that told me I shouldn't be so stupid. "I am, Cole. You know I need to fill that space as soon as possible. You should've contacted me weeks ago. You know there's a list at least fifty students long who would love to live in those houses instead of the dorms."

"It's not my fault he moved out early."

"Cole."

I sighed and scuffed my shoe on the ground. Of course I knew he was right. "Sorry. I guess I was stalling. Do you think I could look for my own roommate?" I gave him the most pathetic pout I could muster and tipped my head to the side. I hoped he would give in. My pathetic look always worked on my mom. The term "puppy-dog eyes" didn't hold a candle to my expression. Of course he caved.

"Okay—but only because you keep the neatest apartment on campus. God help me if I assigned someone who messed up your routine and dropped Cheetos on the carpet."

I smiled and said heartily, "Thanks, Stan. You're the best!"

"But, Cole, I can only give you six weeks to decide on someone. By August 15 the other bedroom in your apartment needs to be filled. Got it?"

I cringed internally. I hated deadlines. I know, I have them all the time with projects and exams, but having a deadline that was not school related made me nervous. "August 15, got it!" I assured Stan the housing man with a nod.

He turned and walked off, and I was left with a cold sense of dread that whoever applied to live with me would turn out to be a slob, or a drum major, or the worst of the worst—a jock! I wasn't looking forward to it.

So, I made a flyer.

> *Male roommate wanted to share a two-bedroom apartment off campus. Must be clean, friendly, quiet, and study-oriented. Preferably* not *a freshman. Must love books, games, and spy movies. To apply call: 717-782-1969 and ask for Cole.*

I posted the flyer all over campus. I thought for sure I'd have loads of inquiries. I was so dead wrong. During the summer, students went home. During the summer, students were not thinking of housing unless they *were* freshman and didn't *have* housing. No one called except one *girl*. Did she not *read* the flyer? I am not living with a girl. I had enough of that growing up with an older sister. Still, I was disappointed. Not even a nibble. Did I come off too controlling on the flyer?

Needless to say, Stan the housing man came knocking on my door August 15. "Did you find someone?" Stan asked.

He really was a great guy; I couldn't fault him for doing his job. "No," I huffed, crossing my arms over my chest in a gesture of aggravation. No matter what, I wasn't going to be happy with whoever he picked from his list, so I thought I'd start off right with full-out petulance.

"Cole, come on," he pleaded, trying to coax me to see the bright side. "We've known each other for three years. I think I know you pretty well by now. No one else would have noticed the lab was painted two shades of gray except you. No one but you caught the typo on the theater marquee last year. And you are the only guy I know who can quote both *The Bourne Identity* and *P.S. I Love You* word for word." He lifted his eyebrows and grinned.

I exhaled noisily. "Fine. Just… don't pick a jock, okay? You know I'm not good at sports, and watching football all winter might kill me."

He chuckled. "I can't promise anything. The list is long, and I have to pick someone today. I have my job instructions too, you know."

"Okay."

I shook his hand, and he left the apartment.

I closed the door and leaned against it, looking at my little home away from home.

Jon and I picked out the green sofa the first year. The coffee table was sitting by a dumpster in town, and he refinished it for me when I said I disliked the color of the stain. My mom gave us the Oriental rug and the Van Gogh print that hung by the breakfast bar. We bought the television together, and he said I could keep it when he moved out. Things would change soon. Maybe the new guy would hate the dishes or spill sugar on the kitchen floor?

I started to panic. I was good at working myself into a tizzy. I flattened my body against the door, closed my eyes, and took deep breaths. *I can do this, I can do this,* I repeated to myself. *Change is good.*

Twenty minutes later I got a call from Stan—he'd found someone.

"Seriously?" I asked in a higher than normal pitch. I rested one palm on the kitchen counter, and my wandering eyes noticed a raisin hiding behind the flour bin. *What is that doing there?*

"Yeah," Stan said. "I told you I have a long list."

I tossed the raisin in the trash. "Is he a freshman?" He had to be!

"No."

"Does he wear Hawaiian shirts?" Why I asked that, I'll never know—it just slipped out.

"No."

"Does he know any three-syllable words?"

"I believe he does. He's an English major."

"Hmm." I contemplated the possibility that Stan had picked someone I'd approve of as I strolled into the living room and sat on my sofa. An English major was promising. "What's his name?"

"Ellis."

"Ellis?" I know it came out bad, the way I questioned his name, but it wasn't like I was talking to *Ellis* about his unusual name. I'd never known anyone by that name. Ellis. It sounded nerdy. Maybe I really would luck out with a great roommate. I did with Jonathan.

Stan then confirmed the name again as if I wasn't listening. "Ellis. Don't worry. I'm sure he'll be fine. I spoke to his mother today."

"His mother? I thought you said he wasn't a freshman."

"He's not. He's a junior, but he's been commuting from home because housing is so expensive. This year he sold his car to pay for housing and applied. Listen, Cole, I got another call coming in. Don't worry. He'll work out."

Sold his car? *That sounds desperate.* Then again, if I still lived with *my* parents, I would probably turn desperate too. "Any idea when he'll be here?"

"Should be anytime now. He said he was leaving home thirty minutes ago with a buddy."

"What?" I panicked, looking around frantically for anything lying on the floor or inexplicably out of place.

"Good-bye, Cole." Stan politely yet abruptly hung up.

A roommate. He was on his way. I could do this.

Someone knocked at my door and I jumped.

Shit! I'm not ready yet!

I set the phone in its cradle on the breakfast bar and walked over to the door. I smelled my pits—passable. I fingered my hair and gave my body a good wiggle to release tension right before I took a hold of the handle and reminded myself to breathe. Everything would be all right. I turned the handle. This was the moment of truth.

A bright white smile greeted me as I opened the door. "Hi. My name's Ellis Montgomery. Are you Cole? I was told you had a room available."

I know he was speaking, but my brain shut off the moment I looked into *the* most beautiful blue eyes I'd ever seen in my life.

Oh boy, am I in trouble!

Chapter 2
Why I Hate Jocks

THE guy in the doorway held out his hand and waited for a response. Any response. When none was forthcoming he repeated himself. "Um, am I in the wrong place? I was told a guy named Cole had a room available."

"I, uh, yeah," I stammered, like a fool. "I mean, *yes*, I'm Cole, and I have a room." I swept my arm toward the interior, and he entered without more prolonged and awkward hesitation.

I could tell right away that his living here was going to cause me some undue stress. For one thing, his old, ripped-up jeans hung low on his well-designed hips! And for another, when he bent down to put his bag on the floor, that round butt of his was two seconds from being squeezed when a loud rush of noisy frat boys swooped in behind me and tackled him to the floor.

Exactly what I wanted to do!

"Hey, guys! How'd you find me so fast?"

One guy, the one with red hair and a baseball cap turned backward, answered, "Good news travels fast, my friend. Plus, Mike texted."

I pushed my glasses up my nose and watched them wrestle. *Too bad chocolate pudding wasn't involved.* On second thought, *watching* was a bad idea. It was obvious to me he was just another gorgeous straight guy that I was doomed to cohabitate with. Watching Mr. Blue Eyes wrestle would give other parts of my anatomy ideas I wasn't able to follow through on. Nonsexual thoughts were best. Platonic thoughts. Even "he's my cousin" thoughts were better than the ones zipping through my brain as I weaved my way around the heaving pile of arms and legs that moved around my living room floor.

This new roommate was only a friend—yeah, a friend; I could talk myself into believing that. It had worked all the other times I had to be around straight guys who were hot as hell!

"I brought beer!" yelled someone new from the doorway. He joined the fray, and hooting grunts soon filled my nice quiet apartment. Now there were six loud, muscular fratheads passing around beers, singing the school's theme song, and chanting "Mon-ty! Mon-ty! Mon-ty!"

A second later, a soccer ball materialized and Ellis started dribbling it in midair. Three bounces to his knee then his inner sole, a quick reverse and over his shoulder and then he popped the black and white back over with a contorted appendage. His feet seemed to hop so fast the ball barely had a second to descend before it was propelled upward again, dancing in the air around his body as a second skin. He was kicking the ball with such controlled manual dexterity that my normal tendency to cringe at the thought of something in my apartment getting knocked over was momentarily stifled. I was stunned by his sheer brilliance of foot.

Wait a minute, I said to myself as the revelation hit me. *He's a soccer player! I told Stan no jocks. Fuck!* I snatched the phone off the breakfast bar and fled to my room.

Stan answered on the first ring. "Hello."

I paced my room like a Jack Russell terrier on crack. "Stan! I told you no jocks. What's with the gang of frat boys wrestling all over my mom's rug and bouncing a soccer ball everywhere?" *A small embellishment never hurt anyone.*

"Oh, I guess I didn't catch that." His tone of voice told me he was lying.

Stan always had smugness to his voice when he was caught doing something he shouldn't be doing. Like when he kissed a freshman nursing student in the press box of the stadium, he replied to the dean, "Oh, so that's *not* acceptable behavior? Had I known it was frowned upon, I would have resisted her advances. I am so terribly sorry. It will never happen again." How he retained his job is anyone's guess. I'm just glad I got the lowdown on the whole story.

But I was in no mood to mess around. This could really end up screwing me if I had to spend my senior year with a jock! "So what are you going to do about it? I need a different roommate."

"No can do, Cole. He's the last one."

"What!" My voice came out a bit shrill so I piped it down. "What?" I repeated. "I thought you had a list of fifty students to house."

"Not exactly; I had six. But they're all taken care of. Ellis is the last one. So what's your beef against jocks, anyhow?"

"My beef?" I asked, but then the little movie camera in my brain started running in reverse and I was transported back to *that day.*

CUE flashback....

I was in high school when I discovered the kind of trouble the "jock" crowd would cause for me. It wasn't because I hated sports, and it wasn't because I sucked at sports. I avoided "jocks" because of the types of people who played the sports!

I suppose my introduction to the cruelty of adolescence could be traced back to middle school, where name-calling and humiliation were the staples of life. Middle school kids had no qualms about calling boys gay for no reason and for every reason. The word "gay" was a derogatory statement for any behavior that didn't fit the accepted norm. For instance, if any boy student chose an instrument other than guitar he was teased for being gay. Choosing soccer over football—gay. Taking cooking over woodshop—gay. Even some guys taking honors English were teased, which I found completely ludicrous because every kid took English, so why would someone be gay if they happened to be smart enough to take an honors class? Stupid! Middle school was stupid!

But living through those brutal years hardened me.

I wasn't popular, and therefore the "in crowd" called me "gay" all the time. Me and one-third of the boys in my class! I wasn't the most coordinated guy either; and being basically a nerd,

I would have rather played chess, but since I wasn't the only one who missed a pass and got hit in the head with a basketball, I dealt with the ridicule and made it through PE with at least a B. And the name-calling—I started not to care.

And to be clear, back then, the word "gay" never meant homosexual. For the longest time, I sincerely thought it was a made-up term created by bullies to denigrate the less popular, weak, and dare I say "smarter" kids in school. There was rumor of what it meant, of course, but no one had actually met *a homosexual.*

Enter me!

It was high school that confirmed homosexuality as reality. More precisely, high school gym class and the dreaded, yet appealing, showers.

I remember one year when baseball *proved to be my nemesis. (Or rather baseball* players!*) My dad convinced me to try out for the team, again, because he had this notion that I'd excel at athletics if only I tried hard enough. So, because I wanted to make him happy, I went. Much to my chagrin, I made varsity.*

Don't get all excited! I only made it because they lacked players. It seemed many of the boys in the school didn't like the coach, so they all went out for lacrosse that year. Varsity baseball had just enough players to play that season as long as me and one other sophomore committed. (Junior varsity, by the way, was made up of mostly ninth-graders and some sophomores who turned out to be less coordinated than I was! Amazingly.) Most of the time, though, I played right field and I can't remember the ball ever coming my way.

The moment that stood out in my memory was during practice. I was fifteen. I was up at bat and a baseball was lobbed in my general direction. I swung and missed by three feet!

"Hey, Reid, you swing like a girl!" someone in the outfield yelled.

The pitcher lobbed another ball. Noticed I said "lobbed"; not zinged, or whipped, or even threw. Point being, he was trying his best to help me hit the ball by tossing it slow and deliberately in the strike zone. I swung the bat and missed it anyway.

"Strike three!" the umpire bellowed.

The pitcher—whose name was Brad—smiled and shrugged at me. He was trying. I gave him a half smile in return and trudged off the field, dragging the bat.

"Next time, Cole," the coach encouraged, patting my shoulder. "You just need to keep your eye on the ball and follow through with your swing."

"Thanks, Coach." I nodded and took my seat at the end of the bench.

Coach Witts was a nice enough guy, but he always said the exact same thing. Every time I struck out he uttered the same advice for improvement, as if he'd run out of creative ways to say "you suck" and stuck with a generally optimistic "try harder next time" approach. I appreciated it, even if I doubted his sincerity. Come to think of it, maybe that was why everyone went out for lacrosse? If you couldn't count on the coach to "coach," then what good was he?

Anyhow, it was hot for late April, and sitting on the bench in the sun made me sweat almost as much as when I stood in right field, hoping nothing would sail my way. After, like, six hours in the grueling sun (I exaggerate), practice was finally over. The team picked up the equipment and lumbered across the fields to the school locker room. This was the part I hated the most—showers!

High school gym-class showers confirmed for me that I was indeed gay.

The difference was that in middle school, boys didn't shower, and if they did it was half-clothed or over so fast that the stink didn't have the chance to leave their bodies. In high school, boys are more aware of the need to look and smell good for the ladies. We sweat more and stink more because we are more aggressive and competitive. (I use the term "we" very loosely.) We need to shower after gym class and especially after baseball practice. It didn't take long for me to realize I was the only one getting stimulated from being in the presence of half-dressed, muscular boys.

Not ninth- and tenth-graders—they were mostly feeble like myself; we're talking seniors! Fourteen- and fifteen-year-olds had nothing interesting to show (normally), but the seventeen- and eighteen-year-old boys, the ones with enough facial hair to order drinks at a bar without getting carded, they had muscles I would die for. The locker room became for me the equivalent of an all-you-can-eat buffet to a ravenous glutton. I yearned for those twenty minutes after practice as much as I dreaded them. The complication was in how much my parts noticed their parts, and how very different the very same sexual organs could appear to someone who happened to be attracted to said organs! So, that particular year, when Brad the pitcher walked past me in the locker room, strutting his god-like naked body into the shower, I looked.

I thought I was discreet. I knew enough not to ogle the curve of his ass or study the swing of his genitals as he walked past me. It was dangerous. No other boys did this! I knew because I always scanned the crowd for others scanning the crowd like me. I carefully enjoyed my view until someone shoved me from behind and startled me.

"Hey, what do you think you're looking at, Reid?" Josh Green asked gruffly. He was one of the linebackers from the varsity football team: huge, intimidating, and another body I enjoyed fantasizing over. "Hey, Foley!" he called after Brad. "Reid's eye-balling your ass!"

"No, I wasn't," I protested.

"Yeah, you were. I saw you," he asserted, shoving me so my back was plastered against the metal door of my locker, thereby exposing my front for all to see.

"Oh shit!" Jeremy Sterner gasped as he pointed. "He's hard!"

Josh Green's fist connected with my marshmallow abs and every oxygen molecule exited my lungs like rats from a sinking ship. That first punch is all I can remember. The rest is in the abysmal, black recesses of my subconscious, never to resurface, else it would damage my now out-and-proud persona. I do remember talking to a counselor about "bullying" and being the recipient of what was basically a hate crime, but to this day it's still a blur.

I blacked out when Josh hit me. The next thing I knew, I opened my eyes and saw Nurse Pennell. She was pretty and kind, and always attended to my various stomach ailments without too much comment about hypochondria. She was the one who recommended a counselor, and she was the one who kept tabs on me after the baseball team voted me off the team.

My dad was disappointed, of course, and it took him the next two years of high school and a year of college to figure out how to talk to a gay son.

I learned my lesson the hard way and was officially outed in high school because of my lack of self-control. So, I kept my eyes to myself. I allowed my very boring, nonpopular self to blend into the background so that no one noticed me. I also suppressed all emotion, which kept me from getting beat up. Boys called me gay, but no one messed with me after a while because they couldn't make me cry over it. They eventually gave up trying. I was left alone by everyone, even the people I thought were my friends. Maybe they thought homosexuality was a disease and they might "catch" it. I don't know. School got very lonely after that.

After high school, I resolved to avoid "jocks" altogether to make my life easier. I figured if I avoided those I was most attracted to, then my overactive libido would stay in check. (Guys for the most part are touted as visual creatures, and I fit the stereotype.) Self-control by avoidance became my creed.

WHAT was my "beef" over jocks? Stan had asked. *Oh, nothing big—not!*

Just like that, he hung up and left me listening to the *beep, beep, beep* on the other end. I was staring at the phone, wondering what the hell I was going to do next, when someone knocked on my door. I knew it was rude not to answer it so I stood up, but my door opened before I reached it, flooding my room with light around a single silhouette—Ellis's silhouette. Anger flared. "Um, haven't you heard of privacy, or were you raised by a tribe of hedonistic Vikings?"

Ellis stammered, obviously unaware of my normally blistering sarcasm, "Uh, I-I'm sorry."

He started to close the door and I stopped him. "Whatever. Say what you came in here to say." I could see a shadow flow over his abnormally gorgeous face. I think I hurt his feelings, but I wasn't about to alter my behavior for a guy I'd just met. Especially a *jock* I'd just met!

"I only wanted to introduce you to my buddies, but if you'd rather do it another time, I understand."

He looked hurt, and sounded hurt, and that made me feel like shit. *Fuck!* I knew one of these days my tongue was going to get me into real trouble, and this was the first time I almost cared. I did the unheard of—I apologized. "No, I'm sorry I snapped. I'll come meet your friends."

His expression immediately changed to hearts and sunshine. "Great!" He clapped me on the back and ushered me into the living room, calling to them, "Hey, guys, I want you to meet Cole…."

He let the "l" sound stretch out impossibly long and it was apparent to me he was searching his memory for my last name.

I filled in the blank when the answer didn't come on its own. "Reid."

"Reid," he reiterated. "Cole Reid, my new roommate!" He smiled and hugged me from the side across the back of my shoulders.

"Reeeeeid," the Neanderthals hollered.

My knees shook as they descended upon me like vultures, squeezing the life out of my fragile bones. Never had I witnessed such a loud group of guys who got wound up so high over nothing. All they did was hoot over Ellis's new apartment and belch the school's theme song. Joy.

When they released me from their greeting huddle, I walked over to the breakfast bar and observed them with as much enthusiasm as… well… a nonenthusiastic person. If this was my life for senior year, Lord help me!

Chapter 3
By The Way, I'm Gay

IT ONLY took a day or so for the celebrations to noticeably calm
down. Was I ever thankful! Ellis's friends didn't hang out as long or
as often as I originally imagined. Apparently they had other places
to be and other people to annoy.

Ellis himself turned out to be quite quiet on his own. And tidy
so far. Not a sock or notebook, or an item of any sort of his, was
displayed anywhere.

After his gang left that first day, he retired to his room and
presumably unpacked. For several days following, I saw him briefly
in the morning and then at night before bed. Either I made him
nervous, or he didn't like me. Or it could have been his initiation
into Reid 101, where the motto is "if it isn't snide or contemptuous,
it isn't worth the time to say it." Let's face it, calling him a
hedonistic Viking wasn't the greatest way to say "howdy" to the
new roommate.

By Monday, I decided to be a fraction more affable than I
tended to be, if only because classes started in a week and then, if
our schedules conflicted, we might never see each other. Ellis was
sitting on the couch reading instead of closed away in his room, so I
approached on cat feet. He looked up.

"Hey," I said with a tilt of my chin.

Ellis's ice-blue eyes held my gaze a few seconds before he
replied, "Hey."

This is going well. "Um, can I get you a drink?"

He wrinkled his brow and shrugged. "Sure," he said, as if he
was unsure why we were talking about it in the first place.

He hates me! I know it. I walked to the fridge and opened it. In
the door, I had Pepsi cans lined up. On the bottom shelf sat a six-
pack of twenty-ounce Cokes—his. I pulled one bottle off the plastic

carrying rings and walked back over to my indisposed roommate. There had to be a way to prove I wasn't a total ass. I took a coaster out of the wooden box that sat under the coffee table and placed his bottle of soda within reach.

"There you go." I bobbed my head, searching for something else to say.

Ellis, who slouched in one corner of the couch, book in his lap, eyeballed me. "Do you want something?"

He sounded defensive. Why was he being defensive? I hadn't said anything regrettable in days. "No, not especially." I continued to stand there, arms crossed over my chest, slightly rocking onto my heels. *Dum dee dum.*

"You want to sit?"

I jumped at his offer. "As long as you don't mind." I plopped down at the other end of the sofa.

Ellis straightened up and reached over for his bottle of Coke. After taking a swig, he set it back on the coffee table—*next* to the coaster.

I let it sit there for a full minute before I felt the need to correct the situation. "Um... I.... How do I say this?" I was tugging hard to restrain my OCD, but every second the bottle sat there and sweat built up on its exterior was a second closer to having a ring on my table. "Could you just...." I pointed in the direction of the bottle and hoped he would catch my drift without me spelling out my issues with glasses—or in this case, bottles—resting on the table's surface.

I saw Ellis's eyes shift over to where I was pointing before coming back to look at me. "What?" he asked.

"Could you just...," I stammered, trying hard not to offend him. I leaned forward, almost righting the error myself. "It's just that I don't want a ring to...."

Ellis reached out and placed the bottle where it belonged just before I touched it. "I got it." He looked back at me with a smirk on his face.

I didn't like his smirk. "Is my pain enjoyable to you?" I asked indignantly.

"Pain? That's a bit of an exaggeration, don't you think?"

"I—" I cut myself off and swallowed a retort, probably for the first time in my life. It was hard to argue with his adorable face. That damn smirk—the one I hated a second ago—lit up his features in the most wonderful way! "You're right."

Ellis gave me another look, one hard to decipher, and went back to reading his book.

"You're going to read, then?" That was about the stupidest question I'd ever asked.

"Uh, yeah, unless you have a problem with that. This is required reading for this semester, and I tend to read slow. I need this head start."

"Ahh." I nodded. His desire to do anything but talk to me came across loud and clear. I stood up, gesturing to my room by pointing my thumb over my shoulder as I stepped backward. "I'll just… head to my room, I guess. Don't mean to bother you."

I left Ellis to his reading.

In my room, all I could think about was the guy in my living room. It was bad news to dwell on his blue eyes, and I knew it. Jon had great eyes, no doubt, but they were a dark hazel. I favored blue. It wasn't exactly a manly trait to have a thing for eyes, but I did. Eyes and feet. I know that sounds corny, but it was a little personal quest I had going on to prove one way or another if a guy's foot size had any correlation to the size of other body parts. With only a few specimens to compare, the verdict was still unconfirmed. I also had a thing for chest hair but that was mainly because I lacked my own.

Ellis's eyes also did something to my stomach I wasn't accustomed to. They made me queasy. And not in a sick I'm-gonna-puke way, either. From day one I knew I needed to be extra careful around him.

Normally, I waited until I was clear on a person's stand on gay rights before I burst forth with the truth. Not that I was hiding my homosexuality. That'd be stupid, because I was out to the general public, but I liked to know if my stand was going to make things difficult. For instance, I would never wear a gay pride T-shirt to the Young Republicans Club. Not unless I wanted to be pounded senseless or harassed to no end. I was nonconfrontational at heart, my biting comments aside, and I avoided arguments if I could. *I realize this is a conflict of character traits, but what can I say? I'm a complex guy.*

Ellis had just moved in! I wasn't going to hit him with, "by the way, I'm gay" until the time seemed right. For all I knew, he could be fine with it. Jonathan had been. Jonathan and I had a great relationship, and never once did my sexuality get in the way. He even teased me on occasion by strutting his stuff around the apartment, and he didn't get offended when I grabbed his ass in reply. It was all good clean fun. We had drinks together on many occasions, and he wasn't bothered when I wore my "Even My Protons Have Pride" T-shirt. ("Pride" printed in rainbow colors, of course.) He'd laughed.

How would Ellis react? I didn't know.

What I *did* know was that fantasizing about him was going to get me in trouble. I shouldn't do it. We were roommates. If he knew I was in my room holding a staff meeting over the intensity of his eyes, he'd probably move out. If he moved out, Stan might assign someone horrible to my apartment. I didn't want horrible. I wanted comfortable, even if I was uncomfortably turned on being around him.

Still, against my better judgment, I couldn't help touching myself. "Just once," I rationalized as I cupped my junk.

I closed my eyes and imagined exuberant aggression on his part. He might possibly be a gentle lover, but for this fantasy he was going to be rough. With only a small pause to grab the lube from my nightstand drawer, I was back to visualizing his smirky smile descending around me. He would play with my testicles with one hand while he gripped my cock with the other to hold it steady. Ellis would loop his tongue, serpentine, around my shaft as he gripped my length with his lips.

"Oh God," I moaned softly.

His eyes would close as he melted into the enjoyment of the act.

"Ellis," I whispered, pretending to watch him suck the very marrow from my bones as the friction coaxed me closer to the end.

I bit my lip as I came, hoping I hadn't made too much noise. And as I lay there waiting for my heart rate to slow down, I heard his bedroom door close. *I hope he didn't hear me.*

I SLEPT peacefully, and in the morning I walked out of my bedroom wondering if *today* was the day we might actually have a meaningful conversation. As I stepped into the kitchen, my stomach seized and my heart palpitated. I audibly choked and Ellis looked up. He was on the floor of the kitchen with paper towels in hand.

"I dropped the milk carton."

Logically, I'd figured that one out since milk was everywhere; my brain instantly spewed forth statistics on bacterial growth and dairy products. "My floor!" I cried, dashing to the broom closet.

"I'm wiping it up," Ellis assured me.

I took out my Lysol disinfecting cleaner and rubber gloves. "I'm sure you're doing a grand job, but I'm mopping the floor when you're done, to remove the microbes."

"It's just a spill."

"But milk sours quickly and gets sticky when not cleaned up thoroughly. I don't want a contaminated cooking environment."

I noticed Ellis's incredulous look. "Fine. You clean it up." He dumped the wet paper towels into the trash can and left the kitchen.

Whatever. If he didn't appreciate my attention to detail, then it was easier for me to take care of it myself. I filled the mop bucket with the hottest water possible and then reshined my floor. *Perfect.* I nodded in approval.

I heard the front door close, signifying Ellis's exit. I hung my head; this friendship wasn't going anywhere.

LATER on, Ellis reappeared—sweaty and out of breath.

"Out for a jog?"

He nodded.

Subconsciously I expected a snide remark about my intelligence or ability to state the obvious, because so far it was reaching stellar levels! No such comment came. Instead he disappeared into the bathroom and I heard the shower turn on.

I was in the kitchen, making myself a mug of tea, when he entered the room soaking wet, towel around his waist. My heart stopped—strike that, my heart accelerated to keep up with the sudden rush of blood to my groin. (Hello? Visual creature here!)

Ellis took a glass out of the cabinet and looked at me. "Are you okay?" He stared. "What did I do *this* time?" He put his glass under the faucet.

I gulped as I let my eyes slide down his chest, over his abdomen (resisting the towel-covered area) to rest at his feet. "Y-you're... d-dripping water all over the floor."

He let out a huff of air and shook his head. "You're really a piece of work, aren't you?" He drank his glass of water, and I stared as his Adam's apple moved up and down, water droplets still clinging to his skin from the shower. His collar-length hair was sticking to his neck as he tilted back his head. He placed the empty glass in the sink. "If you don't want me here, just say so. I've never met anyone as anal as you!"

(Pun *not* intended? If he only knew.)

He strutted back to his room and shut the door none too quietly.

I nearly collapsed but caught myself on the counter until my legs stopped wobbling. His eyes were no longer an issue; now it was that gorgeous body! Good Lord, he was ripped. Not to mention the bear-starter-kit amount of hair covering his pecs. It made my mouth water with a deep need to lick his nipples. No way was I going to keep from picturing him as I whacked my whistle. Ellis was the physical equivalent of every dream guy I'd ever imagined, and more. And if he packed more than your average Joe, then hurray for me!

Only....

We weren't exactly friends, so amping this nonrelationship up to lover status was far from likely. I seriously had no idea how to cohabitate with Ellis without my sexuality causing problems. I'd never felt such a strong sexual attraction to anyone before. This was going to be my biggest challenge yet.

THE afternoon dragged on, night came, and the next morning held no more clues than the day before. I didn't know if he hated me or not, and he showed no signs of *wanting* to do anything together. Talking was out; silence in separate corners of the apartment was in—that is, when he was home. Ellis seemed to disappear often. I was pretty certain he went jogging because he always returned sweaty, but how much could one guy run? There were only so many hours in the day.

I stepped out to the grocery store for some milk, bread, and toilet paper—no, there wasn't a hurricane expected—and came back to find him on the living room couch. His blue eyes connected with mine briefly, and then I spotted the balls of paper on the floor. I almost had an anxiety attack as I juggled the bag in my arms. "What are you doing?" I shrieked. "Were you raised in a world without trash cans?"

"I...."

I know he started answering me, but I wasn't listening as I hurried into the kitchen to set my stuff down. I returned quickly to pick up the papers and deposit them into the wastebasket I brought with me.

"I was going to do that, you know. I'm not a slob," said Ellis.

I didn't believe him. So far the evidence had proved my first impression of him being tidy was completely wrong. "Yeah, right." I sneered. "And I can tell by the milk on the floor, and the puddles you leave walking through the house soaking wet, and the mud tracks you left on the carpet when it rained that morning you went out running."

Ellis jumped off the couch, notebook in hand. "Which I cleaned off the carpet, thank you very much! Have you always been a jerk, or are you notching it up just for me?" He stormed out the front door and left me speculating whether he'd return.

I HAD just opened my bathroom reader, searching for something interesting to occupy my time, when I heard the phone ring.

"Shit," I grumbled. "Fucking Murphy's Law!" It never fails: every time I get settled to take a dump, someone calls. Why? It wasn't like I was doing all that much with the rest of my time during the day. It was only when my bodily functions decided to function that the outside world's sixth sense kicked in. On the second ring, it stopped. *Hmm, maybe it was a wrong number?* I had the answering machine set on five rings.

I took my time and finished up as nature allowed. When I opened the door, I heard talking. Ellis. Ellis was talking on the phone. Why this bothered me, I'm not sure, but I found myself listening in. I closed the door to all but a crack. He hadn't received a call at my house before, so I just assumed he took his calls on his cell. Or texted, like 99 percent of the student population.

He was laughing. I unwittingly grinned as the sound tickled my ears. He had a pleasant laugh that made my skin tingle.

"Oh yeah? I find that hard to believe," he said with voice so relaxed that it washed over me like sipping chamomile tea. It felt warm and nice, really nice. Who knew I could be visually *and* audibly stimulated? I leaned closer, yearning for more. "No. ... He is! ... Oh, completely. ... Okay. I will. I won't forget. Hold on...." He turned in my direction, and I pulled my head away from the crack. "Hey, Cole! How long are you gonna be in there?"

Irked at his insistence, I opened the door and stepped into the room. "Some might find it rude to rush elimination since it can cause the formation of hemorrhoids."

"Sorry. Jon wanted to talk to you while he had a second. He said he texted but you didn't respond."

I hurried to the phone. "You're talking to Jonathan?" My shock and disapproval was not lost on him.

"Relax, he still has time to talk to you."

"That's not the point. You were talking to him? What'd he say?" I snatched the phone he extended to me. "What'd you say?" I demanded of Jonathan.

Jonathan snickered. "Nothing."

"It doesn't sound like nothing," I growled.

"Don't you trust me?"

The innocent tone. *I hate his innocent tone.* "No."

"Come on, I didn't give away all your secrets, Cole. Ellis is a nice guy; I simply gave him some needed advice." His voice was all chirpy on the other end. He was way too happy! Almost like he sounded after Cathy gave him a blowjob. Happy and content. *I wish someone would give me a blowjob.*

"I wouldn't know." I glanced at Ellis and then vanished to my room and closed the door. Ellis didn't need to hear my ranting. "I never talk to Ellis."

"He said you're impossible to live with."

"What?" I shrieked. "Me? He's the one who hangs out with barbarous hooligans and can't seem to do anything without making a mess!"

"Cole."

I waited. He didn't say anything. "What?"

"Have you tried congeniality, or are you sticking to your usual porcupine approach?"

"You know I hate when you call me that."

"It's true. And you have more quills."

"The average adult porcupine has over forty thousand quills."

"Then you have two-hundred thousand. Look, stop pointing out all the negatives around Ellis and get to know him first."

"I wouldn't have to do this if you were still here."

"Ahh, now I get it," he said. I heard the light bulb above his head flick on. "You're still mad that I left. Cole, I graduated. I moved in with Cathy. You're going to graduate too, unless you stay on for your master's. Life is about moving on, growing up, and finding your purpose. I have. It's time you get over your fears and make other friends."

"I don't want other friends," I said, pouting.

"Yes, you do."

"No, I don't."

"You'll like Ellis. I can tell. I knew Stan would find you just the right guy to live with."

"Stan? What does he have to do with Ellis?" It freaked me out a little to think there was a conspiracy going on without my knowledge or consent.

"Relax, Cole. I paid Stan fifty bucks to scout out the prospects and assign a roommate that wouldn't drive you crazy."

"Um, did you *not* hear the part about him being a slob?"

"Look, I have to go." I could hear in his voice he was making excuses. "I want you to promise me you'll take the time to get to know Ellis."

"What do you know?" I grew suspicious of his previous conversation.

"Nothing," he assured me. "We only talked for fifteen minutes. All I'm saying is that he seems like a great guy. It's only until June. Give him a chance. Be nice, and maybe you won't mind so much that I'm gone."

"I doubt it." Now I was sulking. Stupid Jonathan and his stupid logic.

"Go charge your phone and text me later. Good-bye, Cole."

"Bye."

I sat on my bed and stared at the phone as he hung up. Then I glanced at my cell and it was dead, just as he indicated. He always knew when I didn't text back my battery was dead. I plugged my cell into the charger and pondered over what they talked about. Me? The college? Ellis's major? *And I can't believe that Stan was in on it!* Did Ellis know?

I had to know what they'd been talking about!

I stomped back into the living room and found Ellis messing with my television. He had a box of sorts, like a DVD player but not, and cables running everywhere. I sat on the couch after setting the cordless phone in its cradle. "What did he say to you?" I asked directly.

Ellis kept up his tinkering. "Nothing."

Okay, that word was grating on me now. "I doubt it was nothing."

Ellis stopped long enough to peer at me from behind the forty-two-inch screen. "Jon gave me some insight into our... situation."

"Which is?"

Ellis plugged something in and the screen lit up. "Xbox Live" something, something. He then stepped back around the television and picked up a controller. "For one thing, our living together."

"And that's a problem... how?" I genuinely wanted to know his take on things.

"Jon said not to take you so literally. He said you exaggerate, which I already figured out. He also said you view this place as *yours,* and I shouldn't hesitate to make it *ours.*" Ellis sat on the couch next to me and pointed to the TV. "Which is why I hooked up my Xbox without asking your permission."

"Jon told you…. But I…. You hooked up…," I sputtered.

Ellis turned his smirk my way. He had a devious twinkle in his eye that made my insides flutter. "This is *our* place, Cole. It's campus housing; you don't own it. You have every option to move out, same as me. But I think we can make it work. How 'bout it?"

I gaped. I couldn't believe my ears. He was all assertive and direct and insinuating ultimatums. Live with him or move out; that's what I heard. "But I…."

Ellis reached over and patted my knee. "Relax. I'm not hard to live with. Yes, I spill things—sometimes—but my mom taught me early on how to clean up after myself. I like to party, but I also want to keep my four-point-oh. True, I can be loud, but most of the time

I'm reading or writing papers." He relaxed into the cushions. "I love my friends, but I purposely didn't want to room with them in the dorms because they're too wild. I need quiet to study. I'd seriously like to be an English professor one day, and maybe coach soccer on the side. I'm down to earth, and I don't expect much from you other than a chance."

This was the most I'd heard him say at one time since he moved in. What the fuck was I supposed to do with that? It was the kindest argument against my pessimistic tendencies I'd ever heard. I couldn't argue. He was 100 percent correct. "Fine." I sighed.

Ellis chuckled. "Fine. Play against me?" he asked, handing me a controller.

"I've never played."

"What? No way!"

"I live under a rock, what can I tell you?"

"Try anyway, it's easy. The game is FIFA. It's a soccer game. I got it last year for Christmas from my sister."

I looked at the controller and pushed some of the buttons.

"I like your shirt, by the way." He looked at me again and grinned.

I was really beginning to get used to how nice that grin made me feel. Of course I was attracted to him, but the more he talked and the more he smiled, the more I simply enjoyed being near him. Jon was right—he did seem nice. I looked down at my shirt. I was wearing the T-shirt that read "Particle Physics Gives Me A Hadron." I smirked and said, "Thanks. I forget which one I'm wearing sometimes."

"I also liked the one you wore yesterday: 'If you're not part of the solution, you're part of the precipitate.' I had to look that one up to understand it." Ellis stood up. "I'm gonna make popcorn. You sit here and fiddle with that until you get how each button moves the player." He took a step and then hesitated. "I'm not going to spill anything. And I'm not going to let anything explode in the microwave." He held out his palm. "Chill."

He made me nervous, but I had to say I liked his assertiveness. Maybe this would turn out to be fun after all?

TWO weeks went by and we sank into a very nice routine. Classes started, and we agreed that I wouldn't rag on him for making a mess now and again, and he wouldn't get huffy when I pressed him to allow me to clean things up. Whatever Jon said to him that night had produced a one-eighty in the way he spoke to me. I couldn't deny I liked it. He was open and honest, and I appreciated that. There was only one "juice incident" that invoked my wrath, but after I calmed down, we both agreed never to speak of it again.

His friends came by a couple of times to play Xbox, and he seemed to dribble that soccer ball nonstop when they were here, but for the most part Ellis quietly read, as promised. He was very serious about studying, and I think it made it that much easier for me to study as well.

One evening, while trying to make dinner for the two of us, a lightbulb popped in the kitchen. It wasn't dark, but having one bulb instead of two made everything dingy-looking. I needed full light! I grabbed a bulb from the broom closet and set my small stepladder under the light fixture. Just then, Ellis strolled in.

"Hey, what's up?"

"Bulb burned out."

"I'll do it for you," he offered, holding out his hand.

I gave him the fresh bulb and watched as he stepped onto the ladder. He stood on the topmost step, which meant his butt was very close to my face. I stepped back and removed my glasses to distract myself. I figured wiping the lenses was much safer than lusting after Ellis's fine physique. It had been a while since I'd found myself tingling in all the wrong places. Over the past couple of weeks, I'd learned to suppress my desires and think of him purely as a friend. It had worked well… until now.

The kitchen got brighter, and his movement caught my attention. Just as our eyes locked, his socked feet slipped, and he stumbled off the ladder in my direction, slamming into me and crushing me against the stove. He stopped his momentum by planting both hands on either side of my body, but not fast enough to keep from smashing up against me. Heated stares and meshing body parts made every inch of my nervous system aware of Ellis's presence. I swallowed hard and Ellis swiftly pulled away, dashing from the room. I put my glasses back on and reached out in his wake, but it was no use.

"Crap!" I cursed my luck, or lack thereof. If ever I was going to break it to him that I was gay, feeling my erection through my jeans with his groin wasn't on the David Letterman Top Ten.

I knew he could feel me—he had to! I lost the fight with my hormones the instant he got up on the ladder. I couldn't help it. Now he'd fled, and I had no chance to explain myself, nor could I pretend "friendship" was all I had in mind. "Fuck!" I cursed again. I looked down. "See what trouble you get me into!" I wagged my finger at the one part of me that was far from innocent, and yet had no choice in the matter on most occasions. "Argh," I huffed, and I gave up.

I trudged into the living room, not expecting to find Ellis sitting on the couch. *Good! He didn't leave.* But now what should I do? Explain?

He wasn't looking at me when I sat down, but he also didn't bolt. *Should I not sit so close? What if he's pissed? He might punch me. What if he's freaked? He might throw up on me.* I was suddenly glad he was looking the other way because it would be easier talking to the back of his head. I had to try.

"Ellis, we need to talk." I hoped stating the obvious would alleviate tension instead of sounding stupid. "I'm gay." I paused, letting him take in the blunt truth. "I know that's something I should've told you when you moved in, but frankly, I didn't think it mattered. I've never had a problem before. I've lived with guys for years, and my sexuality never came into play. Jonathan never cared. I've had friends that were straight and friends that were gay. It's not like I have a huge secret or anything; I've been out since high school, and not telling you was an oversight."

I ramble when I'm nervous, so rambling now came easy. "I bet you and your buddies don't introduce yourselves by saying, 'Hi, my name is Ellis. I'm straight.' I know that sounds ridiculous but it's how I feel sometimes. I never think to say, 'Hi, I'm Cole, and I like guys.' It's weird." I seriously wanted to touch his knee so he'd bring his attention to my face and not the wall. I needed to know he was listening. "I'm only telling you now because I think that you might have felt… well… that I was…." I exhaled loudly in exasperation. "Ahh! Why is this so difficult to say to you?" I really just needed to rip off the bandage in one quick motion. "Ellis, I got an erection looking at your ass." *There, I said it.* "I'm sorry if that freaks you out. I'll try harder to control myself next time, only, please, don't move out. I really like having you as a friend. Very few people put up with my shit like you do. Forgive me?" I couldn't believe I was practically begging, but I couldn't stop myself. "Please." I was starting to really care for him, not just lust over his body, and here I'd messed things up by allowing my carnal thoughts to linger. I knew it wasn't safe!

I waited, but he didn't speak. I could hear him breathing, but that made me think he was really freaked out and maybe my little chat should have waited until he'd had time to calm down first.

Just when I thought I'd made a mistake by telling him the whole truth and nothing but the truth, Ellis turned sharply and firmly affixed his mouth to mine. One hand appeared at the back of my neck, holding it fast as he pressed me against the cushion, and I felt his other hand sliding up my inner thigh.

Holy shit!

His lips were soft as he kissed me repeatedly, coaxing sweet sighs from my throat and unexpected flip-flops in my stomach. Automatically, I reached up and held his sides gently, touching his solid body but not doing anything rash enough to break the spell we were under. My head was spinning. Ellis's kisses melted my insides, and the feel of his body up against mine made me hot and jittery all at the same time. It was a feeling I hadn't experienced before. I heard a soft moan come from deep within his throat as I parted my lips and flicked my tongue out, attempting to coax him into deepening our kiss. I'd never wanted someone so bad in my life.

Without warning, he pulled away and left. No sooner had I opened my eyes than I saw his bedroom door close and heard the lock click.

I shook my head and wondered out loud, "What the hell just happened?"

Chapter 4
Is It Me Or Is It You?

I STARED at his bedroom door for an hour but it never opened. Ellis didn't reemerge. I was left wondering if I'd imagined everything, but when I licked my lips, I tasted cinnamon toothpaste. Not mine!

Shit! Ellis kissed me. What did that mean? Was he gay? Why didn't he tell me? Or was he messing with me? No, Ellis wouldn't do that. *Maybe he* is *gay? Should I knock on his door and ask what's going on, or should I wait?*

I chose to wait.

I DIDN'T see him until the next morning, and all I caught was his shadow following him out the front door. He vanished much like he had when he moved in. It made me worry. What if that kiss was a mistake? Or maybe kissing me was a horrific experience and he regretted it. *Shit, I hope not.* I thought it was a terrific kiss!

I was in my room at my desk working on an essay on Archimedes's principle when I heard the apartment door close. *He's home.* I could have rushed out but that might have seemed desperate. If he needed space, I needed to give it to him. (That's what I would want.) After another hour, when I was finished and hoping to get some sleep before classes in the morning, I heard a knock at my door.

"Come in," I said.

The door creaked open, but Ellis didn't enter. He stood at the threshold in his sweat pants and a ratty white T-shirt. He looked divided or confused. What did he want?

"You standing there all night, or are you testing my telepathic abilities?"

At least that changed his expression from bewildered to irritated. I'd take any reaction. "I wanted to know if you'd play Xbox with me?"

Ah, direct. Good. "Xbox?" I asked dubiously. "You know I suck, right?"

He lifted the corner of his mouth. "I don't care."

He didn't look like he'd leave without a "yes" in response. "Fine," I said, tossing back the covers. I followed him to the couch and sat down next to him. The couch. All I really wanted to do was pick up where we left off. We'd kissed, after all. I seriously wanted to do it some more!

We didn't. We played Xbox until two in the morning. It was fun, actually. Ellis laughed at me because I'm mentally challenged when it comes to video games. (I loved his laugh.)

I didn't have an Xbox or PSP or DS growing up. My dad is an arborist, and we spent a lot of time out-of-doors hiking, fishing, and exploring for native plants. By all accounts, I should have chosen botany or horticulture as a major, but when I started taking science classes I excelled at physics more than any other.

Ellis was patient, though, and I enjoyed being around him even if it was to play pointless video games. He made no move to repeat the other day, and he also didn't bring it up. Maybe it *was* a mistake. The thought disappointed me.

A MORNING or two later, after nothing noteworthy had occurred, Ellis came out of the bathroom showered and fully clothed. He wore a tight blue muscle shirt, which challenged my self-restraint since his biceps were three times the size of mine. And by God did I want to touch those muscles! He waltzed into the kitchen as if nothing was amiss and smiled. "Good morning," he said pleasantly.

I wasn't sure how I was supposed to react. My brain kept looping the question, "Is he going to say anything, do anything, lean in and kiss me again, maybe?" But I got nothing. He had to know how hot he was! Right? Did he expect me to act like nothing happened between us?

"Uh, hi." I said it kind of bewildered-like.

"Listen, I called Rob to see if he wanted to do breakfast. He's up for it. So I was thinking maybe you'd like to come along—hang out with me and my friends. I know you don't normally eat breakfast, but I thought it could be fun."

"Wait…." I paused, trying to let my brain catch up with what he proposed. "Is Robert the one who can belch the alphabet?"

He chuckled and shook his head. "No, that's Mike. Rob is the big guy who's always smiling. But his name isn't 'Robert'—it's 'Robin', hence why everyone calls him the Boy Wonder."

"Ah, makes sense now."

"But he prefers Rob."

I nodded, thinking over his invite. "I guess I could. It's not like I haven't met them before." I shrugged indifferently, but inside I was a bundle of nerves. If Ellis was asking me to go to breakfast, and we'd kissed before, was this a date? Would he expect me to act a certain way? Or hold his hand? And what would his friends think? "Your friends aren't going to drink beer this early in the morning, right?" *I pulled off nonchalance to perfection by asking that one.*

"No." He smiled. His eye contact lingered. "So, I'm going to find my shoes, and we can head out when you're dressed. Okay?"

I looked down, having forgotten what I was wearing. I guess pajama bottoms weren't appropriate to wear out. Although I have to say, I have seen many a college *gal* walking around campus in bottoms that looked suspiciously like pajamas. I think there is a double standard going on here!

I grabbed a T-shirt out of my drawer and pulled on the jeans that lay at the foot of my bed. Ellis was waiting for me in the living room when I was done.

"Ready?" he asked with more excitement than I had seen in him before. He walked over to the door and opened it. "Shall we?" he asked, motioning for me to exit.

He's holding the door for me. Oh God, this is *a date.* "Yeah," I said, stepping out the door. "Where are we going? Do you need me to drive?" I asked, still playing along with the casualness of it all.

"There's a little diner around the corner from Mike's brother's house. And no, Russ is driving." Ellis seemed very relaxed, and I was anything but. He *really* invited me to hang out with his friends. I wasn't sure if I should be excited or terrified.

"Which one is Russ?"

"The tall redhead."

"Got it!" Details helped pull things together for me.

Outside, Ellis's friends were waiting for us at curbside. I saw Rob's beaming face and felt oddly comforted. Ellis said he's always smiling, and even if I hadn't spent much time with him, I could imagine it being a winning personality trait. "Did someone call for a taxi?" Rob asked, opening the rear door for us.

"And you're right on time!" Ellis said, high-fiving him before crouching down and slipping into the backseat.

When it was my turn to get in, only then did I notice how much room it *didn't* have, and that was mainly because there was already a passenger besides Ellis. It was a Ford Fiesta, not exactly made for three in the backseat.

I skeptically asked, "And where am I supposed to sit?"

Russell leaned his head back so I could see him from outside the car, and said, "Sorry, dude. I didn't know you were coming. Mike was hungry and jumped in, and I didn't think it mattered."

"Sit here," Ellis gestured, squeezing over against Mike as far as he could.

I slid my glasses down my nose and peered over the frames at him. "Although I appreciate the fact that you think I can fit into the four inches you provided by smashing Mike into the other door, I still don't see it happening."

"Then sit on my lap," Ellis offered easily, stunning me into utter silence.

Luckily Mike broke me out of my flabbergasted shock by saying, "You turning queer on us, Monty?" Mike used what I suspected was a shortened version of Ellis's last name, Montgomery. I could tell he jested, but Ellis didn't look so happy about it.

"Either that or I sit on you, Foster!" Ellis lifted his butt in Mike's direction.

"Stop, stop, you dickwad! Get your ass out of my face." Mike shoved at him until he gave up and sat back on the seat.

"Torture any cats lately?" Ellis asked.

"Fuck you! Shaving a cat isn't torture."

Rob emphatically gestured. "Can we *not* talk about Mike's sadistic fascination with furry animals right now? Drop it, or get out."

I'd never heard Rob so stern but it worked—Mike shut up.

When the adolescents were finally settled, Ellis looked at me again. "Getting in?"

I lifted an eyebrow and pushed my glasses back up my nose. I wasn't sure what was going on between us, but if he was offering, I'd be damned if I was going to turn him down. I tried to go in headfirst, but that was futile. Feetfirst sort of worked, but I ended up with my legs all up in Mike's space. It's not like I'm *that* tall at five eleven, but factoring in Ellis, who was probably six foot plus, and Mike, who was taller still, going to breakfast became vaguely similar to a world-record video I'd seen of nineteen female students cramming into a Smart car! Biggest difference (discrepancy in number of people aside?) I was crammed against Ellis, and his hard body against my side felt very nice.

As Russell drove down the road, Rob started talking randomly about humpback whales, which morphed into humpbacked animals and then on to camels. (Apparently he's deranged like that. I'm sure he was dropped as a child.) He rattled on for the entire ride. "Cole, you're the science guy," Rob addressed me from his spacious front seat. "What's the difference between a one-hump and a two-hump camel?"

"Ah, I'm pretty sure that's a math question."

Ellis whispered to me. "Don't."

I glanced at him. He lifted his brows slightly, pleading with me to contain my sarcasm. Could I be swayed so easily? *Oh God, yes!* As I took a nanosecond to consider it, I felt him caress the small of my back. I shivered and closed my eyes at the sensation. He was doing this *here*? Did his friends know he was gay?

"No seriously," Rob continued. I opened my eyes and tried to pay attention. "I didn't know if there was a major difference other than one hump. And can you have a three-humped camel?"

I was about to make different remark, about needing a zoologist this time, when Russell added, "Are camels mammals or dromedaries?"

Rob punched Russell in the arm as he drove. "A dromedary is a mammal, moron. Now stop interrupting. I'm doing research."

"What kind of research?" Russell asked.

I whispered to Ellis as the banter continued in the front, "Are they always like this?"

Mike answered, "Pretty much."

"Genetic research," Rob replied. "I want to know if you can genetically alter camels to create more humps?"

"Ah, like on a wump." Russell smiled as if finally satisfied with Rob's line of questioning.

"Exactly! If Mr. Gump has a wump—which is basically a mutated camel—then somehow he figured out how to multiply the humps to get seven. But why seven?"

Russell snapped his fingers. "One for each friend. Maybe he only has seven friends?"

Rob continued his hypothesis. "But if you have a seven-hump wump, then it stands to reason you could possibly create wumps with all different number humps once you figured out the basic difference in the genetic code for one- or two-hump camels."

Oddly, this argument sounded insanely familiar, but I didn't know where I would have heard of a "wump."

Russell chimed in, "Which is why Dr. Seuss had to be a mad scientist in order to genetically mutate the animals in his laboratory!"

Rob beamed, "Exactly!"

"I wonder if Mr. Gump is related to Forrest Gump?" Russell asked innocently.

Oh my God! I looked at Ellis. "Are they arguing over a Dr. Seuss book?"

He nodded. "Uh-huh."

"Shoot me now."

Ellis chuckled, and as he did so he rested his very warm palm just to the back of my hip and squeezed. I could have died. I closed my eyes again and swallowed hard. I swear if he moved his hand any lower it would be on my ass, and at that point, I would be kissing him like crazy whether his friends were present or not!

Russell and Rob continued their discussion in the front seat, oblivious to Ellis's stealthy affection. I relaxed my body into Ellis and prayed there would be road construction on every turn to delay us on the way to the restaurant.

I have no luck—the roads were clear.

In the restaurant, we were seated at a large round table sort of in the middle of the floor. I didn't think Russell and Rob could contain their shenanigans long enough to eat, but I hoped that since we were in everyone's view—not like being in a booth—that they'd show some decorum. I sat between Mike and Russell, with Rob and Ellis across from me. The waitress came and poured us all coffee and took our orders: Rob ordered pancakes; Russell, French toast; Mike and Ellis got the house special with an omelet; and I asked for the waffles and hash browns. In a short time, we got our food, and everything seemed like breakfast would be a pleasant and calm experience, unlike the car ride here.

Ellis kept looking at me and then looking away. I think he was trying to portray an air of casual observance as he checked out the décor and made eye contact with each of his friends as they ate or spoke, but I had a feeling I was the only thing on his mind. What gave it away was when he surreptitiously poked the tip of his tongue out for a split second when Rob bent down to retrieve his dropped fork. Ellis kept a straight face, yet I could see a gleam in his eyes every time they made contact with mine.

He was flirting with me, and I hoped to God I wasn't blushing.

Then Russell tilted his head to the side, listening. "Do you hear that?" He asked, a forkful of syrupy French toast inches from his mouth and dripping onto the table. I had the urge to grab a napkin for him.

The waitress gave Rob a new fork and refilled our coffee, ignoring how we all sat—heads cocked to the side—straining to hear the music. I wasn't sure what we were supposed to be listening for, but I angled my head toward the ceiling like the rest.

"What?" Rob asked, with a cheek full of pancakes threatening to explode. (Note: I hate when people talk with their mouths full.)

"The music," Russell insisted, spewing French toast bits out. (What a pig.)

It was an old Madonna tune from the '80s. I wasn't sure why it was significant, but something in Ellis's glare made it clear that someone was going to get pounded later.

"They're playing your song, El," Russell answered, grinning like a proud papa.

I strained to hear the quiet elevator music coming from the speakers in the ceiling above our heads, but Rob's protest was louder than the background music. "Russ, you dork, how many times do I have to tell you 'Like a Virgin' isn't about virgins. It's about *feeling* like one all over again. You can't categorize this as Ellis's theme song when it's completely erroneous." Rob jumped suddenly. "Ouch! Who kicked me?"

Ellis glared again. "Shut up, Rob."

"What? Why? Are you worried about Mike? He knows. Remember he found out last year when that girl at the pool party got drunk and tried to kiss you." Rob had a way of rambling on a whole other level than I ever did. He could have done it professionally. He stared at Ellis, who wasn't talking, and then his eyes glinted with an unspoken understanding. "Oh... ohhh! You don't mean Mike. You mean Cole!" Ellis still didn't answer audibly, but if his eyes could shoot poison darts, Rob would have been a pincushion.

Rob looked across to me. "Hey, Cole, did you know Ellis is a virgin?" Why Rob felt the need to tell me must have been under the *Jeopardy* category heading "How to Embarrass Your Friends" for eight hundred, Alex.

"I *am* going to kill you," Ellis snarled. Ellis might have *sounded* like a seething wolverine, but the placid look on Rob's face told me he knew Ellis was all bark.

"No, you won't. Besides, what are you going to do? You and I are the only two virgins on campus. Practically everyone knows anyway."

"They do now," Ellis grumbled.

Mike spoke up. "I heard yesterday James is one." I found it interesting how he referred to "virgins" like a secret club or something.

Russell dropped his fork. "What? No way! I thought he was dating Tina."

"Dating, but they've only kissed. James said she wants to wait until marriage."

"Ha!" Rob threw a piece of biscuit at Ellis. "At least James and I can brag about kissing a girl. Young El is pristine green."

Mike laughed. "Loser!" He placed his hand to his forehead, fingers in the shape of an "L" against it.

Ellis groaned and laid his face on the table.

"But, Rob, that girl you kissed was ten, it doesn't count," Russell remarked, ignoring Ellis.

"Yes, it does! We were both ten."

"Nooo," Russell stressed with an air of sarcasm. "Kissing a girl means kissing with the intention of dating or other 'extracurricular' activities. When you're ten, neither one of you knows what that means."

Rob quickly retorted, "*You* don't know what that means!"

I smirked, genuinely amused by their banter as well as Ellis's embarrassment. But as I thought about it, this actually explained a lot! If Rob's pronouncement was indeed correct—that Ellis had never kissed a girl, then I might very well have been the first person he'd kissed. Wow! *I was Ellis's first kiss.* He might be completely mortified over it, but I was feeling rather special.

AFTER the car ride home, during which Ellis sat stiffly silent and did *not* caress my lower back or any other part of me, Russell dropped us back at the apartment and Ellis went, predictably, to his room. I understood the embarrassment factor, but he couldn't slip into his room every time and lock the door. So far, his method of dealing with uncomfortable situations was to leave the apartment all day or lock himself in his room. I felt excluded. I get that girls are way better at talking about their emotions than guys, but—being a guy—I know we're not emotionless abysses existing without need of compassion. Sometimes emotions simply got tangled up on delivery from the post office.

I knocked and waited and then knocked again.

After the third time, he opened the door. He looked drained. He didn't speak; he merely stood there in the open doorway analyzing the ground. (Or my crotch, but I have the feeling that was only me being hopeful.)

"Is it true, what Rob said earlier? You never even kissed a girl before?" I tactfully inquired when it was clear he wasn't going to communicate without prompting.

He nodded the slightest of nods.

"Does that mean…. Was I your first kiss?"

His gaze flicked up to mine and then back to the floor. Another slight nod.

I felt a flush of heat in my belly. It was true and I was thrilled. I stepped closer and boldly cupped the side of his neck, extending my fingers into his hair and touching his cheek with my thumb. Ellis looked up. "Good," I said, using my eyes to assure him waiting until now was a positive thing. Then I leaned forward and kissed him gently.

One kiss. I made my point. I backed away to allow him his space. Being embarrassed by all your buddies was a shock to a man's pride. I got that. We'd talk another time.

Chapter 5
Getting To Know You

ROBIN MCAVOY met Ellis Montgomery on his first day of college. Ellis was waiting to see the registrar, and Rob was in line in front of him. Rob wouldn't have taken notice at the time except Russell Davenport came out of the office and tripped over his own feet, crashing into Rob and pushing Rob into Ellis. The result was a pile of legs and arms and books and papers, and they all tried to right themselves and sort out the mess before they lost their place in line.

"Nice, Russ! Way to be smooth in front of the ladies," Rob commented, noticing several girls nearby giggling and pointing.

"Sorry, I told you these shoes were too big." Russell scrambled to retrieve his papers before passers-by stepped all over them.

"A half inch doesn't negate agility. You either have it or you don't." Rob shook his head and offered a hand to the poor schlep he fell into. "Sorry about that, man. My friend isn't used to walking on these legs yet." Rob noticed the guy with hat-shaped black hair glanced at Russell's legs as he took Rob's offered assistance to his feet. "It's a joke; they're not prosthetics." Rob snagged a ball cap off the floor and handed it back to him. "I'm Rob McAvoy. This is Russ." He held out his hand again, more formally this time.

"Ellis Montgomery," Ellis said, placing his hat on backward before clasping Rob's hand.

"Are you changing classes already?" Rob asked, pointing to the change request form in Ellis's hand.

"Yeah, one class conflicts with the fall soccer schedule. I can't miss soccer."

"Soccer? Cool!" Rob was genuinely excited.

"Are you on the team?" Ellis asked.

"Nah, too much running involved. I have asthma. Not bad, but enough to keep me from playing sports. I like to watch, though, or play FIFA for Xbox."

"You play?" Ellis's eyes sparked.

"Yeah. Maybe we can get up a tournament sometime. Russ loves to get beaten." He reached over and rubbed the top of his friend's head.

Russell shoved his hand away and protested, "Shut up! Just because I can't get my guy to kick when the ball drops in front of him doesn't mean I'm inept. It was the controller, not my player!"

"Yeah, yeah. Keep saying that and maybe one day I'll believe you." Rob looked to Ellis and asked, "Are you staying in the dorms on campus or the off-campus housing?"

Ellis frowned. "Neither. My parents can't afford it. I got a partial scholarship for soccer so that covers two-thirds of my classes, but I can't pay for housing. I'm commuting from my parents' house."

"Too bad. Well, anytime you want to crash, drop by. Russ and I are in the residence hall for freshmen."

"Okay."

"Listen, it's my turn to go in." He pointed to the open registrar's office. "But I'd like to chat some more if you want to grab a cup of coffee with me later. What'cha say we meet outside this building in about thirty minutes?"

Ellis smiled. "Okay."

"Are you so hard up for a date, McAvoy, that you're asking a *guy* to meet you for coffee?"

Rob looked in the direction of the voice he recognized. "Bite me, Mike. I'm surprised to see you out and about. I thought you'd be in jail for knocking over that girl in the wheelchair."

"They couldn't prove it was intentional," Mike said proudly.

Rob shook his head in disgust. "One day your malicious nature and aversion to people who *aren't* like you is going to bite you in the rear." To Ellis he said, "Ignore him. Mike's got a God complex and feels the need to put others down to feel better about himself. Not to mention how jealous he is that I can get a date and he can't."

Ellis paled instantly. "W–what? I—"

Rob laughed. "Chill, man. I didn't mean you. I'm only messing with Mike because I've known him forever. I assure you, I'm not gay."

Mike piped up. "Are you sure about that, Boy Wonder? All those girls you're friends with, and I hear you're still a virgin."

Rob wasn't laughing with him. "Ha ha. Say whatever you want. But just because I don't want to desecrate this temple"—Rob gestured to his body with a sweep of his hands—"doesn't mean I'm homosexual; it just means I have higher standards than you."

Russell looked positively ill. "Desecrate? Why would you want to desecrate on yourself? That's disgusting."

Rob rolled his eyes and threw his hands up in surrender. "Oh my God. I'm surrounded by morons." He looked right at Russell and explained, "*Desecrate…* not defecate, Russ. You're thinking of the word *defecate*."

Russell snapped his fingers and smiled. "Oh! I knew that sounded wrong."

Rob looked at Ellis. "These are the people I'm friends with. If you still want to have coffee with me, I'll see you in thirty."

"Okay." Ellis nodded in confirmation.

ELLIS sipped his coffee and asked, "So you knew Russ before you roomed with him?"

Rob smiled. "Yeah! Best friend since the third grade. Isn't that cool! And being assigned the same dorm room was totally random." He grinned and nodded at a girl who walked by. He forgot her name, but he knew she was in his literature class. The coffee house was frequented by most of the college, and being the person he was, Rob recognized many of the patrons. He came here often to have coffee, study, or just chill in a pleasant atmosphere. It was the best hangout spot around.

"That's cool. I mean, unless you can't stand being around him that often."

Ellis seemed like a really easygoing guy, and Rob was really grateful for Russell's two left feet. "No. It's fine. Russ and I are together most of the time anyway. We hang out, play Xbox and card games, study, run the campus youth group together, practically everything."

"Youth group?" Ellis asked.

Rob was used to being questioned about youth group, so he'd figured out quickly that honesty was the best policy and being up front about his life made having friendships easier. "Yup. It's an on-campus ministry. Russ and I help organize activities for a married couple that lead Bible discussions," Rob answered openly. "That's how I know so many people that go here even though this semester just started. I was here a lot in May and June getting acquainted with the campus and learning the ropes from the guy who was graduating. They needed someone new, so Russ and I volunteered."

"Oh." Ellis's eyes darkened. Rob was also used to skeptical confrontation and could tell there was more going on behind that simple grunt. He waited for Ellis to go on. After sipping his coffee, Ellis asked, "Bible? You mean like a Christian thing?"

People milled around the coffee shop and took no note of their conversation.

"Yeah," Rob said, shrugging like it was no big deal. "But you don't need to look like you've run into a satanic cult. We don't sacrifice babies, and we don't require your first born to join. It's just a discussion group. This is a college campus—lots of people from all walks of life. Sometimes people want to know about Jesus, and I help with a group that facilitates that. No agenda. You come or you don't—our friendship doesn't depend on that." Rob truly meant it, but Ellis still looked doubtful.

"Then... what does it depend on?"

Rob grinned and replied, "Honesty." He felt the need to explain a little something about himself. "You see, Ellis, I read people. Not like magic or anything, and I don't believe in clairvoyance. It's more like I see things, feel things, and sometimes I get a sense of a person by a handshake. I can't always explain it, but I *do* think it's a gift from God. When I helped you up off the floor by the registrar's office, I got these calm vibes off you, compelling me to get to know you more. I can't base that on anything but a warm feeling I had in my gut, but trust me—I'm never wrong." Rob held up his hand when he realized what he said. "I know that makes me sound gay, like Mike said, but I'm not. I just sense things."

"I guess I can believe that."

Ellis still looked skeptical, so Rob continued. "People talk to me all the time. Randomly, sometimes. Like, I'll be standing in line at Walmart and someone will spill their life story and I have no idea why. People trust me. I'm a magnet for things I can't explain outside of the God equation. I see it that way because I'm also a Christian. I view life from a biblical prospective. I'm not trying to freak you out; I'm just saying this is who I am. I like to be open, and I tend to say what I think. I'm not friends with people just to recruit them into anything, and I never have a hidden agenda. That would be dishonest and cultic. I'm just me. So what I want to offer you is friendship. I know a lot of people on campus, and if you're a freshman, like I think you are, I can introduce you around."

Ellis smiled gently and the hard edge to his eyes began to fade. "Okay. I'd like that. I don't know anybody. But, so you know, I don't really want to know about the Bible. If that's okay."

"Dude, that's totally fine." Rob finished his coffee and took the last bite of his scone. "I'm about getting to know people for who they are. I'm a Christian. I'm not going to hide it any more than Mike hides being a douche."

Ellis shot coffee out his nose.

Rob laughed heartily. "See, I knew I could be myself around you."

Ellis composed himself, wiped his face, and smiled back. "Yeah, I kind of felt like that when you held out your hand to help me off the floor. So what's the deal with Mike?" Ellis asked. "Why'd he call you 'Boy Wonder'?"

"Mike gets his jollies through intimidation. He thinks it's a riot that my name's *Robin*. Not *Robert*."

"Oh. What a jerk. I mean, Robin Williams is a pretty famous person."

Rob gesticulated. "Exactly. Thank you very much! And if I was half as rich as Robin Williams, no one would jest about my name again."

Ellis then added, "Besides, Batman and Robin were always my favorite superheroes growing up. I think Robin is a good name."

Rob's heart warmed. "See? This friendship was meant to be!"

Ellis smiled back and nodded in clear agreement.

SINCE then, Rob had seen Ellis almost as often as Russell. He watched many of his soccer games and helped him study. They even went to a few campus bible group outings together. They became close friends during the first two years of college, and Rob was pleased. So when Ellis showed up curbside with his new roommate, Cole, Rob knew something was up.

It wasn't as if Ellis couldn't have any other friends. It was that in two years, Rob thought he knew all of Ellis's friends: Russell, Mike, James, a guy named Geoff on the soccer team, and himself. Ellis had friends in high school, but they all went to different colleges and barely spoke anymore. Ellis was shy by nature. Ellis liked predictability. Ellis had a hard time opening up. Now he'd moved in with Cole and suddenly, in a couple of weeks' time, Ellis was allowing Cole to sit on his lap for an entire car ride to breakfast? Rob was blown away. True, he kept his shock in check, but he still felt like saying, "What the hell?"

Over breakfast he carefully observed Ellis. He was quieter than usual, like he was nervous. His eyes darted to everyone as if waiting for them to do something uncharacteristic, except it was Ellis who was acting out of character. And he kept looking at Cole with a bemused expression glued in place. *Why?*

And then the Madonna song came on and Ellis turned ghost white, even before Russell's comment. Ellis was seriously upset and embarrassed beyond anything when Rob outed him to Cole about his virginity. *Why would he care?* The guys always ragged on Ellis and Rob about it. It was like a quest they had to get the two of them laid. Ellis never caved to peer pressure, which was one thing Rob admired about him. What was it about Cole that had gotten him shaking on what used to be solid ground?

When they left the restaurant, Rob started gathering the clues.

ROB went to class like usual, but then, instead of hitting the library with Russell, he thought he'd shoot over to Ellis's. He rang the doorbell and waited.

Cole answered the door and arched his eyebrow up. "Ellis isn't here."

Rob got straight to the point. "Alright. Can I come in and wait? He's probably still at practice."

"I suppose asking you to wait in the corridor would be uncouth." Cole opened the door wider. "Hold on, you're not a vampire, are you? If I don't invite you in, are you forced to remain outside?"

"No." He couldn't think of anything else to say. Cole had never joked with him before, and the vampire comment threw him.

"Then I guess I'm obligated to bid you enter." He swept his arm wide. "And wipe your feet, please."

Rob walked in and felt an unexpected chill. Either Cole was hiding something or he was Satan incarnate. (Rob leaned toward the secretive side since he doubted Cole was Satan.) He wanted to feel him out, but had to think of what to talk about first. "So, Cole, are you going to watch Ellis's game on Tuesday? It's a home game."

"Ah, I guess." He sounded uncertain. "Ellis didn't invite me."

Rob wanted to laugh but didn't. "Ellis doesn't have to invite you—it's open to the public. Five bucks to get in for students."

"But what if Ellis doesn't want me there?" Cole asked, as the door opened behind them.

"Doesn't want you where?" Ellis asked.

"Oh, hey, El." Rob greeted him with a cheery wave. He wished Ellis had been a little slower to return home, but oh well.

"Hey." Ellis nodded, walking right up to Cole. "Want you where?" he asked again.

"At your game," Cole said.

"Oh," Ellis answered solemnly.

Rob could swear Ellis looked like he'd been put on the spot about some dire decision. What was the big deal? It was only a soccer game. And Cole seemed nervous. Why? Cole was Ellis's friend, right? Why wouldn't he want him to come?

"I assumed he knew. Sorry," Rob said to Ellis.

Ellis flicked his gaze over to Rob. "No, it's fine. You can come," he said to Cole.

Rob clapped his hands together. "Great! It's settled. Soccer and then pizza here after you win."

Ellis grinned. "Don't be so confident. We're playing against the best team in our division." Ellis placed his gym bag on the floor by his bedroom door and headed to the kitchen. Rob followed him.

"So?" Rob shrugged. "You're awesome. I've never seen a striker with as good footwork as you. Plus, when you pass, the ball falls right in front of the wing—that guy doesn't even need to look up!" Rob pointed to Ellis as he addressed Cole, who had followed them into the kitchen. "I'm telling you, this guy could play professionally. He rocks!"

"Stop." Ellis blushed. Rob didn't think he'd ever seen Ellis blush.

AFTER the game, Rob and Russell went back to Ellis's place with Cole. They waited for him to get back before ordering a pizza. Once

Ellis lumbered in, he disappeared into the bathroom for a shower with less than two grunts at his friends.

"I told you this was a bad idea," Cole grumbled. "I'm a walking black cloud of negative energy, I could have told you he'd lose."

"No, it wasn't you," Rob disagreed. "Ellis said they were good. And this is just what he needs after a loss like that—friends, fun, and pizza. It'll be here in thirty minutes. In the meantime we can play Uno or Yahtzee?" Rob offered. Ever striving to be a peacekeeper, he prided himself on knowing what would cheer his friends up.

"Yahtzee?" Russell asked. "No one plays Yahtzee. Phase 10, Rummikub, or Chickenfoot is where it's at."

"Are you a middle-aged housewife now?" Rob joked. "Rummikub?" he scoffed.

Russell punched his arm. "Hey! I'll have you know these games are fun. I play them all the time with my mom."

Rob nodded and looked at Cole. "Who is a middle-aged housewife."

Cole snickered. "I actually have Phase 10 in my room."

"See?" Russell excitedly pointed.

"And your encouragement will only ensure he never leaves your house. You know that, right? Russ already likes your company."

Cole winced. "It there an antidote to counter the effects?"

Rob grinned. Cole's sense of humor was unusual and often dry, but Rob liked his style, even if he came off gruff and unpersonable at times. "You mean a surefire way to keep his Russness at bay?"

"Yeah."

"Hey!" Russell was offended.

"Put ketchup on his hotdog and he'll never grace your presence again."

Russell huffed at Rob. "If he does that, I'm never talking to you again! I mean it!"

Cole ignored Russell and kept talking to Rob. "Is he allergic to ketchup?"

"No, he's a condimentaphobiac."

Cole's voice went up in perplexity. "A whaaat?"

"A person who's afraid of condiments." Rob explained.

"I've never heard of such a thing, and I've memorized a long list of phobias."

"Wave a bottle of mustard in front of him and see what happens."

Russell placed both hands on his hips and scowled at Rob and Cole. "You think you're funny, don't you? I'll have you know that hotdogs are perfect just the way they are, plain, the way God created them! They don't need sauces or spicy mixtures to hide their doggy goodness."

"God didn't create the hotdog, Russ. It was some German guy in the 1800s who sold them on the streets of St. Louis."

"Whatever! You don't always have to correct me, Rob."

"I know, but it's fun." Rob blew off Russell's irritation. Just then, Ellis joined them in the living room. None too happy, Ellis's shoulders slumped and disappointment exuded from him. "Hey, El, you want to play Phase 10?"

He shook his head. "Not really." He slowly walked to the kitchen. Cole jumped up to follow him, which interested Rob immensely. Something was going on, and Rob was determined to find out.

"I'll be right back," he told Russell.

"Get me a Coke while you're up."

Rob cringed at Russell's loud voice. "Okay," he said, trying to appease his friend but internally hoping he wouldn't ask for anything else. He slinked across the room while Russell was fiddling with the television and attempted to eavesdrop on Ellis and Cole. He knew it was wrong, but curiosity was wriggling in his stomach like crazy.

"I told you I shouldn't have gone," Cole said, as soft as a caress. "Everyone says how terrific you are. I go and you lose for the first time."

"It's not your fault. I'm glad you came. I'm only sorry I didn't invite you sooner. I should have. I liked knowing you were watching, even if I sucked." Rob couldn't see Ellis, but his voice was... different.

Rob peeked around the corner carefully and caught a glimpse of Cole tenderly stroking Ellis's shoulder blade. Then he dared to finger the strands of Ellis's wet hair. *Guys don't do that!* He and Russell were very friendly at times, but something in the way Cole touched Ellis went way beyond the open affection he and Russell shared. It was... tender.

Rob couldn't see Ellis's face, but he *did* see Ellis move his hand and rest it on top of Cole's where they stood by the sink. His thumb made little circles on the back of Cole's hand just before Cole cleared his throat, and Ellis pulled his hand away. Rob knew he'd been spotted. He walked into the kitchen boldly, swinging his arms to clasp his hands behind his back. "So," he said casually, "is it going to be Yahtzee or Xbox?"

Ellis replied, "I think Russ should choose since you gave away his condiment phobia." Ellis acted as he typically would, but Rob didn't think the touching he'd secretly witnessed was normal at all.

"Ah! Really?" Rob moaned, throwing his head back in defeat. "Alright." He wanted to say something about their behavior, but if he pushed, then he might end up alienating his friends. Rob couldn't handle that. He'd wait and let things play out as they may.

Still, he couldn't resist the urge to meddle. "Hey, Cole. Do you like camping? There's a group of us going next weekend if you're up for it. Ellis is going."

Cole looked puzzled. "Camping?"

Rob apologized. "I know—squirrel moment—but I was just thinking about how fun it's going to be and I thought you might like to come."

Cole seemed unsure how to answer. "I guess." He darted his gaze to Ellis and then back to Rob. "If you want me to."

"Of course!" Rob confirmed. "It'll be great! You'll see. Right, El?" He slapped his buddy on the back.

Ellis looked ill briefly, but managed a thin smile. "Yeah, great."

Rob congratulated himself. Of course he'd allow things to "play out as they may," but giving a little nudge wasn't unheard of. If something was going on between Ellis and Cole, he was sure a weekend together would bring it to the surface.

Chapter 6
Rainy and ~~Whet~~ Wet

CAMPING was something I hadn't done since I was a kid. I remembered going with my parents and smelling bacon in the wee hours of the morning. Although, when my mom cooked bacon, one side was still raw while the cooked side was black as tar. She was terrible with the cook stove in the middle of the woods. Still, we always had fun. My sister would collect wildflowers and present them as a gift to my mom, and she would make a show and thank Bethany profusely for her wonderful offering. Meanwhile, my dad would try to catch dinner and return with a fish smaller than an appetizer at a fancy restaurant. We'd all laugh, and Mom would pull out a container of chili she'd prepared ahead of time and heat it up for us.

Those were the days!

Not so much now.

I arrived with "the guys" late in the evening. We're talking *late*. Pitch black, freezing cold, and starting to rain. Not my ideal list of camping essentials; *these* were the reasons *not* to go camping, in my book. Apparently, Ellis's friends hadn't received that memo, so we all went.

Much to my surprise, there was a group of campers there to greet us and help with our gear. See, when I went camping, it was "car" camping. My dad pulled the SUV up to a campsite and we pitched a tent. All our stuff was right there. In this campground, the sites were a hundred yards away because it was for group camping—something I had never done. It was nice of these people to pitch in and help, because I was in no mood to haul all my crap through the woods in the dark!

"You didn't tell me about all these other people," I griped to Ellis when the others weren't paying attention.

"Oh, I didn't?" He seemed surprised by his lack of detail sharing. "Well, this is Rob's church group. I think he said maybe seven families were camping here over the weekend and about fifteen people from the college. It should be fun!" He said this with a grin and nudged me with his elbow.

Chirpy. He was always chirpy and pleasant. Why? I gave him a scowl in reply but he only chuckled. "Terrific," I said as I rolled my eyes.

Classes had been intense the past two weeks, so between papers, projects, and soccer, there hadn't been any time to explore whatever was happening between us. We simply settled into a fond friendship. You know, one of those friendships with a little more affection than most, since he did touch me more than anyone else, but not enough affection to be considered a "public display." I liked the "A," don't get me wrong, but I wanted the "PD" part of it as well! So far, not so much. Ellis seemed shy, and I'm not a person to push for anything that doesn't happen naturally. We'd only known each other a short while, so I figured I could take it one day at a time and one flirtatious glance at a time.

The gear-unloading process took literally minutes as each person took a bag or two, and before I knew it, our tent was set up and there was a fire burning. I was impressed. I didn't think they'd mentioned being Boy Scouts, but they could have been.

"Who is sleeping in that tent?" I asked, pointing to a smaller tent next to the big tent.

"That's for our gear," Ellis explained. "Rob and Russ were going to sleep in it, but we decided to all sleep in the big one I brought and put our stuff in the little one. That way, we stay warmer and the bags stay dry. I think it's supposed to rain every day."

"Seriously? Then *why*, exactly, are we still here?"

Ellis gave me that charming smile of his that lights up the universe and said, "Because it's going to be fun. You're wearing Gore-Tex; I wouldn't worry about being wet. Just make sure to put on layers and stand by the fire. You'll be fine."

"Hey, guys!" Rob called from across the path. "There's food over here. Hotdogs and s'mores! Come on."

Russell stopped poking our fire and nodded to Ellis. "Coming?"

"Yeah," he said. "In a second."

I watched Russell scamper off. "Gee, you guys go all-out on the nutrition scale. Are we having scrapple for breakfast?"

Ellis stepped in front of me before I'd taken two steps toward the other campsite. Sometimes I forget he's taller than me, because most of the time he's lying on the couch playing Xbox, and sometimes I forget just how incredible he smells. But just now, with him peering down at me those few inches with just enough light from the fire behind me to flicker in his eyes, my breath caught in my throat. I hoped he hadn't heard me gasp.

"Cole, you'll have fun," he said in that deep, mellifluous voice of his—the one that could be used for voice-overs if the animated characters ever needed to be sensual or debaucherous. (I suppose that's not a word. How about "lecherous"? Yeah, that will do.) I tried hard not to make any of these mental notes out loud as he continued talking. "I promise. No need for sarcasm, no need to point out that it's warmer and drier back in the apartment. This weekend is about relaxing and enjoying our friendship."

I had to ask. "Yours and mine? Or being friends with everyone else? Because I'm not sure I'll *like* everyone else."

Ellis smirked. "Everyone else," he said, briefly stroking the whiskers on my chin with his thumb and forefinger. "I'm pretty sure you and I don't need a camping trip to enjoy being friends. Come on."

His bold move, however fleeting, left me weak in the knees. He was three steps ahead of me before my brain kicked in and told me to move. I hurried to catch up, wobbling my way over tree branches and weaving around rocks and ferns. Ellis looked back and smirked at me. And even though that gleam in his eye didn't help me to focus on walking straight, I was glad he was waiting for me to catch up. He's courteous like that.

We walked over to the other camp together, and sure enough, there were hotdogs a-roasting and s'mores galore. Ellis slapped hands with several college-aged kids and then, much to my chagrin, turned my way. *I like fading into the shadows, Ellis, remember?*

"Hey, everybody, this is my roommate, Cole." He patted my shoulder, and the group around us waved and gestured cheerfully. He looked at me and pointed to each person respectively. "Cole, this is John, James, Tina, Lisa...." He paused as he turned to the other side of us. "And Tim, Mike—you know Mike—Maggie, Alex, Nick, and Sandy." Why he bothered with all their names I'm not sure; it wasn't like I'd remember them beyond this weekend, anyway.

Then Russell extended his hand and added, "And I'm Russ and this is my buddy Rob." He slapped Rob's stomach as he took my hand and shook it.

"Ha ha," I mocked.

"Cole doesn't get out enough, guys, so we gotta make this a memorable adventure." Ellis was so very good at pointing out my flaws.

"Shut up," I grumbled, elbowing him.

He snickered in that annoying way he does and walked over to a man standing under an easy-up canopy, leaving me alone with the group of merry churchgoers.

I never went to church myself. My mom and dad never attended when I was young, so it wasn't something I thought of doing as I got older. I wasn't against church, necessarily, but it was the whole part about homosexuality being a sin that I tended to avoid. I'm gay, remember? God's wrath pouring down on me for something I had no choice over didn't seem very fair.

But being here, with them, I had to admit they seemed like a nice group. They laughed and joked just like everyone else. I even forgot how tired I was. And how cold.

Sinking into my sleeping bag was the pinnacle of bliss. I couldn't believe it was almost midnight! Rob was on the far left of the tent, then Russell, then Ellis, and then me—squished up against the other side of the tent. Rob was squawking at Russell in the dark.

"Stop touching me!"

I laughed quietly to myself, thinking about how they acted like a bunch of twelve-year-olds.

"I'm not doing anything. That was Ellis," Russell weakly defended himself.

"Don't drag me into this," I heard Ellis say.

They'd agreed on lights out five minutes prior so that no one had a flashlight beaming in their eyes when trying to fall asleep. It was a good plan, but no one seemed ready for the call of Morpheus. They were still play-fighting.

"Get your finger out of my ear, you dipwad!" Rob murmured angrily, although I guarantee he wasn't angry at Russell—he never was.

"I didn't do it!"

"Get off!" Rob said louder. And then I heard rustling, the shiny fabric of the tents and sleeping bags rubbing together in that audible way they do when cotton never makes a sound.

Ellis, who was facing the other way, took the opportunity to roll over and look at me. I couldn't really see him completely. It was very dark, yet as I stared, I could make out his face and nose and finally his eyes. There must have been a strong moon, or maybe it was the fact that when your eyes dilate in the dark you can eventually see more, but I could see his expression after a few minutes. He looked serene.

When he noticed I was looking at him as he was looking at me, he stuck out his tongue. When I smiled, he crossed his eyes. Then, when I rolled my eyes and minutely shook my head, he crossed his eyes and stuck out his tongue as he crinkled one side of his face. He was so funny sometimes. I really enjoyed that part of him.

Our relationship might not have gone where I'd have led it, if given the choice, but after the initial angst over learning to live together, and then the whole uncomfortable Bermuda Triangle of uncertainty after the kiss, I was simply glad to joke and laugh with him. He was so cool to laugh with!

Then Rob must have gotten tired of fussing at Russell and given him a shove, because Russell collided with Ellis, and then Ellis was pushed closer to me.

"Get away!" Rob said.

"Gladly," Russell replied.

I didn't say a thing. Neither did Ellis.

Ellis was practically nose to nose with me, lying partially over my body, and all silly expressions vanished from his face. He was suddenly serious. I felt his breath on my chin and noticed how hard he was breathing. I swallowed the lump in my throat and wished the lighting was better to see him by. I loved his eyes, and considering the fact they were, like, an inch and a half from mine, I truly wished I could see the color more.

If this was any indication of what the next few days would be like, I wanted to go camping every weekend.

I DIDN'T know how long we lay there like that—staring at each other in the dead of night—but morning peered over the horizon faster than I deemed possible. I looked around, but Rob and Ellis were gone. Russell was snoring. And I was feeling the hunger pangs of someone in desperate need of coffee and sausages.

I slipped through the tent opening and breathed in a lungful of cool, mountain air. It was crisp and clean and refreshing. Not too bad. I could see smoke rising from the fire across the way, and lots of people already milling around at... clock check: 7:02 in the morning! I spied Ellis wearing his Steelers sweatshirt and smiled to myself.

Yeah, it's time to get up and greet the day, I sighed as I took a fresh pair of socks out of my bag.

I wasn't sure why we even had a fire at our camp, because it was seriously superfluous. This camp across the path, and I forget which family it belonged to, seemed to have everything! Literally. Well, except for maybe the kitchen sink. They had two easy-ups and a table laid out with muffins, hash browns, sausages, bacon, and even doughnuts! The coffee was piping hot and they had three different types of creamer. *What kind of camping is this?* Except for the lack of beds to sleep on, it was like a five-star hotel. I snagged a piece of bacon as I heard someone trotting up behind me.

I turned to find Ellis—cheery as ever—standing there. He grabbed me around the shoulders with one arm and squeezed. "Morning, pal!"

Pal. I guess I could settle for that if nothing else was on the menu.

I lifted my eyebrows and tilted my chin slightly in response. No need for me to be all Pollyanna and pretend to be something I wasn't. He knew I wasn't a morning person. If everyone else needed to be warned, well, I wasn't going to be bothered about that. They'd figure it out soon enough.

Ellis took a Styrofoam plate and piled on some eggs, fresh off the skillet. "You want eggs? Dave makes great eggs!" He pointed to the guy next to the Coleman stove.

"Hi," the guy named Dave (apparently) said with a smile.

(Is it me? Or do all these people just seem too nice? I'm not used to large groups of genuinely nice people. There has to be a catch!)

I replied, "Yeah, I'll take some eggs."

Why fight it? Ellis had a "thing" for breakfast, and if I tried to explain my normal tendency of skipping "the most important meal of the day" he might have a conniption. I didn't want to upset Ellis; not when he wore the most adorable smile on the planet right now. He looked positively tickled. Perhaps coming camping with him really did mean more than he'd let on? He was adding things to my plate left and right. Bacon, potatoes, a muffin, two sausages and some eggs—of course, can't forget the eggs.

When he was done, I just stood there, waiting for him to make eye contact. "What?" he asked with an innocent glint.

My inner snark took over. "Um, are you planning on helping me fulfill my dream of becoming a sumo wrestler? There's no way I can eat all this."

Ellis didn't look offended at all when he beamed back at me. "No, silly. You eat whatever you want. I'll finish the rest. Come on." He turned and motioned for me to follow him to the campfire, where it seemed all the same people from the night before sat. *Did they ever go to bed?* They all had plates balanced on their laps, which was fine for the agile crowd, but not so much for the nimbly challenged, such as myself. (Or Russell, for that matter.)

Ellis sat next to me and put his cup of joe on a rock at the edge of the fire ring. He greeted Lisa and Sandy with a smile as he munched on his eggs and hotcakes. He wasn't talking. And he wasn't looking at me. But the whole time we ate and listened to the little conversations around us, I had the distinct impression his eyes were on me the whole time. And when that guy named Dave, the one who cooked the eggs, mentioned something about a hike later in the morning, Ellis nodded and agreed for us to join them while at the same moment reaching over and stealing a piece of my bacon off my plate without any hesitation at all. Did guys really do that? Did *we* do that? I didn't remember him eating off my plate at the apartment. Separate plates. Separate glasses. Separate everything. And here he just took a slice of bacon out of the blue! What was going on here? I thought only couples did that.

Internally I was flipping out, but on the outside I continued to eat as if nothing was amiss. No need to draw undue attention our way if no one cared to begin with. Ellis *was* a friendly person; perhaps he did this with all his friends? I didn't know. I'd only met a few of them. He kind of did his own thing at home, and what he did with the soccer crowd, I had no clue.

As everyone ate, the guy named Alex came over with his guitar, took a seat, and began to strum. It was nice. Several people must have recognized the tune, as it prompted a spontaneous sing-along among the campers. Ellis included. I'd never heard him sing before—aside from occasional snippets from outside of the bathroom door. He had a deeper voice than I imagined. Baritone. Sexy. I had almost gotten caught up in its melodious allure when a little birdie told me to stop staring.

Thank God for that little birdie!

I shifted my eyes back to the dancing flames and concentrated on all the little things that *didn't* give me an erection: the Gettysburg

Address, my mom's blueberry pie, midterms, Newtonian Mechanics—no, that actually *did* give me a hard-on; point being, I needed to control myself or this day could end badly.

Besides, I didn't know what Ellis was thinking. So he'd kissed me? Once! It didn't mean anything. (Oh, wait, I also kissed him that time after breakfast.) And he liked touching me sometimes—no big deal. Rob and Russell touched all the time! And so last night we shared a "moment"? So what! It didn't imply that anything was going to happen between us.

Moreover, Ellis had said these were church people. Unless they all attended the Unitarian Universalist Church of Love, I was pretty certain they wouldn't appreciate my homosexualness. Some people did, some didn't; but I wasn't in the habit of spewing out personal facts in a church setting. While I was here, I was bound and determined to keep it to myself. If no one was going to stand up and shout, "I'm straight," then I wasn't going to wave my Pride flag.

A SHORT time later, people started cleaning up and discussing possible hike scenarios. True to his word, Ellis cleaned my plate after I had finished. Not a word about it, he just took it from my grasp and gobbled the rest of it down. I swear I don't know where he puts it, because he's built like a brick wall.

Apparently there was a lake nearby with a dam, and the consensus was to check it out. Twelve people were going, which meant only two cars were needed if we crammed. I got stuck in the back next to Tina and Sandy. (I'm always in the back because I'm so skinny.) Ellis opened the door and popped his head in.

"Got room for one more?" he asked.

I tried sliding over to make room but there really wasn't much. Then James from the front seat offered to switch. He jumped out and let Ellis have the passenger seat. James was small. I couldn't blame him for taking pity on Ellis's long legs and wide shoulders. Still, a part of me protested his graciousness on the grounds of jealousy. I coveted that front seat! Not the seat itself, but the idea that Ellis's body was pressed all over it, and not a bit of him was pressed against me! Damn seat.

James was nice-looking but he had nothing on Ellis, so the ride to the lake was bearable. We got out of the sardine can and stretched before deciding on the best trail to take. Rob voted for adventure and chose a trail that went all the way around the lake. Russell tried to point out that there was no way of knowing if the trail extended that far around, but Rob put his foot down and started walking. I guess we were a bunch of lemmings because everyone else followed suit. Good thing there wasn't a cliff in sight!

After about thirty minutes, it started raining. The sound of the rain was peaceful. I could hear it hitting the leaves above with small pit-pats, but the canopy was enough to keep it off my head. No one was discouraged because of the rain; if anything, it brought out the kid in all of us. Rob and Russell chased each other with long sticks, pretending to sword fight. Alex picked up stones along the way and threw them at trees down the trail. Sandy and Lisa picked flowers and found the largest mushroom I'd ever seen. And Ellis? Well, Ellis tended to skip ahead and then drop back and circle around like a border collie herding in the flock. I guess he liked to keep tabs on people or something. He was chatting with everyone.

"How ya doing, buddy?" he asked me a few times.

And after I answered, "Fine," he kept on flitting.

Then we came to a large impasse, and the group stopped cold.

No one sat and scratched their chins, but they might as well have. You could see several of the men working out just *how* they were going to cross the little rivulet that ran across the path. We could see where we needed to go, but the water looked deep and probably very cold.

I knelt down and stuck my finger in. "Oh yes, very cold."

"I figured it would be," Lisa said, standing next to me.

"How are we going to cross, Boy Wonder?" I looked to Rob for the answer. "Do you have a grappling hook inside a gadget on your belt?"

"I wish. Um, I'm working it out." He said it, but the look on his pursed face didn't agree.

"Look!" Russell pointed. "We can step across on that row of rocks."

Ellis, who'd slipped in beside me quietly, commented, "They look slippery, and there aren't enough to make it all the way across without getting wet."

I looked at Ellis, he looked at me, and then we both studied the water's edge.

"I'm going to look farther up," said James, trotting off.

Our group scattered, and when I wasn't paying attention, there stood Lisa on the opposite side. "Wait... how did you get over there?" I called across.

She smiled and held up a pair of shoes and socks. "I took my shoes off."

I felt a cold shiver travel up my legs from the mere thought of walking through the water. She apparently had! I could see her pink little feet as she dried them off with her socks and then put her shoes back on. Then Rob stood on the opposite bank, holding Sandy on his back. Russell walked up behind him holding James. Each rider hopped off their taxi and waved across to those of us still wondering how we were going to cross.

Alex and that Dave guy stepped across on those slippery rocks Russell had pointed out earlier but hadn't utilized on his own. Their feet were a little wet, but they made it. I figured I'd give it a go, too, but Ellis grabbed my elbow.

"What?" I asked.

"You aren't going to try that, are you? It's slippery." Ellis objected.

"And you ask because you have a better suggestion?"

"Up there," he said, gesturing. "A bunch of the others went across those rocks and made out better than Alex and Dave. You don't want cold feet, do you?"

"No, but that spot is just as sketchy as this one. I'll be fine." I proceeded to grab hold of a branch and steady myself as I tentatively toed the first slime-covered rock in the water.

Then Rob scowled and chastised Ellis by saying, "Dude, are you seriously allowing Cole to walk across that! Have you seen him walk? He makes *me* look elegant."

I grinned in a way that said "bite me," but I answered as politely as I could. "Thanks, Rob. Appreciate it, man."

"I'm just being honest. I don't want you falling in and trudging your soggy self up the trail to *my* car. And did I tell you, El, about the other day? I saw Cole literally fall *up* the steps. I mean, who does that? *Up* steps. I mean, really." He held his hands out to the sides and shook his head. His bewildered expression even made *me* snicker, and the whole thing was *about* me.

"Then what do you suggest?" Ellis asked.

"Carry him. Like Russ did James. You have Gore-Tex boots on, your feet will be fine."

"You can't be serious," I said, looking at Rob and then back to Ellis. The thought of wrapping my legs around Ellis was too much. There was no way I was going to let him carry me. I didn't give him the chance. I quickly stepped out onto the first rock and wobbled onto the second. I nearly got to the forth before I felt cold water on my toes.

"Ellis, it figures—he's just as pigheaded as you!"

I heard Ellis chuckle behind me.

I made it over and turned around to see Ellis following the same path. After he stepped ashore, I pointed at my Converse All Stars. "See, only one got a tad wet."

Ellis grinned. "I thought a 'tad' was half a million miles in space terms?"

I scrunched up one eye and stuck out my tongue. Ellis laughed even more. But then… so did I.

BACK at camp, we stood around the fire again. By now it was pouring. Water was coming down in buckets, but no one seemed bothered at all. There were about twenty people huddled around the fire, singing and roasting marshmallows. Everyone was so wet that steam rose off our jackets and our hair stuck to our faces. I stood there thinking this was about the best camping trip I'd ever taken.

Then Rob starts up a new song that required gestures. *Gestures, good grief!* "Repeat after me, and move like I move," he instructed. "I have a piece of cookie dough." He held out his hand like it really had dough in it.

Everyone repeated, "I have a piece of cookie dough." (Complete with hand gestures.)

"I put it in my pocket." Rob put his hand in his pocket and waited for everyone to do the same.

The little song went on for about twenty minutes. The cookie dough—evidently—had the growing power of a test-tube science project gone wrong. It grew to humungous proportions and stuck to everything in sight. People around the fire were hopping on one leg pretending their hands were stuck to their ankles. Everyone was laughing, even me. It was simply hilarious to watch everyone joining in, no matter how ludicrous the action. Rob was undeniably a showman and a leader and knew how to work a crowd. He had everyone forgetting about the pouring rain. I almost didn't want the night to end.

But then it did, and we plodded back over to our camp and the dark, cold tent.

When I returned from the bathhouse after brushing my teeth, I noticed the sleeping bags had been rearranged. It appeared that Rob didn't want Russell sleeping next to him, so he took the opportunity in Ellis's absence to move Ellis in between them. I felt a twinge of disappointment, but it was no big deal. It was dark and we were going to be sleeping! I crawled in and got myself comfy and waited for Ellis's reaction.

"Oh no, no, no. We're not playing musical sleeping bags," he said.

Rob explained his side of the story. "I'm not sleeping next to him. He snores."

Ellis cocked his head. "Dude, we're in a tent. The snoring doesn't magically disappear if he's on the other side of me!"

"Well, it won't be in my ear!"

"I'm not happy about this, but whatever." Ellis made his way in and zipped up the flap of the tent. I watched him shimmy his body into the sleeping bag and adjust his pillow before lying flat and therefore disappearing from my view. "Good night, Cole." His voice drifted to my ears.

I smiled. "Good night, Ellis."

"Good night, John-Boy," Rob said. My smile grew wider.

Russell replied, "Good night, Sue Ellen."

"It's *Mary* Ellen," Rob corrected Russell.

"Really? I thought it was Sue Ellen?" The flashlight flickered across the top of the tent.

"No. You're getting *The Waltons* confused with *Seinfeld*."

"No, I'm not!" Russell lifted up and leaned over Ellis's body, pointing his flashlight at Rob. "They are totally different shows. Why on earth would I get them confused?"

"Because you're a deranged and confused person. Now turn that thing off and go to sleep."

Russell plopped back down and turned off his light. Quiet. Nothing. Then, seconds later, I heard him ask in the darkness, "So… who were the other Walton children?"

"Go to sleep, Russ," Ellis mumbled.

"I can't," he whined. "Rob, sing me a song?"

Ellis protested, "You better not."

I know I shouldn't have been amused by their antics but I was. In fact, the interaction between them was growing on me like the comfort of my favorite slippers. Rob chuckled softly and began singing, despite Ellis's warning. "All right, you chipmunks. Ready to sing your song?"

Russell quickly responded, "I'll say we are!"

Ellis's deep groans of disapproval rumbled through the air, adding to my secret enjoyment.

"Okay, Russell?" Rob asked, substituting Russell for a chipmunk. (Which I thought was humorous.) Russell could be a chipmunk. I could picture him scurrying around looking for acorns and foraging in the underbrush with all his energy.

"Okay!"

"Okay, Cole?"

"Um, I'll pass," I answered politely.

"Okay, Ellis?"

"Go to sleep, Rob," Ellis grumbled.

"Ellis?" Pause. "*Ellis!*"

"I said no!" Ellis was growly tonight, wasn't he? I felt movement and heard the sleeping bag fabric again. I turned my head and saw Ellis's cocoon lift up and roll over. (My eyes were adjusting nicely to the darkness.)

Rob was not bothered by Ellis's mood. "Not a fan of the 'Chipmunk Song', eh?" he quipped. "I could sing Bob and Doug McKenzie's version of 'The Twelve Days of Christmas'."

"Please don't," Ellis moaned. "It's practically October, for Pete's sake!"

Russell piped in singing, "Four pounds of back bacon, three French toasts, two turtlenecks, and a beer...." He leaned his body over Ellis. On the last line, Rob joined him. "...in a tree!" They stopped, and Russell asked, "How does the beer stay in the tree? Wouldn't it fall out?"

Ellis's irritation got louder, although muffled from his position of lying facedown with Russell's body draped over him. "Stooop. Go. To. Sleep."

Rob and Russell ignored him. "I don't know. I guess you could tie a string around it."

Ellis lifted his head. "This is worse than singing. Russ, get off me." He wiggled around.

"Oh, so you want more singing?" Russell asked rhetorically.

"Oooh, how about some Bob Rivers?" Rob chirped, full of excitement.

Russell laughed, still leaning over Ellis, still ignoring his wiggling and whining. He crooned leisurely, "Lacy things, the wife is missing…."

Rob chimed in and sang the next line, "Didn't ask for her permission…."

They alternated lines until they got to the chorus and then harmonized together, singing, "Walking Around In Woman's Underwear," which was also the song's title.

I started laughing. I remembered hearing the twisted tune played over the college radio one Christmas, but it was even funnier now hearing the guys' rendition. I think the song was about a cross-dresser or something, and when Rob sang the line about "handcuffs at night," I about died. I couldn't control the quaking of my body. I think I even snorted. These guys were so bad!

Ellis was not amused. "Rob, quit it. Russ, get off!"

Russell lay back down and continued singing.

"Stop singing in my ear, Russ," Ellis griped. I wasn't sure why he was in such a bad mood. Earlier he was just fine—laughing and joking. What changed?

The song didn't bother me, and I was the gay one of the bunch. They were just being Russell and Rob. Goofballs. If I didn't care why should he?

Russell proposed a solution. "If you don't like it, switch spots with me. I'd rather sleep next to Rob anyway. Cole is too quiet and you're too grouchy."

"And how do you suggest I do that? I can hardly move in here!" Ellis growled.

"Roll over me, you grumpy grizzly."

"What?"

"You heard me. You're in a sleeping bag. Pretend you're a log and roll over my body. I'll roll in the opposite direction and we'll switch spots."

Seems logical to me.

I heard some grunting and watched the darkened shapes lift and twist. Ellis wormed his way over Russell and rolled down as if off the side of a steep hill. All the way into me! Suddenly, we were nose to nose again, but this time I had a hard time believing it was purely accidental despite it being Russell's idea and the difficulties of maneuvering in a bag.

I heard Russell and Rob faintly as they quietly sang together. "Have yourself a merry little Christmas." It was lovely. They really did harmonize well together.

But no matter the pleasant air the singing gave to the night, I was distracted by Ellis's proximity and aroma. I kept my eyes squeezed shut and pretended to be asleep.

His breath smelled cinnaminty, and my mouth watered involuntarily. This was so not fair. If he knew how hard this was for me, he would never have invited me along. His mouth was scant inches from mine, his breath drifting over my face, and his body was practically touching every part of mine. Sure, there were layers of Thinsulate and polyester in between, but I could still feel his weight on me.

Why didn't he make a move to slide off?

Minutes passed and yet there he lay. The singing duo quieted down, and a little while later I heard Russell snoring as usual. I didn't dare move. I loved his weight on me, but I didn't understand. What was going on? Ellis knew I was gay. Why would he be so cruel as to lie on top of me? Didn't he know how turned on I'd be? Not that simply having a *guy* lie on top of me assured anything, but this was Ellis. Ellis! The guy who kissed me. Ellis! The sexy soccer player who invaded my dreams every night to press my naked body against the wall as he….

I swallowed hard. I was seriously seconds from a panic attack. I needed to calm down and think logically. *Breathe, breathe.* Maybe Ellis really didn't know what he was doing to me. Russell was just lying all over him and he didn't seem to care too much. The three of them were always wrestling in the living room and carrying on like crazies. They were touchy people. I just wasn't used to it, that was all. I came from a family of nonhuggers. The cramped sleeping arrangement would end in the morning. I could handle it.

Oh God, no, I can't.

Just when I thought I couldn't take another second of this titillating torture, Ellis shifted his body weight, and I involuntarily popped open my eyes. I caught a glimpse of Ellis's eyes shutting as he leaned in the rest of the way and touched his lips to mine. I couldn't believe it, and I almost jumped back in shock. (I know I flinched as I sucked air in through my nose.) However, my brain is often overridden by my libido, and I found myself kissing him back without a conscious decision to do so.

Kissing Ellis! It was wonderful.

Unlike before, when he kissed me on the couch and then pulled away and began a week's worth of bizarre mood swings, this time I could feel his tongue flicking in and out, licking me as he claimed each soft kiss. These were restrained kisses, I could tell. After all, his friends were sleeping right there, and we couldn't risk getting caught. I let him run the show and enjoyed every second. I was somewhat surprised by his boldness when he widened his lips and probed mine for entrance, but I didn't resist one iota. I was willing give him whatever he asked for.

And the feel of his tongue gliding over mine was heavenly.

Then he pressed closer to me, meshing his lips firmly to mine and fully engaging in an exploration of the contours of my mouth and throat. I could feel his foot rubbing my leg through the sleeping bag, and I had to remind myself not to groan for fear of being overheard.

I faintly heard a zipper before his hand—warm and toasty—cupped my jaw. Oh God! I wanted him so bad, but if I didn't keep reciting the lyrics to the national anthem in my head, I was going to start moaning into his mouth and pull his body completely over mine.

Ellis tasted so good.

Oh shit! I think he just thrust his pelvis into mine. No, no, no, this is not happening. I could feel small movements. This was turning into a nightmare. I could feel my throbbing groin taking notice and desiring to thrust back. *No, no, no! I can't do this quietly. I can't do this at all. I don't want to grind against him until I spurt, I want to roll him over and rip his clothes off!*

Ellis must have felt my tension. (Perhaps through my hesitance.) He slowly withdrew his tongue from my mouth and kissed me a few more time before leaning back. I could barely breathe as I looked into his eyes. He stared at me. What was that look? Longing? Desire? Confusion? Hard to tell in near darkness. Just when I opened my mouth to whisper a question, Ellis rolled off me.

He lay there very still.

Then Russell snorted really loud and woke Rob up. "Russ!" I heard rustling and then all was quiet again.

I closed my eyes and hoped I would dream all night of that kiss we'd just shared.

Chapter 7
Where We Left Off

GETTING back to the apartment was *loud*. I swear I thought camping was supposed to be relaxing and all naturesque—this was anything but. Between the rain and the rain and the—oh yeah, more rain—I thought I would have gills by now. Still, looking into Ellis's eyes was awfully nice. And the feel of his lips and tongue was a definite plus! If given a choice, I'd go camping again.

I guess my main complaint was the car ride, with five other guys who hadn't showered all weekend crammed in Russell's mom's Pilot. Add in all the wet gear, and the smell was noxious. I don't know who started the singing, but somehow they made their way around to Christmas songs and by the time we pulled into the college, I never wanted to hear "Silver Bells" again!

The volume followed me up to my apartment, because of course they couldn't remain in the car *or* go home to their own residences. The lunatics had to sing and joke and act all *happy*. I was getting tired of happy. I was on happy overload. Where was a nice cynic full of gloom and doom when you needed one? Oh, that would be me. Except, I wasn't feeling very cynical. I was feeling… placid.

I'd say it was inexplicable, but I knew exactly why I felt like that—Ellis! The whole ride home, memories of his lips against mine blocked my normal tendency to complain. I lost interest in griping about the seasonal discrepancy of song selections and went with the flow. They probably forgot I was even in the car because I was oddly quiet. Ellis was in the front seat and I stole glances at him as often as I dared. God, he was so hot, but I'd be a fool to think anything would develop between us. I was *so* not in his league even if he wasn't straight.

So when all the guys finally exhausted their stay and decided to head out, I wasn't expecting anything more from Ellis. What had happened between us must have been a dream, right?

I was standing by the dryer, folding my shirt, when Ellis walked up beside me.

It was late, but I wanted to fold the last of pieces laundry I'd done because then my shirts wouldn't wrinkle overnight. He leaned on the washer and folded his arms across his chest. He was fresh out of the shower, all wet hair and soapy scent. I suppressed the desire to breathe in a lungful of "Ellisness."

"So… fun weekend." Leave it to Ellis to keep the conversation brief.

"Yeah… and wet," I countered. After placing my folded shirt on the pile, I grabbed some socks.

Ellis stood there, awkwardly silent, slightly nodding as if he was thinking of what to say but hadn't figured it out yet. "So… you like my friends?"

I placed my socks on the pile. "Yeah, but I told you I liked them before we went. I wouldn't have agreed to go camping all weekend if I hated your friends."

"Ah! But you weren't familiar with the entire experience of being with them for days, let alone all those other people. And you lived!"

I rolled my eyes and grinned. "Barely," I halfheartedly grumbled.

Ellis smiled back.

Damn, that smile. It got me every time. It was casual and genuine and made his eyes light up in ways that stuck with me for hours after he'd gone to class. I couldn't take much more of that smile making me hard. Ellis needed to make a move on me, or move out, because living in limbo was no longer an option.

"So… do you want to play Xbox? I got a new game—FIFA Street Soccer."

I could tell he was fishing for an activity. That was a good sign. At least he wasn't disappearing into his room and acting strange, like the first time we kissed. Only, Xbox wasn't the activity I had in mind. I shook my head.

"A puzzle? You like puzzles."

Okay, now he was grasping. "Ellis, you're trying too hard," I said as I shut the dryer and faced him. *Here it goes—I'm making a move. It's now or never, but not knowing might give me a stroke.* Suddenly, I was glad I'd grabbed a shower while the guys were reliving stories of the weekend, because I was sure my pits were sweating. Nervously I broached, "Ellis, can we... do you want to... pick up where we left off?"

He shoved against the washer and practically jumped in my direction, eyes all wide with anticipation. "Yeah, sure!" he said. Then he eased back, as if rethinking his initial reaction. "I mean, if you want to."

"Ellis, it was *my* idea."

"Oh yeah." His voice was soft; he lowered his eyes, gazing at my chest. He looked as if he wasn't sure where to begin as he tentatively lifted a hand and traced my collarbone with his fingers. As soon as his eyes met mine, they glazed over in a lustful sort of way, and he leaned in the rest of the way.

His kiss was strong and sweet as he gripped my shoulders and stepped into my body. It wasn't until I opened my mouth and licked his lips that he let go of the hesitance that kept him from fully engaging in whatever activities were playing in his imagination. As soon as our tongues touched, he let out a heady grunt of desire and wrapped his arms tightly around my back.

This kiss was not the tentative exploration I took part in as we lay in the dark of night half freezing over the weekend. Oh no! This was all need and want, and finally having the fortitude to give in and take without restraint. I felt his erection against mine for the first time as his body molded against me. My jeans and his sweatpants not withstanding, it felt promising. At least kissing me turned him on, so my wonder over his sexuality had hope. I felt him rock his hips as he started a slow grind, pulling me tighter to him and then sliding one hand up the back of my shirt while he squeezed my butt with the other.

He reluctantly pulled away, sucking on my lip before letting me go, and then slipped my shirt over my head. I removed my glasses and placed them on my pile of laundry and then turned back to face him.

Ellis was staring at my chest.

Why? I'm not sure. I know for a fact I lack his definition, and the sparse amount of hair attempting to grow on my skin was far from sexy. Still, he studied me. He lifted his hand and circled my left nipple with his thumb. He pinched me gently, and I gasped, enjoying the sensation. He looked into my eyes briefly before placing his other hand over my right pec and thumbing my nipple. He dipped his head and licked me there. He swirled his tongue around my now fully erect nipple, and his teeth grazed me just to the edge of pain.

My dick pulsed.

I stepped back and his eyes questioned my reaction.

"Come on," I prompted, taking his hand and then leading him into my room.

Ellis stood there watching me as I removed my jeans. Either he got off on watching guys strip, or he was nervous to follow suit. I stepped closer and lifted the hem of his shirt. "May I?" I asked.

Jolted from a dreamlike state, he nodded and answered, "Oh yeah, sure, of course."

Once shirtless, I ran my hand over the hair on his chest and trailed my fingers down to his waistband. I watched his eyes in the dim light of the room, waiting for fear to flash by, before I slid my palm down over the massive rod that strained to rip the fabric. When the fear didn't come, I touched him. Instantly he closed his eyes and gasped. He shuddered as I stroked him. His panting reminded me he was not as experienced like I was. He wasn't used to being touched by anyone, let alone a man. I needed to ask what he wanted to do. I might not be the authority on gay sex in America, but I wasn't going to force a newbie to do something he wasn't absolutely ready for!

I let go and asked, "Ellis, what exactly do you want to do tonight?"

He looked at me with that same nervousness he'd had for the past twenty minutes. "I, um, I don't know... stuff." Timid stammering wasn't convincing me he was ready for intercourse.

I took a stab at what I assumed he was too prideful to admit. "You aren't ready for sex, are you?"

He looked at the bed and then shifted his gaze to the floor. In an almost imperceptible voice, he replied, "No.... Maybe.... I don't know."

Oh fuck! was my initial thought. I'd never considered myself a take-the-lead type of guy. Virgins, I could handle, as long as it was a mutual desire and the prospective partner was most definitely gay. Ellis? I wasn't so sure *he* was sure he was gay. I'd only heard him talk about girls. I'd only seen him out with girls. (Well, the girls on the camping trip.) If this was an experiment on his part, it could totally screw up our friendship. *That* I wasn't about to risk for a fuck.

I remembered my first time none too fondly as the misadventure of a naïve eighteen-year-old "looking for love" in all the wrong places. First sex in the front seat of a Ford Escort, while parked in a graveyard in the middle of the night, was *not* romantic. We didn't talk. It was purely sexual, and I don't remember his name. What I remember was my ass hurting so bad I thought he tore my colon. I wanted to protect Ellis from a bad experience at all cost!

"Ellis, we don't have to do anything you're unsure of. I like kissing you, and as far as I'm concerned, we could lay here and kiss all night if that's all you're comfortable with."

"No," he said, gliding his strong hands over my shoulders and then gripping my virtually nonexistent biceps. "I want to... do stuff... with you. I can't stop thinking about you." He stepped closer, and then the bare skin of my stomach was touching his. *Oh*

God, it feels so good! He explained, "I lay awake at night thinking about sneaking in here and touching you." He swallowed hard, and I heard myself whimper as he wrapped his arms around me, holding me tight. "I don't know *exactly* what to do, but I know I want to try. Being around you...." He paused and kissed me. "Being around you makes me...." Ellis paused again to kiss my neck. "You make me so fucking hard." He nipped my neck and squeezed my ass with both hands. "I want you, Cole."

He sounded desperate, almost pleading. How could I deny him when he'd practically begged for this? His statement—as well as his tongue in my ear—was all the confirmation my body needed. Testosterone flared and I pressed against him, rocking my groin into his. Ellis moaned and backed me toward the bed. We fell onto it, and he roamed over me with his hand, exploring my chest, stomach, and groin. He rubbed me through the fabric of my boxer briefs as I groaned into his mouth.

After several minutes of kissing and touching and holding each other, Ellis eased back, and I watched as he stood up and pushed his sweats and briefs down his muscular thighs. His cock bounced free. It was so magnificent that I had to remind myself not to drool! I practically had to tear my eyes away as he crawled back over me. If he noticed my stunned and awed expression, he didn't say, he merely tugged on my underwear and assisted me out of my last shred of clothing. Then, without hesitation, he lined his body up against mine and pressed his manhood against my hip as he kissed me again.

After a while, it became apparent that Ellis was unsure of the next move. He rocked into me a little, but not enough to come. He kissed me leisurely and touched me affectionately from my thighs and groin up to my nipples and neck, yet his groping lacked the desperation of a man who wanted to fuck. Ellis wasn't frantic; he was gentle. Even as he licked down my neck and playfully swirled his tongue around my nipple, I could tell he was hesitating. That was when a little voice inside my head suggested I take the lead, no matter how unnatural it felt to do so.

I nudged Ellis onto his back and maneuvered my way on top of him, straddling his thighs and kissing him ruthlessly to ramp his expectations. He slid his hands over my back like a blind man reading Braille—memorizing me. I'd never felt so treasured as I did with Ellis. Here I was trying to amp up the sex so we'd actually get to the fucking before morning, and Ellis was caressing my skin and massaging all my parts as though I would vanish any second. I hesitated to push him for more. It felt so nice to be touched like this. Maybe this was what true foreplay was for? Or maybe I was so used to random sex that I'd missed out on what it was like to be with someone you cared about?

I was contemplating the possibilities when his fingers grazed my entrance. A tingle shot through me. That was the signal—I wanted to fuck and I was damn near the breaking point. I took his dick in my hand and started stroking. Ellis's gentle touch turned to vise grips that squeezed my ribs. He was writhing beneath me, moaning and panting as I wiggled lower. I lined my mouth up with his throbbing crown and licked the precome from his slit. I'd never seen someone come so unglued by the slightest of touches. Ellis was practically screaming by the time I sucked him down. *What would he do when he came?*

But he wasn't going to, not yet.

I sucked up and down his beautiful erection for several minutes, and then used my hand when I needed to breathe. I had to restrain myself from laughing as I watched his expression. His lips quaked and his eyes moved back and forth under his closed lids. He shook a few times and held his breath. I could be torturing him if I went by the little whimpers and slight cries escaping his larynx. He gripped the sheets and tilted his hips; it was exhilarating to know I'd made him like this.

When I let go, his eyes flew open.

I wiggled my way back up to his lips and grinned. "Just checking. I was beginning to wonder if you were capable of any other sounds." I fingered through his layered hair and looked deeply into his heat-filled eyes.

Ellis growled in response and rolled me onto my back. He came over me aggressively this time, pinning my arms above my head as he sucked on my neck. I felt the sting; I knew he'd left a mark and that knowledge pleased me more than I had words to express. He kissed his way down my chest and licked my throbbing penis from my balls to my tip. No hesitance there. Maybe he was dominant after all, or maybe it was to prove a point? Either way, he grabbed me at the base and pulled me to his lips.

I watched as he closed his eyes and went down.

It was my turn to moan, and moan I did! I hadn't been sucked in ages. *Remembering* how it feels to get a blowjob and actually *receiving* one are two different things. There was nothing like having a hot, wet mouth engulf the most sensitive part of your body to make every trace of the world disappear and every nerve you possessed dance in ecstasy. That was, until teeth scraped against said nerves and the ecstasy screeched to a halt!

"Ah!" I winced. "Easy there, killer. If you bite it off, there won't be anything left for later."

Ellis let go and repositioned himself next to me. "I'm going to choose to ignore how unnecessary that comment was." His hurt came across loud and clear.

Instead of shrinking away from embarrassment, Ellis kissed me. I knew I didn't deserve such a warm, gentle kiss in light of the biting (literally) remark I gave him. I felt horrible. When he released my lips, I whispered, "I'm sorry."

He didn't answer verbally, but pulled me close so that we were positioned on our sides, erections lined up and rubbing together nicely.

I had to give him credit. I think I would have called it quits if a guy I was with said what I just said to me. I needed to do something, something nice; something unexpectedly stimulating that would let Ellis know how wrong I felt for chastising his first attempt at sucking a dick.

I started my nonverbal apology by cupping his balls—he sighed.

As he relaxed onto his back, I scooted down his body and nestled myself between his legs. I know he was probably thinking

I'd suck his dick again, but there are more ways than one to get a guy off. Testicles are extremely sensitive and often overlooked. *Ellis has a nice set of balls*, I thought as I nuzzled his sac with my nose. I kind of liked the fact that they were hairy. From my experience, gay guys kept things clean and shaven because they knew what to expect when having sex. They anticipated mouths and tongues slipping and sliding in places where hair grew and wasn't always appreciated. Sucking on Ellis's hairy ballsac reminded me that no other guy had been here. I was his first. Little ol' me and my predisposition to blurt out inappropriate comments during Ellis's introduction to Gay Sex 101.

This needed to be good!

I took his testicles into my mouth and rolled each one around with my tongue. Ellis groaned my name, giving me an unexpected thrill. *He groaned my name!* I pushed his legs wider, and he bent his knees on cue, opening himself to me willingly. I caressed his ass as I suckled him and then grazed his entrance with my thumb. Ellis jerked, groaning some more.

Licking as I was, and slobbering all over his private areas, gave me more ideas how to please him. Besides the sensitivity of his scrotum, I knew Ellis would also enjoy a good rim job! Granted, I'd never actually done it before, but how hard could it be to eat a guy's ass?

I sat up and grabbed a pillow. "Here, let me put this under your hips," I instructed.

Ellis didn't question me. In fact, the glazed expression of hormonal intoxication that exuded from his eyes was more than enough to convince me he was enjoying himself. Without delay, Ellis allowed me to elevate his hips, and he unquestionably exposed himself by pulling his knees toward his shoulders.

Casually, I resumed my slippery treatment of his scrotum before inching my way down. I licked and sucked and then released his balls, flicking my tongue around the skin underneath. I jutted the tip of my tongue down further and tickled my intended target. Ellis gasped, and the pink pucker before my eyes eased open a smidgen. I licked again, and Ellis cooed—fucking cooed!—as his sphincter relaxed. Right then I let loose and teased his hole with my tongue for as long as humanly possible.

I couldn't believe I was doing this. I'd never done something so intimate. Sure, fucking could be considered intimate, but there was also a huge detachment quality to it if you closed your eyes and imagined something else. (Like getting fucked in a parking lot and imagining it was a hot actor, or even wanking off in bed with your roommate in mind.) I tongued Ellis and felt more turned on than any other time in my life.

I sucked and I probed, but as I did so, my own body reminded me that holding back was damn near impossible. *I need to penetrate him.* The thought stunned me. Me. I, Cole Reid, was about to fuck my friend. Would I be good enough? Could I sink into him deep enough? I wasn't exactly endowed. I *did* fuck that one guy that one time and he hadn't complained, but I didn't want to be bad for Ellis.

One step at a time, Cole. One step at a time.

First I had to prepare him. That would be the courteous thing to do. Sucking his cock was the best distraction I could think of while preparing him for entry so I positioned myself and pulled him into my mouth. I took my time conducting oral sex as I let my saliva drip from the corner of my mouth and coat my fingers. This had to be perfect for him! On second thought, lube was way better. I moved fast to snag the bottle from my drawer before Ellis questioned why I stopped. Saliva is good, it's fine, but lube is slippery and designed not to dry up quickly. Ellis deserved a smooth experience for his first penetration.

I coated my fingers and rubbed them over his pulsing ring of muscle and hoped I wasn't pushing my luck as I forced one finger inside. As he tensed up, I sucked extra hard on his crown and swirled my tongue along the ridge. That seemed to work. His hips rested once again on the mattress, but I *did* notice him fist the sheets as I pumped and twisted my finger.

"Cooole...." My name came out as a desperate plea to stop— or maybe keep going, I wasn't sure. I twisted my finger again, and he repeated, "Cooole." Maybe two fingers would tell me for sure if this pursuit was welcome or not? "Ahhh," he cried, squeezing his sphincter as tight as it possibly could get with two fingers inside.

I let his shaft slide from my lips and pumped it slowly with my fist. "Ellis, relax," I said. "I won't hurt you."

He was breathing hard, but he succeeded in relaxing enough to allow my fingers room to move. This was my last chance. I needed him to feel that last known secret among gay men; the one that straight men never understood and therefore taunted us foolishly by calling us butt-fuckers. Of course we were butt-fuckers! Do you know how incredible it feels to get your butt fucked? No! You're straight.

I curled my fingers and searched out that one spot that gave gay men the edge in pleasure-educing positions. Ellis's hips buckled. "Cole!" His cry hit soprano. *Bingo! He's not going to struggle against this sensation now!*

I brushed over his prostate again, and he panted, "More."

I pumped and twisted my fingers before inserting a third, hearing his grunt of surprise as I gave his sweet spot another nudge. He rewarded my efforts by touching my hair and rasping, "Oh God, Cole, that feels so good."

I was done. I'd prepped him as best I could, but I'd be damned if I was going to wait any longer. I needed release so bad and I didn't want the explosion to happen all over my bed—it was going to be inside of Ellis! I grabbed a condom out of the nightstand as Ellis watched me. He let go of his knees and tenderly held my waist.

I positioned myself and looked into his eyes before pressing in. I could feel him shaking beneath me. I saw anxiety in his face, but not fear. I rested my weight on him and kissed his mouth as I slowly breached his opening. He quivered and cried out.

I searched his eyes as he panted. "Are you okay? Do you want me to stop?"

"No. Just give… me a second." Ellis closed his eyes and seemed to will away the pain.

I complied, not so happily. Holding still as his ass gripped my throbbing penis was not optimum pleasure for me. It was like holding a chocolate bar between your lips and not being allowed to eat it. Oh, man, I wanted to devour it!

When he opened eyes again, he urged, "Go ahead, move. I want to feel you move." So move I did. Slowly, of course—I didn't want to scare the shit out of him any more than I already had. I pumped in and out several times before picking up the pace. He lifted his legs and locked them around my waist, and I swiveled my hips.

Ellis cried in a pitch that only dogs could hear, and I knew things would go smoother from there on out—no way he was going to fight that. He thrust his hips up to meet mine and tugged me down for a bruising kiss. I hammered in and out, harder and harder, until we were both moaning from release. I couldn't believe my own aggression as I fucked him. It scared me. I was an animal, and yet Ellis took every bit of it! He gripped my ribs, leaving his fingerprints as permanent tattoos, and groaned so loud I swore the police would be showing up any second to cite us for disturbing the peace.

Spent, I sprawled on top of his heaving body and felt the wetness between us. Sticky and delicious. I'd made him come so hard it felt like a pool of lava oozing from where our skin connected. I hated pulling out. I wanted to lie there for hours feeling him all around me, smelling the musky thickness of sex in the air, and listening to his steady breathing. I knew I couldn't.

For one thing, a condom dried to my genitals was about the least appealing thing I could wish for after sex. Another was the uncertainty of knowing whether he would stay and snuggle or grab his things and go. When I returned from the bathroom with a towel, my answer was given to me. Ellis was asleep. This was *my* bed. I had every right to remain in my own bed! If he wanted to leave, he was free to. I wiped the wetness off his abdomen and retrieved the extra blanket from the closet.

As I turned out the light and settled against my pillow, Ellis rolled over and snuggled against my back. He pulled me close, and I felt his breath in my ear. I swear he sighed in a way that melted my heart.

Then the unthinkable occurred. Somewhere between after-climax euphoria and ejaculation-enduced sleep, Ellis whispered in my ear, "I love you, Cole." My eyes snapped open in the dark.

"What did you just say?" I asked none too politely.

Ellis didn't say anything else. He hugged me and murmured nonsensical things. That was when I knew the morning was going to prove interesting.

Chapter 7.5
Ancient History

I'VE never been one to enjoy the "life of Riley," as they say. As far as I am concerned, my life has been an uphill battle in an ice storm with no crampons. Nothing goes right for me—at least not without effort. When I came out to my parents, it was a forced event. I wasn't ready to admit my sexuality, but that option died the moment I was caught ogling Brad Foley's ass. Since then, it seemed like I never had it easy.

My dad didn't talk to me for a long time. He used to take me on "garden tours," as he called them and spout Latin names for plants and pick up bugs for me to identify with our insect encyclopedia. After I was a known homosexual, there was a three-year gap in our father-son outings. Thankfully, the silence ended, but to this day I am unsure what changed.

My mom and I have never been very close. We talk, and I guess the communication is about the same as it always was, but she favored my older sister. That's just the way it was.

I hear there are families that are affectionate by nature, but that wasn't mine. We didn't hug. And we didn't talk about our feelings. I learned early on to suck it up and take things like a man. Of course, as I got older, that cliché got harder and harder to understand. I wanted affection. I longed for a hug now and then when I fell and scraped my knee, but that wasn't acceptable in the family I had. We didn't cry over cuts and bruises! At least not out in the open.

I remember running to my room and hiding in the corner between the bed and the wall, crying until the pain went away. I'd pretend my mom came in to smooth my hair out of my eyes and kiss my nose. She'd tell me, "You'll live." But it was all in my imagination.

Don't get me wrong, I love my family, and we *did* have fun together. We camped when I was little (like I mentioned before) and went crabbing on the Chesapeake Bay. My dad taught me how to clean fish, and my mom taught me how to cook. (Although, when I moved out and asked how to cook hotdogs, I thought she'd die from laughter. I'll never live that one down!) We were a good, normal family, I guess, with the exception of those few years during high school.

After high school, life got worse.

I had to get a job. I worked at Giant Food for four whole weeks before my mother decided I needed to go to college "stress free." That was a joke. She thought that giving me money would be easier on me so that I'd keep a four-point-oh and land a high-paying job when I graduated. *Thanks Mom, I appreciate that.* Not having to work was nice, but it didn't make everything easy. My grades were not hard to maintain; it was having extra time on my hands that I didn't need. If I had a job, I wouldn't have time to worry and obsess over my personal life.

The one I didn't have.

I tried talking to people on campus, but they looked at me like I was a nerdy freak. (Which I suppose I am.) I didn't really have great social skills given my nonaffectionate family, and the fact that I am gay and was basically shunned from the age of fifteen. I'd never had close friends; my best friend was always my dad.

(Which is why I am socially awkward after he ignored me for a couple years. Maybe I need to talk to a professional about that? It could *not* have been beneficial to my emotional development. *Hmm.*)

I'm convinced that meeting Jonathan was a fluke. I mean, he's, like, awesome, and I didn't have to work for his friendship at all. It just fell together! Things like that don't just happen, at least not to me! Still, our friendship came on fast and strong, like a summer storm, only it didn't die out as fast as it came. It endured for three years.

During that time, I developed a small crush on Jonathan. He knew about it. He laughed about it. And he helped formulate a game-plan of communal discourse that would lead to relational bliss. At least that was the plan.

My disastrous date to the cemetery, he had no control over, but date number two? He could not contemplate the reason for failure.

"*SERIOUSLY?*" *Jonathan questioned shrilly.*

"*Seriously,*" *I replied for the second time, without a hint of sarcasm or humor to my tone. "You better not ask me that again.*"

"*But... guys really do that?*" *he asked, flummoxed by the activities of men in America, as though being gay made them so different from straight guys.*

I flopped back on his bed after closing the door behind me. The noise from the other boys in the house was deafening. I was glad we were comfortable enough around each other not to have to "pretend" for the sake of appearances. Do you get my drift? He was fine if I was in his room with the door closed and others were in the house. He didn't care if they said something about his sexuality. He was secure enough to know he liked women. And he was also secure enough to know he could be near me in a comfortable, lay-on-my-bed type of way and know I wasn't going to make a move on him.

I wasn't stupid. I'd acquired some *self-control. I could be near him and not think thoughts that made me get hard and sweaty.*

"*What can I say? Some guys are pigs,*" *I admitted with a sigh.*

"*Well, yeah, but he didn't seem like that to me when we met him,*" *Jonathan replied. He crossed his outstretched legs and just about kicked me in the head. He was leaning up against his headboard, and I was at the foot of the bed with my legs hanging over the end.*

We had discussed my single status a week or two prior and he'd told me I was good-looking enough to be able to find an interested party anywhere. When I laughed out loud, he considered it a personal challenge and we ended up cruising for guys everywhere we went. It was sort of fun, so I went along with it. He'd point at some random guy, and I'd say, "No way," or "Maybe," and his guesses would get more and more accurate to what I liked in a guy. The problem was, every guy he pointed out was straight.

This time, the guy we discussed as we lay on his bed, was not. Another fluke! We were in a mini-mart and this cute guy was squeezing the honeydew melons. Jonathan pointed, I nodded, and the cute guy, his name was Eric, smiled our way. I froze, but luckily Jonathan thought fast on his feet. He had me over to Eric in a flash, and he was—to my shock—interested!

So we went out.

He took me to the movies, which was nice. I liked movies. And he bought me popcorn. Then, after the movie, at the remote end of the parking lot, next to his car, he kissed me a few times and asked me to suck him off. I didn't question it because I happen to like sucking cock. I might not remember the guy's name who fucked me the first time, but I remembered his dick. And I remembered how much I liked sucking it!

Just before Eric came, he pulled his dick out of my grasp and milked it the rest of the way all over my face. And that was that. No reciprocation. No exchange of phone numbers. No kiss good-night. He drove me home in silence and then sped off.

I sighed. "This is the luck with guys that I was telling you about."

"Cheer up, Cole. So, this date was disappointing. At least you didn't get pregnant." He chuckled and I appreciated his attempt to make me smile. "I admit it's less than encouraging, but the right guy is out there. I know it. You'll find someone." He sounded so hopeful. I only wish I felt the same optimism.

"I can't believe you are okay with me talking about it."

He replied honestly. "It's no different than listening to other guys talk about eating out a girl's pussy. It's just sex. It's not like I'm there watching it."

"I guess. But I don't really want to hear about pussy, if you don't mind."

He laughed and nudged my shoulder with his foot. I shook my head and grabbed at his ankle. Jonathan waved his foot around, evading my snare until we both jumped due to a loud noise in the hallway.

"We have to get our own place," he said.

"Definitely."

IT WENT on like that for the next three years. I officially met one guy per year due to Jonathan's point-them-out method while we were around town. (And *unofficially*, I hooked up with Eric twice to give him head. What can I say? I'm pathetic.) I liked the sex, but it was clear that sex wasn't my sole purpose in dating. I wanted a relationship, and I didn't see that logistically happening while I was at school. Gettysburg just did not have a gay population large enough to support my needs. I was resigned to giving up.

"YOU can't give up. Not yet. What about the guy you met in Lancaster?"

I gave him my you've-gotta-be-kidding-me glare. "Garrett?"

"Yeah, Garrett. You went out with him twice!"

I shrugged lazily. "I don't feel anything for him."

"Did you give him a chance?"

"Yes."

Jonathan gave me "the look."

"Yes," I reiterated with more conviction. "I gave him a chance, but he doesn't do anything for me. His kissing is... blah."

"Really? Is that the only reason? Because I remember when he showed up at our door you could not get past his attire."

"Plaid on plaid in not fashionable!" I couldn't believe he was bringing it up again. "And... he slurps when he drinks. I can't stand it!"

"You are going to have to let go of these nitpicks eventually. No one is perfect."

"I know." My shoulders sagged. I knew he was right. I was too demanding. I sat next to him on the couch and told him, "He called

yesterday and asked me to a party tomorrow night. I said I'd think about it."

"He did?" Jon was very excited. "Then you should go!" He slapped my knee and playfully punched my shoulder.

"But he seems so boring," I pointed out.

"And you sum this up from two dates? Give him a chance. Maybe he'll surprise you."

I LISTENED to Jonathan, and I called Garrett back. That was the last date I went on.

"What happened?" Jon asked with great concern as I entered his bedroom at nine thirty Friday night. (I would have pointed out the sadness of being in bed at nine thirty on a Friday night, but I knew Cathy was at her parents' house.)

I stood still by the doorway. Numb. "He...." I couldn't form the sentence in my head. I was too stunned.

Jonathan got out of bed and walked over to me. He touched my shoulder and I jumped. "What is it?" he asked, concerned.

"Garrett... he...." When I stopped again, I could see the alarms going off in Jon's eyes. I touched his comforting hand. "No, he didn't hurt me."

"Then what happened? You look really shaken."

He urged me forward and we sat on his bed. He allowed me time to gather my thoughts and caringly rubbed my back. This is why I can't find someone. No one measures up to how great Jonathan makes me feel. *"Garrett took me to a sex party."*

"What?" Shocked, Jon stopped making small circles on my back.

"Yup. Boring, plaid-on-plaid Garrett is into orgies." I looked at him and felt my emotions flooding in. However, I refused to cry. I would not cry. I hadn't cried in almost five years, and I wasn't going to let Garrett break me.

"I can't believe that. Wow. I guess you never know about people," he mused. "And you're sure?"

"Oh yeah. Naked people throughout the apartment, fucking and sucking anyone close enough to touch, the smell of come and latex chokingly thick in the air—yeah, I'm sure."

I knew there was nothing really to say to that. Jon's response was, "I'm sorry."

"Me too." I leaned my head onto his shoulder. "Are you sure I can't simply date you? I could get a sex-change operation and you could eat my pussy all you want."

He chuckled. "Don't you think you'd miss your dick?"

I sighed again. I touched my genitals reassuringly. "Yeah, I would. I don't want to be a girl. It would merely make it easier if I could have you and not try to find someone in the vast seas of mediocrity. Are you sure you have to graduate in a few months? Can't you stay with me next year until I graduate too?"

"Nope. Sorry. But I promise you'll find someone special. I bet it'll happen when you least expect it and when you aren't even looking. You'll see!"

JONATHAN was always positive. And, he always supported me. But when he told me I'd meet someone special, I didn't believe him! Six months later, I met Ellis.

Chapter 8
Was I Dreaming?

WHEN daylight flooded my room, I knew it was time to face the music and see if our friendship had survived a night of—from my perspective—awesome sex! But I wasn't the virgin here. Ellis was. *Did Ellis hurt like I did my first time?* I hoped not. I tried desperately to prep him as best I could, but there was still no guarantee that today he wouldn't feel the repercussions, despite my careful planning. To his advantage, and to the detriment of my ego, I was on the low side of average. He should be fine.

I rolled over. Ellis was gone.

Shit! Why does every guy leave me? Either he was fixing me coffee or he'd freaked out entirely and left. Or, as my cynical subconscious whispered, his butt was still throbbing and he regretted every second. No matter what the answer was, an empty bed made me feel used and all my other bad experiences taunted me with *I told you sos.*

I grabbed some underwear and hurried into the living room. No one. Kitchen? No one. I made myself some coffee and mulled over what I could possibly say if and when he returned. I was no stranger to guys leaving in the middle of the night, but I'd never slept with a friend before. I wanted to kick myself.

Why didn't I wait?

TWO hours later, Ellis bounded through the door, sweaty, out of breath, and wearing my "What Is The Speed Of Dark?" T-shirt.

"Hey," I greeted him, like I normally would. "Where ya been?"

"Out. I ran four miles and then played basketball with Russ."

He said it like *Duh!* was attached to the end of the sentence. Was it me, or was he acting like last night didn't happen? "Oh, okay," I said. "I was just wondering where you were. That's all."

"You're not my mother. I'm a grown man. I can go out if I want to!" Ellis barked.

Wow! Attitude. Not the optimal reaction I longed for. His defensiveness told me he wasn't too thrilled with last night's experience. Did I flat-out ask, or let it go? I went with my current trend and let it go. "Yup, you sure are."

He narrowed his eyes. "What's that supposed to mean?"

I didn't like the growing hostility. I hadn't done anything. "Nothing. I'm just agreeing with you. You can do whatever you want."

"Damn right," he huffed as he stormed to the bathroom and slammed the door.

I called after him, "Although you could ask before taking my shirt!"

I heard the shower come on. A moment later, the door opened and my shirt came flying toward me. Ellis was angry, and I was not about to stick around. While he showered, I took the opportunity to grab my coat and leave.

I WALKED to the ever-popular coffee shop around the corner, where everyone loved to sugar themselves up on oversized chocolate muffins and cinnamon sticky buns, and ordered some comfort food of my own. (A chocolate chip scone and a cappuccino; I'm not original.) As I stormed out of my apartment and walked over here, I felt a sudden turmoil of emotions flooding my heart that I'd never experienced and didn't understand. Did Ellis feel like this?

He regretted last night, I was sure of it. And what I lamented was fucking a friend who obviously wasn't ready.

I took a sip of my drink and wiped the foam from my mustache—I really had to trim this thing—and fought the heat rising up the back of my neck. *Was I going to cry?* Oh, fuck no! I'd never cried over a guy before, and I was sure as hell not going to start now in the middle of Gossip Central. Me? An emotional train wreck? Wasn't going to happen! But it was painfully clear that our friendship would never be the same, and that was what I honestly regretted the most.

I really felt like we'd had something wonderful developing between us. Way different than Jon and me, what Ellis and I had was... *special.* (I can't even believe I used that word.) But it was. He *knew* me. Even in this short time, I really felt like he knew me deeper than Jon. It was in his eyes when he looked at me. Like he didn't see a sarcastic hypochondriac with OCD and controlling tendencies, Ellis saw *me*—the real me. The one I hid behind a wall of cutting remarks and manipulative suggestions. How could I get that Ellis back after sleeping with him and ruining the remarkable start we'd had?

While throngs of cheery coffeehouse patrons milled around me, my mind flashed images of last night like a PowerPoint presentation of photographs flipping from one to the next.

Ellis was beautiful.

His voice moaning my name was beautiful.

The taste of his skin, the pulse of his private muscles against my sensitive tongue, the quiver of his hands as he touched my face; all these memories collided against my painstakingly built façade of callous malcontent and roared, "Beautiful!"

I was not as prickly as people believed.

Jon told me eight months ago—after I declared celibacy following my last horrific dating experience—that I would, one day, take it all back. He knew I'd find someone. He said it would happen when I least expected it and when I wasn't looking. Damn if he wasn't right! Ellis just happened along when I was resisting the change that had occurred when Jon graduated. Ellis ended up with me after Stan....

I looked up, and there he was.

"Stan? What are you staring at?" I asked. He was looking at me, but I wasn't sure I appeared any different than before. He'd never stared at me before. "Do I have foam in my goatee?" I quickly inspected my chin by running my fingers over the hairs. I didn't feel anything.

"May I?" Stan asked, gesturing to the seat across from mine.

"Sure." Stan sat and studied me as if he knew something. I hate when people do that. "If my grandmother died, please spit it out. I can't stand the ominous anticipation." I pointed across the table. "And if you start out with the anecdote about my cat falling off the roof, then I will personally stick a piece of scone up your nose."

Stan didn't grin. *Uh-oh.*

"What is it?" I asked again, trying my best to sound interested.

"You had sex with Ellis, didn't you?"

I nearly choked to death. As I coughed out the last dry crumbs from my lungs and grabbed for the cup of water Stan held out to me, I nervously checked the surrounding tables for shocked stares. None. Good. "Holy shit, Stan, can you say it any louder?" I was not pleased.

No reaction from him.

"He told you?" I asked, incredulous that Ellis would broach such a personal topic with someone other than myself.

"No. I watched him doing suicides this morning as I remarked the field for the game on Wednesday. I've never seen a man do suicides on his own without the coach threatening him at every sprint."

"So?" I acted like it was no big deal. Ellis was a dedicated player; perhaps he felt some extra work was best for his stamina.

"Cole, let me tell you something. I raised six boys; one of whom was gay. I've seen all kinds of reactions to anger, confusion, and even love. When I saw my boy Ellis running suicides at full tilt, I knew something was up. He didn't have to tell me anything."

"But he could be upset about anything," I rationalized. "It didn't have to be about me."

Stan nodded. "True. But he was wearing *your* T-shirt."

"That doesn't prove we had sex."

"No, but I think I know him pretty well. And besides, you have a huge hickey on your neck."

I self-consciously covered my neck and protested, "How? He barely talks. Well, I mean, he used to not talk much before… he and I…." This was more complicated to explain than I thought. "Ellis and I became really good friends, and he started talking more as we hung out. I think I know him better than *you* do." I don't know why I got defensive over it, but the notion that Stan knew something about Ellis that I didn't struck a nerve.

Stan sat there calmly. "I know everyone around here thinks I'm only the groundskeeper and housing administrator. No big deal, right? Well, that's where you're wrong. Housing has only been a recent addition to my job description, but I've been groundskeeper here for over thirty years. In that time I've learned how to gauge people. All people."

"What do you mean, gauge people?"

"I figure them out by observing them."

"You think you know Ellis because you *watch* him?"

"Exactly."

That didn't seem like enough to me. "I don't think you can know someone simply by observing their behavior a few times. You need verbal intercourse." *Shit, bad choice of words.*

Stan smirked and leaned forward, crossed his arms and rested them on the table. "Joke if you will, and tell me I'm full of shit. I'm not bothered by your personality flaws."

"Ouch!" I said, sitting straighter and leaning against the back of the booth. I wasn't used to Stan's curtness.

"I've learned over the course of sixty-three years that people don't see me as a threat. I'm invisible for the most part, and they go about their business as if I wasn't standing there at all. So I watch. I pay attention. I see what goes on, and I hear what people whisper about."

"Like a spy?" I asked.

"Maybe. My point is that I've been on the campus long enough, and I've listened to and watched enough people over the years that little things rarely escape my notice. Call it stewardship of humanity, if you will."

I felt slightly awkward, but there was a part of me that needed to know why his "stewardship of humanity" included Ellis and me—more specifically, our personal business. "What does this have to do with Ellis?"

He smirked again! I felt my anger click past simmer.

"Cole, Ellis is working through some things."

"And you think I screwed up his life by screwing him." It came out harsh, I admit it.

Leave it to Stan to reply with calm logic instead of defensive whiplash. "No, what I'm saying is that you need to give him time to work through it. Let me put it to you this way—some men take out frustration on a pile of wood."

"Huh? I'm not planning to become a lumberjack."

"Cole, stop it. Let me speak. Some men take out frustration on a pile of wood. They may have a wood splitter, but when their wives upset them, they'd rather take a hatchet or a splitting maul and hack the heck out of each piece of firewood purely by muscle alone. It's the testosterone in us, I guess."

"What about the ones who don't wield axes for fear of accidental amputation?" I could not resist inappropriate humor.

Stan didn't hesitate to continue. "Some wash their car two or three times. Some take a six-mile run. Some move plants or trees in their garden, which didn't need to be moved. Heck, some men even build a shed, or paint the whole damn house! Point is, it's usually physical."

I could see where he was going. "Like voluntarily running suicides on your day off." I hung my head, and Stan didn't say anything right away.

I didn't run much myself, and I knew every coach had a different pattern of running for what they term "suicides," but from what I understood, it was grueling and nowhere near fun. Suicides are run at full speed. The runner sprints to the ten-yard line, and then back. Then sprints to the twenty and back. To the thirty and back, and so on until they have successfully sprinted to each yard line and exhausted every ounce of energy they have in them. No one *volunteered* to run suicides.

"So Ellis is working through stuff; why conclude *I* was the stuff?" I asked.

"Intuition," he answered with a grin. "Ellis likes you. I saw him a few days ago when I fixed the sprinkler head on the D-lot flowerbed. He thanked me for housing him with you."

"He did?" My aching heart flooded with joy over one small comment.

"He did. I knew he was perfect for you."

"I thought Jonathan paid you to find me a roommate?"

He was unfazed by my declaration. "True, but I knew Ellis would suit you beyond a simple friendship."

"What? How? Wait…. What do you mean *beyond* friendship? Stan, were you playing Cupid?" It sounded absurd, but everything Stan had said pointed to that conclusion.

"Maybe a little. I told you I observe people. I notice things. I'd seen how he talked with girls but didn't quite 'connect' with them. I have a gay son, so I've seen the way at least one homosexual man looks at other men. One day last year, while he was sitting in the quad, you walked by the humanities building and he looked up. He watched you walk all the way over to the library. When you disappeared from view, he grinned and leaned his head against the tree behind him. He sat there in the shade a full twenty minutes with his eyes closed."

I gaped. I was stunned. And while this revelation about Ellis was thrilling, Stan's confidence in his stalking abilities frightened me more than I care to admit. "You're like the college creeper, Stan. This is *not* good. If the dean knew you were watching all the students this closely, you'd probably lose your job! You don't have cameras in the dorms, do you? 'Cause that would be sick!"

"No," said Stan, shaking his head adamantly. "It was to help you. Ellis was searching for his identity, and I hoped to give it a nudge by placing him with you. I knew you wouldn't push, but I also knew you'd be too attracted to him not to go for it if the time was right. Don't look so shocked, Cole. You and I have been friends for a while! Remember the older accountant that asked you out that time? You came back all depressed and rambled on about finding a nice, quiet guy your age instead of a middle-aged married guy having a crisis."

"You remember that?" I cringed. I'd tried everything to block it from my memory since it was that horrible. Telling Stan was obviously not the greatest decision either, but I didn't know he was a stalker.

"I remember everything, Cole. It's a curse. We went for a drink, and after your third beer you said, and I quote, 'A muscular jock would be tasty to wrap my legs around as long as he was smart enough to spell the word *Sanctiloquent*.' I think that was when you were reading a book for your religious studies class and felt pious for ten minutes."

"Ha ha. I doubt it. I remember the book, and I do recall making that comment. But with as many times as I told you not to house me with a jock, I find it odd that you'd do it anyway. What if I was the worst thing to ever happen to Ellis? What if he hates me forever? How could you manipulate our lives like that?" I seriously wanted to know.

"Because you're my friend, Cole. I like you. You remind me of my son." His face darkened slightly, and he whispered, "My son died of AIDS five years ago."

I was instantly nauseated. "Oh my God. I'm sorry." I reached out and touched his hand. "I didn't know."

His lip lifted at the corner. "I know. I didn't mention him to get sympathy, but I hope you can understand. I love working here because I'm drawn to kids. My kids are grown and living in several different states. My son died before I got a chance to know him and accept his lifestyle. I've talked to his partner a few times since the funeral, but I don't feel like I was a part of anything meaningful. When I met you, I felt this resurgence of fatherly pride. I wanted to see you happy. And I hoped I could somehow make amends with my son for not taking the time with him by being there for you." I could see he really needed my approval. He was practically begging me with his eyes.

"I guess I understand. But what am I supposed to do in the meantime? Ellis practically bit my head off earlier."

"I bet he's torn and confused over whatever happened with you. Give him space."

"I am, that's why I'm here. But what if it's not enough? What if he hates me?"

"You had sex with him, right?"

I furrowed my brow. That was not a normal question. "I'm not describing the sex, if that's what you're fishing for."

"No, I'm only making sure. I didn't think Ellis would run himself that ragged over a simple kiss."

I was still dubious of his intentions, so I answered slowly, "No. It was… sex."

He let out a breath and sighed, "Good." And he looked a little too happy about it.

"Stan, I think I'm done here. If you keep talking, I'm going to see you as some old pervert who has nothing better to do than fuck up young gay men by meddling in their sex lives. For my sanity, and the potentially virginal ears eavesdropping on us from the neighboring booth, please leave."

Stan's eyes went wide. "Oh, okay." He didn't look offended. He appeared more worried or astonished at my unswerving dismissal than anything. He stood and backed away. "Then, we'll chat another time."

"Yeah, another time," I answered with a nod. And Stan left.

It was a disturbing conversation, yet insightful. I'm not sure the board of trustees would agree with his behavior or even consider it ethical. It was slightly perverted, if you ask me. But… he was trying to be my friend, and he did say I reminded him of his son. I guess I could forgive him for making me a little uncomfortable. But what Ellis and I did behind closed doors wasn't anyone's business, least of all Stan's!

My ears picked up the college radio station playing softly thought the speakers overhead. It was Maroon 5. *"Put your hands all over, put your hands all over me."* I groaned. I put my head in my hands and allowed the words of the song to slingshot me back into my mental PowerPoint presentation of last night's snapshots. We felt so good together. I had to believe he felt something for me. If I couldn't hope for that, then I might as well move out now. I couldn't live with Ellis if he hated me. I didn't understand why I felt so restless over this *one* guy. Why did my next move depend on Ellis? Why did I feel the need to try so hard with him?

As if on cue, I heard the fading lyrics of another Maroon 5 song. (It must have been a play block.) *"Why does the one you love become the one who makes you want to cry?"*

Love? *Surely not.*

"I simply don't want to lose a friend," I rationalized. I shook my head and walked over to the trash can to deposit my napkin, and placed my empty cup in the appropriate tub. "Love has nothing to do with this," I scoffed and headed home.

Chapter 9

Aftershock

ELLIS was having the most pleasant dream of his life. He was hiking the Appalachian Trail and standing on Blue Mountain overlooking the scenery below. The sun was just rising. The wind whipped around him and he felt free. Glorious. Reborn. He held his arms out to the side and yelled across the valley, "Woo-hoo! Yeah!" It felt wonderful to be alive. He was standing at the highest point in Berks County in any direction, stark naked and yelling at the top of his lungs. A hawk flew overhead and "kee-eee-arred" back to him, and he laughed out loud.

"Are you going to converse with the local wildlife, or join me for breakfast?"

Ellis turned his smiling face toward Cole and then scampered back to rejoin him in their double sleeping bag. He snuggled up to him and kissed his sweet lips, relishing the feel of his scruffy mustache and goatee. Ellis loved how Cole's facial hair scratched at his lips and chin. It was a demonstrable attribute that reminded Ellis he was kissing a man. This man!

Cole reached down and grabbed the curved globe of his ass, pulling him tight against him. Then Cole rolled Ellis to his back and aggressively pushed his legs apart.

That was when Ellis woke up.

He opened his eyes and found he was staring at the back of Cole's head. Not from far away, mind you, but up close and personal! In fact, his lips were mere inches from the back of his neck. Ellis breathed in deeply and detected several smells simultaneously. Sweat. He sniffed again. Body odor—he seriously needed a shower. And—sniff—sex. Like latex and come. His heart sped up.

Ellis went to move but couldn't. His arm was firmly clasped around Cole's midsection, and Cole's arm rested over his. Their bodies were touching from where his nose touched Cole's brown hair all the way down to where his ankle looped over Cole's foot. He could feel every inch of him. Cole. In his arms. He swallowed hard.

Ever since Cole had opened the door and begrudgingly endured the shenanigans of his pals, Ellis couldn't stop thinking about him. He was amused by his gruff demeanor, yet also intimidated by it. Cole's obsessive compulsiveness drove him crazy, yet he found he wanted to please him more and more. Cole, with his vast collection of stupid science-related T-shirts, his tortoiseshell rectangular-framed glasses, and his quirky way of cleaning the lenses every time he was nervous, made Ellis's heart yearn for something it had never felt in his entire life.

He leaned in a fraction and kissed Cole's skin.

Kissing him felt so good.

But as soon as he lifted his knee, attempting to maneuver his body without waking Cole, he felt a twinge of burning pain... *there!*

There! A place that should never burn unless he'd experienced long bouts of diarrhea, which only occurred if he drank too much milk. He shouldn't hurt *there*.

As the events of last night flooded his conscious mind, Ellis started to panic. He could hardly catch his breath as he gasped. He had sex! Cole fucked him! He—Ellis—allowed Cole—a man—to penetrate his asshole! And now he was here in Cole's bed, entwined with Cole's sleeping form and unable to get away. But he had to! He had to run. Ellis needed to escape this bed of vulnerability he'd suddenly found himself in.

Cole had fucked him. Hard.

This couldn't be what it felt like to be gay? This open. This helpless. This emasculated. He thought he'd feel joy, peace, love, warmth, but all he felt was terror.

The room was spinning and his arms felt as though they were trapped in a vat of molasses, difficult to pull free from Cole's vise grip. His legs wouldn't move, either. They were stiff and unresponsive. How could he get out of here when Cole had chained him to the bed?

At once, in one swift motion, Ellis rolled backward and landed on his feet on the opposite side of the bed. He was free. Standing completely nude in Cole's bedroom, while Cole obliviously slept. He had to leave. Now! At once! Ellis snatched his clothes from the bed, the floor, the nearby chair, and left without making a sound.

After yanking on basketball shorts and a T-shirt, he left the apartment, in desperate need of solitude. He jogged to the football field and fell into a casual run around the sidelines. Without thought, he stopped at one goal post and dashed to the ten-yard line and back. That was easy. He sprinted, this time to the twenty. His calves burned, but he loved the familiarity of it. He repeated the exercise by sprinting to the thirty-yard line and back. His thighs burned. Good. But he could still feel a throb in his ass. It felt like Cole was still there—pushing in and pulling out in that seductive rhythm of sexual conquest and domination.

He sprinted to the forty, back, fifty and back.

Cole couldn't control him.

Maybe he—Ellis—wasn't gay? Maybe last night was an accident? He sprinted to the sixty and back. His lungs burned. His thighs screamed. Still, he ran on.

Sure he felt attracted to Cole. Cole was adorable in a nerdy-science sort of way, but did that mean he cared for him in a homosexual way? Maybe Ellis was confused. Cole was insufferable and incorrigible and infuriating—run, touch eighty-yard line and turn—but he was also thoughtful. He never made dinner without asking if Ellis liked all the ingredients first. That was nice. He didn't have to do that. Cole was tender and affectionate but never did anything blatant when they were in public.

Cole was sweet in his own way.

Ellis bent and touched the goal line on the opposite end and nearly collapsed on his return, huffing and puffing on the fifty-yard line. "Then why… why… do I feel… so scared?" he asked himself, but he was too exhausted to think. In his mind, something was wrong. Sex was supposed to bring a couple closer together, but sex with Cole made him feel more distant, more confused, and more insecure. Why?

Across the field, he noticed Stanley White repainting the lines on the field. He glanced his way. "Shit! What if he knows?" Ellis asked out loud. "What if he can look at me and tell I had a dick up my ass?" He often found Mr. Stanley's presence comforting, but today Ellis all but panicked thinking the kindly older gentleman would walk over and chat. Thankfully, he didn't.

Ellis took the moment to leave before Stan changed his mind. "Maybe something's wrong with me?" said Ellis, clambering along, hoping Cole wouldn't be in the apartment when he returned.

Of course Cole was home. And then he lied about shooting hoops with Russell. He hated lying to Cole. Plus he yelled at him! Ellis felt awful about yelling at Cole. Part of him struggled with a need to reach out and hold Cole, but the selfish half fish-flipped in his gut, reminding him how exposed he felt in Cole's presence. He turned on the shower but remained by the door—listening.

Cole bellowed, "Although you could ask before taking my shirt!"

Ellis looked down. *Shit! I'm wearing his shirt.* "I must have grabbed it by accident." He yanked it off and flung it out the door. Seconds later, he heard the apartment door slam. Ellis leaned on the door and fought tears.

He stepped into the shower and felt the hot water cascade over his sore muscles. He washed. He leaned on the wall, thinking about what he'd done last night. *It's not supposed to feel like this.* As the water ran down his face, Ellis watched the bubbles chase each other down his legs, over his feet and into the drain. If only the fear he felt would follow them down. If only the manifest weakness sobbing itself free through his tears would vanish with the bathwater and cleanse him of the shame he felt. Ellis leaned on the tile and cried like he'd never cried before.

FOR almost two weeks, Ellis walked through a fog. Concentrating on school was nearly impossible, yet somehow he'd managed to pull off A's on all the papers he handed in, albeit low A's, but he didn't know how. Everything was so mixed up in his head. If someone asked him what he was studying, he was certain he wouldn't be able to explain anything properly. What was he going to do with midterms approaching?

In the back of his mind, he knew he'd gone to see his parents a few times but what they did or ate on those occasions, he couldn't remember. He could hardly remember anything. Except Cole.

He sat on the couch while Cole was in class and tried with great effort to compose a poem for creative writing. The task was daunting. He couldn't write poetry. He couldn't concentrate on poetry.

And what should I ~~say~~ speak of today,

Of paper flowers and skies of gray?

Or ~~cloudy~~ moon-lit nights, sitting alone,

Candles burning, with no one home.

Ellis crossed off words and crumbled sorry attempts at expressing his feelings. He felt cold. He felt empty. He felt a mountain of guilt and shame, but what was he ashamed of? He didn't know—that part was unclear. Two weeks ago, he would have sworn he felt ashamed of letting Cole fuck him. Then time passed. Days and days. Now, he wasn't sure what was going on in his head. Every time he saw Cole, he could only think of touching him, kissing him, wanting him, and missing the feel of him in his arms. Yet every time he considered giving in to his yearning desire, the fear of strangulation stopped him cold.

The constant conflict was unbearable.

He threw another ball of paper just as the door opened and Cole walked in.

"Ah!" Cole cried. "Again?" Cole was not questioning Ellis's actions in a happy voice; it was his "I can't believe how fucking-stupid you are" voice.

Ellis jumped up. "I'm sorry," he replied, scrambling to grab all the crumbled papers from the floor.

"The logic eludes me why you can't bring the wastebasket from the corner of the room over to where you're sitting, so that each failed attempt at artistic expression can simply be placed into it and not all over my floor."

Ellis looked up at Cole, who was reprimanding his actions with hands on hips. "Maybe if you gave me twenty more minutes, I'd have cleaned them all up and left no evidence for you to find fault with."

"So you're saying it's my fault you're a slob?"

"No. I'm saying you need to stop trying to control my actions to the point of creating a carbon copy of yourself. I'm not you!" Ellis yelled, glaring at Cole before depositing his trash in the can Cole held out. It wasn't like he'd planned on yelling, but it was easy to do when his emotions were so close to the surface. "How many times do we have to go over this? I'm not you! I carelessly make messes and clean them up after. I don't think about ants that *might* be attracted to the sugar on the floor, and I don't care if my clothes get wrinkled when I leave them in the dryer overnight."

"Maybe that's your problem! If you thought ahead—ever, maybe you could avoid all the messes you create!" Cole yelled in return.

Ellis snatched up all his books and went into his room, tossing them onto his bed. He returned to the living room, where Cole stood, and grabbed his jacket. "You're right!" he roared, allowing his frustration to pour from the funnel of his lips. "I *do* need to think ahead! If I did, maybe I wouldn't have slept with *you*!"

Cole opened his mouth, but then stopped. He looked away, and Ellis took that split second between reaching out and fleeing to disappear through the door. Fleeing the scene was easier than apologizing when he wasn't sure which part he needed to apologize for.

ELLIS wandered into the pub feeling… God, he didn't know.

He lumbered over to the bar and took a seat. The bartender gave him an inquisitive look and Ellis didn't bother bickering over his age. "Coke, please," he said.

This pub could be seen as a family pub, if one could refer to Irish pubs as having a "family" style. Lots of people came here for the food as much as the drink and atmosphere. It was comfortable and generally affordable. It was also close to the college, and students could walk over from the dorms. The establishment always carded, so no one bothered trying to get served if they were underage. Ellis knew better. Plus, he figured, in a few months it wouldn't matter anyway.

Ellis sipped his Coke and waited for his sister. He hoped that coming out this evening wasn't going to be a mistake, but what else could he do? Stay in the apartment? No thanks! Earlier in the day he'd entertained the idea of inviting Cole along tonight to meet his sister, but after they yelled at one another, Ellis knew he wasn't ready to get over *that night*.

It hadn't been quite two weeks, but the night he'd slept with Cole had haunted his dreams every night since. Sometimes the images were so vivid that Ellis could taste Cole's sweat on his lips when he woke up. Ellis didn't want to remember what they shared in Cole's bed, but still the images flashed before him... *all the time!* He felt like a hostage of his own memories. Cole's mouth on him. Cole's teeth nipping. Cole's breath panting his name.

"Hey, El!" Ellis blinked and turned toward the sweet voice to his left.

"Hi, sis," he replied, sliding his arm around her waist and then squeezing her tight.

The perky little blond gestured to her side and asked, "You remember Lori?"

Ellis nodded and leaned into her offered hug. "Of course I do. Although I have to say, since you guys decided to make it official, I don't see either of you as often. What is that about? Your straight brother isn't all that interesting anymore?"

His sister protested, "Hey! Gay or straight doesn't matter! I love you either way. But I am sorry about the disappearing act. It wasn't intentional. We just... got... distracted." She gave her girlfriend a devilish grin and blushed as she ran her fingers down Lori's bare arm.

"It's been two years, Sara. I used to see you so much it was annoying. Now I forget what you look like."

Sara looked surprised, but Lori didn't bother playing into his joke. "Stop it," she said, thumping her hand against Ellis's chest. "We haven't changed that much. She's still beautiful, and I'm still the plain Jane with straight brown hair that no one notices anyway."

"Not true!" Ellis refuted. "You've always been beautiful, Lori. Your downfall is having terrible taste in women."

"Hey!" Sara shrieked and slapped him as Lori giggled.

"So, what are we doing? Eating? Playing darts in the game room? What?" Ellis thought getting activities started would help organize his dull evening and help keep him from daydreaming.

"I could eat," Lori said.

Sara nodded in agreement. "Yeah, and play darts after." She smiled as she spoke, continually stroking her girlfriend's lower back.

Ellis was happy for his sister. She'd found true love, it seemed. Lori had always been a huge part of her life. They'd been friends since maybe elementary school, at least in Ellis's recollection. They had always been close and always did everything together. It wasn't a hard stretch to believe they were girlfriends when they told their parents. Ellis remembered his mom and dad looking disappointed, then sad, then understanding, and finally welcoming. They had always liked Lori anyway.

So if Ellis knew his parents were okay with Sara's sexuality, then why was he afraid of his own?

A cold shiver went down his back. "I gotta take a wiz. Be right back."

"Hey." Sara stopped him with a touch on his arm.

"What?" Ellis looked her in the eyes.

"Are you okay? You looked drained."

Her concern was appreciated, but he wasn't ready to spill. "Yeah. Fine. I'll be right back." He turned and strolled off toward the toilets. He could hear Sara calling after him, saying something about a table. He'd find them later; he knew he would.

In the bathroom stall, Ellis leaned against the wall, covering his face with his hands. "What am I doing?" he muttered. "I'm not gay. I like girls. Girls are beautiful. Even the lesbians I know." He chuckled. That was an absurd thought, even if it was true.

He *did* think girls were beautiful, and he could confidently say that he thought *most* girls were beautiful, even the fat ones. There was something about the feminine shine that attracted him. He liked the sound of a female voice. He liked the curve of a female waist. "So what's wrong with me?" His self-examining, one-way conversations were becoming habitual. He couldn't remember talking to himself like an idiot *before* he moved in with Cole. Ellis snapped his hands away from his face. Epiphany strikes! "That's it! Living with Cole has made me batty!"

Flash! Ellis writhing under Cole's body. Breaths mounting. Moans filling the room. Cole's lips kissing his neck. Cole's cock touching something deep inside....

"I'm crazy, all right. Crazy for something I don't want to think about."

He didn't want to think about any kind of attraction to Cole. He didn't want to think about homosexuality at all! And now here he was, having dinner with his gay sister and her lover! "I certainly know how to torture myself, don't I?"

Just then the bathroom door opened, and Ellis went still. He didn't want whoever it was overhearing his external, internal conversation. As soon as the person went into a neighboring stall, he'd leave. He just needed to remain quiet for another few seconds.

"Ahhh!" Ellis jumped as someone grabbed his leg under the stall dividing wall. "What are you—?" He started to question his unseen attacker but stopped when he heard sniggers from the adjacent stall. "Rob, is that you?"

Rob popped his head under the stall. "Yeah."

Seeing Rob's huge smile was comforting, but he wouldn't admit to it being a pleasant surprise. "Idiot!" he said. "What do you think you're doing?"

Rob's head disappeared and Ellis opened his door to join him in the open part of the restroom. It wasn't exactly normal to have a conversation in the men's room, but this was way better than having a conversation under the stall dividing walls.

"I came in looking for you," Rob answered.

"Why? How'd you know I was in here? And what if you grabbed another guy's leg instead of mine?"

Rob's expression said that the notion was ridiculous. "I saw Sara by the bar and she said you were in here. And come on, you've worn the same shoes since I met you. I'd know it was you in the dark."

"Have not!"

"Have too!"

"I just bought these three months ago! So there." Ellis stuck out his tongue.

"And they are exactly the same style as the last four pair! There back!" And Rob stuck out his tongue.

"Oh," Ellis allowed. "But you still couldn't see me in the dark. They don't glow."

Rob wasn't fazed. "Sure they do." He leaned over and pointed. "See that little Adidas symbol on the back? It glows."

"No, it doesn't." Ellis didn't believe him.

"You don't believe me?" Rob asked as if challenged. He reached over to the light switch and turned them off.

"Rob!" Ellis protested in the utter darkness.

"Just look!" Rob insisted.

Ellis couldn't see anything, but he brought his knee up and grabbed his foot, inspecting the heel of his shoe in the dark. Sure enough, a little Adidas symbol glowed in the dark. "Wow. I never noticed that before."

"Never underestimate my powers of keen observations, my friend. My eye spies all!"

The door opened and they turned to see Russell enter. "Why are you guys standing around in the dark? Did the power go out?"

Rob answered, "No, blockhead! If the power went out, then you wouldn't be letting in light from the hallway!" He shook his head. "Jeez, why do I have to be the brains for all of you?"

"You're not *my* brains!"

"Of course not, Russ. That's why you're asking if the power is out when it's clearly *on* in the room behind you."

"Shut up, Rob." Russell looked at Ellis and asked, "So, why are you in here?"

"He's in here inspecting the electrical system."

Russell punched Rob's arm. "Shut up, Rob!"

Ellis breathed out heavily. If this was the type of evening he was going to have, he almost considered going home. Yet, it might prove a good distraction. "I was just leaving, Russ. Do you guys want to join us?"

Rob turned on the lights and answered, "Not if it's going to be a major inconvenience. I saw Sara had a friend with her. Is it just the three of you? Is Cole coming?"

Russell said, "You guys go ahead, I gotta wash my hands."

"Okay." Ellis nodded to Russell, and he left the room with Rob. Ellis nonchalantly answered Rob's question saying, "It's just us. Cole's not coming."

"Huh. Isn't that weird? I mean, I haven't seen him since the camping trip. Is he okay?"

Ellis appreciated Rob's caring nature, but it didn't help him forget about Cole if Rob was going to bring him into every conversation. "He's fine," Ellis said with finality. Suddenly he needed a diversionary tactic to change the subject. *Lori!* "By the way, Sara's friend isn't just a *friend*. Lori's her girlfriend." He knew it was rude disclosing personal information about his sister to Rob, but there was a part of his brain that needed to feel Rob out. (Besides getting the topic off Cole.)

Rob stopped walking about twenty feet from the bar area. "Gay, huh? Okay."

Ellis glanced at him. "Is that going to be a problem? You don't have to hang out with us if it weirds you out."

Rob calmly shrugged. "No, no problem."

"Are you sure? I know you go to church all the time. You lead the youth group and you're way more spiritual than me!"

Rob chuckled. "Spiritual? Is that what you call it? Okay."

"You are. Isn't homosexuality a sin and all?" Ellis didn't *want* to go there, but his mouth wouldn't stop talking.

Rob answered, "Ellis, can't we just have fun? I'm not here to judge people. I like your sister, I just didn't know she was a lesbian."

Ellis stared. *Rob's not here to judge people. Would he judge me?*

"Ellis?" Russell's voice drifted in from the side. "Are you in there?"

Ellis snapped to face him. "What?"

"Ah, you spaced out." Rob shook his head and made a face.

Russell grinned and lifted an eyebrow. "Are we joining you guys or what?"

"We're joining them."

When they walked toward the bar where the girls waited, Ellis noticed a guy at a table behind them that was wearing a shirt that read, "A man and his truck, it's a beautiful thing." *Funny T-shirt,* he thought. *Cole likes funny T-shirts.* He caught himself doing it again! *Shit! Stop thinking about Cole!*

Sara waved at him, trying to grab his attention. "El, are you in there?"

Ellis blinked. "Yeah, I'm here. So what are we doing?"

Lori scrunched her eyes up at him. "Um, getting a table for *five,* apparently. Are your friends joining us?"

Rob chimed in as if Ellis had prompted him. "Why of course they are!" To Lori, he held out his hand. "These are my friends Rob"—he gestured to himself—"and Russ." Ellis glared at him. Rob continued, "Rob is my very best friend in the world, and I owe him everything. If it weren't for his exceptional mastery of sociable intercourse, I'd be an introverted hermit on the verge of academic suicide."

Ellis rolled his eyes. "Shut up."

Russell made a face. "Dude, that makes no sense."

"Yes, it does."

Lori smiled and shook his hand. "It's nice to meet you."

Russell hugged Sara. "I haven't seen you in a long time. You look great!"

"Thank you!" she said happily.

As they exchanged pleasantries, Ellis caught sight of Cole entering the bar. Their eyes met. Ellis felt nauseous and frightened. If he joined them, would everyone know they slept together? Would they judge him for it? Inexplicably, Ellis looped his arm around his sister and pulled her close, kissing her temple. She giggled and planted a kiss on his cheek, cupping his jaw tenderly.

Cole's eyes flashed anger and hurt. He took one step toward them and then stopped. His shoulders drooped right before he shook his head, turned, and fled through the doors, practically pushing a woman over in the process. Ellis felt the damage he'd inflicted by that one small gesture as if Cole had walked right up and slapped him across the face.

Ellis released Sara and hung his head. *Why did I do that?* He shouldn't have. His stomach knotted from the guilt. *I should go after him.* He glanced up and noticed Lori watching him. Ellis cleared his throat and shifted gears. "Should we ask for a bigger table?" He'd wallow in his shame another day.

Sara agreed and held up her hand to the hostess passing by. When she walked over, Sara asked, "Is it possible to change that to a table for five? We had some more friends join us."

"Of course."

They were given a large round table near the corner of the upstairs "game" room, which suited them just fine. It was easier to relax and have a drink, shoot some pool, and then walk back over to the table. Ellis was trying to forget the look in Cole's eyes, but so far it wasn't working. He sipped his Coke and listened to Rob and Sara talking across the table. Apparently she visited his church once.

"You play that drum thing, don't you?" Sara asked.

"Yeah!" Rob said, pleased as punch. "It's called the cajón."

"I knew I recognized you! You play well; I think it adds a lot to the worship service."

"Thank you."

"When were you in church?" asked Lori.

"September, I think," answered Sara. "Remember? Darian asked if we'd like to join him so he wouldn't feel weird going alone with Matt, but you ended up having to work and I went without you."

"Oh yeah, I remember."

Sara kept rambling. "I met Rob a few times at the house and I knew I recognized him but the setting threw me. I didn't expect to see someone I knew at Darian's boyfriend's church. It was odd." Ellis could see similarities between his sister and Cole. Cole would probably like her. *Cole—everything comes back to Cole.* Suddenly he wasn't in the mood to eat dinner.

"Small world," Rob commented. "Next time, come over and talk to me after the service."

"I will, the next time I go," Sara answered.

Russell added innocently, "I wonder if there's any correlation between the Cajon and cojoncs?"

"Only you would think of that, Russ." Rob said, shaking his head.

Ellis found the comment amusing, but his lips refused to smile. He was still thinking of Cole's reaction when he hugged his sister. They'd never met, and she looked nothing like Ellis. He knew he'd successfully misled Cole. Ellis hated himself for it.

"Ellis, would you like to throw some darts with me?" Lori asked.

He shook off his unwanted thoughts and nodded. "Sure." They walked across the floor to the dart area. No tables were in direct line of flight and only tables for two lined one wall so they would not stick out in the middle of the floor. As he picked the darts out of the board, it occurred to him who he was playing against. He turned to Lori. "Are you sure you want to play? I beat the crap out of you last time."

Lori grinned. "I know I have a bad reputation for competitiveness and I don't take losing well, but I promise not to hit you if you play fair."

"Deal," Ellis conceded, handing her the yellow darts. "You can go first."

"Thanks." Lori threw it and managed to hit the outside wedge of thc targct. "Wow, can you tell I haven't played in a while?"

Ellis grinned and took a shot, hitting a double red. Normally each player threw three darts in one leg of the match, but he knew this was just for fun.

Lori aimed and hit the triple ring; she was more satisfied with that. "So, Ellis," Lori asked, "what's the story with that guy?"

"What?" Ellis's alarm carried over into the dart he threw. It stuck into the wood paneling beside the dartboard.

"That guy, the one with the glasses and goatee; the one who gave you the wounded expression when you hugged Sara."

Ellis looked down. He'd been caught. How many other people would pick up on his behavior when the two of them were seen in public together? Ellis would never be able to walk free again. "I don't know what you mean," he lied.

"Ellis," Lori said, reaching up and touching his arm. "I'm not an authority on male relationships, but my best friend, Darian, has been through enough therapy to clue me in on the subtleties that other people miss. That guy was jealous and hurt. And that's coming from a *lesbian* who only saw his face for a second. He cares about you, doesn't he?"

Ellis wasn't ready to share his indiscretions, but from getting to know Lori over the years, he knew her to be compassionate and sincere. Plus, she was gay. If anyone would listen without judgment, it would be her. "I don't know," he answered halfheartedly, looking at his feet.

Lori threw another dart and hit the board near the center. "Your turn."

Ellis looked at Lori. Her features were soft and comforting, telling Ellis with silent encouragement that he needn't fear. He turned to the dartboard and took his shot. Just off the bull's eye. "When did you know you were gay?"

Lori threw her last dart. "Um, I guess in middle school. It's hard to say. It's difficult to pinpoint a time because I've always been a friend to Sara. My romantic feelings developed over years. I'm not sure when it crossed over to sexual thoughts. Sara *is* four years younger than me, remember. I don't think we started messing around until she was at least a junior in high school." She walked over and retrieved the darts for another round. They weren't playing, but throwing the darts gave them something to focus on besides the potential complexity of the conversation. "But being in a relationship with another woman never felt strange. It made me feel... complete."

"Sounds great." Ellis had to admit that was what he wanted. He wanted to spend each moment with Cole. "So... you two... you're... intimate?" He didn't know why he asked, but the words slipped out.

Lori laughed. "What?" Her eyes glinted. Ellis could tell she wasn't offended, but at the same time she seemed shocked to hear the question.

"Sorry, that was totally out of line to ask. You're dating my little sister, for Pete's sake! Forget I said anything." He turned to walk away, but felt Lori snag his arm. He stopped and looked at her. Lori's mirth had disappeared and was replaced by empathy. Ellis felt compelled by the compassion exuding from her eyes to expose his heart for the first time. Something about Lori told him she could be trusted, and Ellis felt a wave of relief. Rob always had the gift of "sensing" people, and for the first time, Ellis knew exactly what he meant. In that moment, Ellis felt Lori's deep concern for him. Plus, he needed to talk to someone or he'd die.

As if reading his mind, Lori led him over to a small side table to give them privacy. It was nowhere near their friends, and so far, no one else was playing darts or sharing a drink in this area. They were essentially alone. "I'll listen," Lori prompted respectfully, "if you want to talk."

Ellis would have loved to sit for a while and bask in the presence of someone who truly cared. He could tell Lori did, even if they'd never shared deeply with each other before. But sitting for a long while to build up his courage to talk wasn't an option. If he waited too long, someone would notice and walk over. He'd have to start soon! He only needed to be strong for thirty seconds and get it out. He took a deep breath and blurted, "How did you know that coming out wouldn't ruin your life?"

"I didn't," Lori said. "But I knew I didn't want to hide either. I liked girls. I liked Sara. Even if she was too young at the time to really explore her feelings, I still figured I'd never know if she liked me back if I hid who I was."

"But didn't you get ridiculed?" The thought frightened him.

"Yes. Girls can be really nasty, and they called me names for a long time. I even found used tampons shoved in my locker once but never found out who did it."

"Holy shit! That's disgusting." Ellis could not imagine the male equivalent of that action. Shit in his mailbox, maybe? More reasons he didn't want to think of himself as a homosexual.

Lori shrugged. "That's life. Sometimes it's not so fun, but you have to hold out for the good parts."

"Which are?" Ellis held his breath, waiting for the answer he knew Lori would give.

"Love. Being loved, and loving someone in return is the greatest gift in the world." Lori's eyes moved from Ellis to the table across the room. "I think I've loved her since I was twelve."

Ellis followed his gaze. He saw Sara slap Rob on his shoulder and throw her head back laughing. Whatever was going on at the table gave the impression they were all enjoying themselves. He was glad. He turned back to Lori when she continued speaking.

"Which sounds completely ridiculous, I know, but she was the one. She's always been the one."

"How do you know if it's right? How do you know if you picked the right one?" It was purely a research question since he loved his sister and knew Lori was right for her.

"You don't. Not really. I waited eight years to take a chance on love, and I was terrified. But life is about taking chances and having faith in something bigger than yourself. I love Sara, and my waiting paid off. She cherishes me and protects me and loves me with more devotion than I thought humanly possible."

Ellis admitted, "I wish I had that."

"Relationships are a two-way street, Ellis. One thing I know for certain is that you have to talk, you and cute guy with the glasses."

Ellis felt his checks grow hot.

Lori continued. "My friend Darian…. You remember Darian, right?"

Ellis nodded. "The emo guy with the piercings and the nail polish? Of course I remember him." He remembered Darian as the guy in high school who came out and always got picked on for it. He was a couple years older than Ellis so they'd never had classes together. "I think he was over a few times playing checkers with you guys, right? I asked if he wanted to knock around the soccer ball with me, and he wasn't coordinated enough to kick it unless it was sitting still. Yeah, I remember Darian."

"Good. Anyway, Darian's been through a lot of shit lately. Because of everything he's gone through, I've learned about the need for real communication. Not just grunting like you *men* are famous for."

Ellis grinned. He knew exactly what she was talking about.

"Especially you! I know you don't talk much. But my advice to you is to talk to this guy. If you care about him, tell him. Moments in life disappear faster than a flash. Don't let him slip away without knowing how you feel." Lori squeezed his hand and Ellis smiled again.

"Thanks." All of what Lori said made sense, but Ellis still felt a niggle in the back of his mind telling him something nameless was wrong. "But… what if… I'm not gay?"

Lori started to grin but stopped, her mirth draining into sincerity. "Oh, you're serious. Are you really asking my opinion?" Ellis felt stupid for even saying it, yet Lori came off so sympathetic. "I'm sorry, I only assumed you were gay because of the way he looked at you, especially considering you never dated girls. I never thought you might be undecided." Lori touched his hand again.

Ellis considered her concern and the tender way she patted his hand. It certainly wasn't flirtatious, but it was way more than casual.

Lori was a beautiful girl, despite her protests to the contrary, and if Ellis really *was* straight, then wouldn't her soft caresses stimulate him? Ellis had to admit he liked it. Lori's touch was without pretense and it felt comforting. Lori's presence was soothing. He was pretty sure any straight guy wouldn't feel so relaxed. If she touched Russell like this, or—God forbid—Mike, Lori would be slapping them across the face right now for their testosterone-fueled advances.

He sighed. He knew he wasn't straight. "So, how did he look at me?" Ellis hated the thought that they were that transparent, but gave in to Lori's intuition.

"Like you betrayed him the moment your lips touched her face. He didn't know Sara's your sister." She said it like a statement, not a question.

"You are too observant for our own good."

Lori smiled. "Call it a gift."

Ellis looked down at his hands where they were folded in front of him. *Admitting the truth to yourself is the first step to healing, right?* Given that to mull over, on top of the idea that he was so intensely attracted to Cole that, no matter how hard he tried, he could not stop thinking about him, Ellis had to conclude he was only trying to fool himself. He'd remained single throughout high school because the notion of dating girls seemed stupid. They were only friends. He'd never felt attracted, sexually, to a girl. Ever. They were nice to look at, and fun to talk to, like Lori, but the only time he'd ever been aroused was when he thought of boys. And now, after meeting Cole, he was experiencing intense desire on a whole other level. He wanted Cole. He needed Cole. The issue in his head couldn't be his sexuality—there had to be another reason for his panic the morning after.

So where did that leave their relationship? He'd treated Cole like shit the past two weeks. They hardly saw one another. And now he'd kissed his sister in an attempt to lash out in anger and fear. What could he do now?

"Well, if I'm gay, then… do you think he'll forgive me?" Ellis asked, even if it felt embarrassing to do so.

Lori smiled warmly. "I hope so. It'd be nice seeing you snuggled up to someone on Christmas. You've been single way too long!"

Ellis smiled and felt his face get hot. He knew he was blushing, but with Lori it didn't matter. She was practically his sister-in-law. Her confidence and observations gave Ellis hope. Maybe somehow he could make it right and talk to Cole. He wanted to talk to Cole… if only he knew where to start. "Thanks."

"Anytime." Lori stood up and held out the darts. "One more round? For real this time?"

"Yeah." Ellis stood up and threw a dart at the target. As they played, Ellis thought about what he could do to earn Cole's favor back without talking. Explaining his previous reaction with words was too difficult, but maybe he could start with good deeds. Actions spoke louder than words, right? Ellis hoped so.

Chapter 10
Soccer Heads

FOR a solid week I managed to avoid Ellis completely. After his little stunt in the pub, I never wanted to see him again. It was apparent to me that when he kissed that girl, he was screaming at me to fuck off. I was right all along—Ellis wasn't gay and sleeping with me was a huge mistake. Only, the knowledge hurt like hell, and I was struggling with every ounce of dignity I had to maintain a noncaring front. He could treat me like shit, but I wasn't about to give him the satisfaction. He would never see me cry!

However, as the week dwindled by, I started noticing little things around the apartment that didn't match up. Like, while I was angry I was blind, but as the days progressed and my anger lessened, I saw details that didn't make sense. Everything in the apartment was neat and I hadn't lifted a finger.

I looked at my bookshelf and each one of the bindings was aligned with the edge of the shelf. The CDs were in alphabetical order, as I liked them to be. The pillows were fluffed, and the picture frames had been dusted.

Weird.

If I didn't know any better, I would have thought Ellis moved out.

On the coffee table I spied a Godiva dark-chocolate bar. *Only Jonathan knows these are my favorite.* How did Ellis find out? What was he up to? Why would he do this? Was it a sick joke to rub it in how great he was, just to laugh in my face and kiss some other random girl the next time I saw him?

I even smelled lemon-scented disinfecting cleaner, the one I used to scrub the kitchen floor. Had Ellis scrubbed the kitchen floor?

I walked into the kitchen and jumped. Ellis was standing there like a serial killer, silent and lurking for no reason. I clutched my chest. "Good God, Ellis! What are you doing?"

"Nothing. Silently hoping you'd go to your room so I could sneak out before my game."

That didn't surprise me! "Pft!" I scoffed. "Figures. Can't stand to stay and face me? I repulse you that much? Thanks. Thanks a lot."

I turned to walk away, but he grabbed my arm. "Cole."

"What?" I snarled.

Ellis let go and backed off. "Nothing." His face wasn't full of disdain like I expected, it was full of *something*, but I couldn't name the expression. Ellis was acting weird. A clean apartment, and a look of... *something.* I didn't know what to say. *"Fuck any girls lately?"* came to mind but I didn't scream it. I was such a coward.

The doorbell rang, which I was grateful for. It gave me something other than seething hatred to chew on. I stormed to the door and opened it. "What!" I growled again before noticing who had come to call. It was Rob, Russell, and Mike, plus a guy I didn't recognize.

"And a *top of the morning* to you too!" Rob quipped, complete with a fake Irish accent. Damn these walking comedians and their tricks!

I glared and left the door open as I walked away.

They came in and slapped each other's hands, grunting and bumping chests. I swear guys have their own chummy "mating" rituals, yet with no romantic inclinations. Like football players who pat each other's butts—why? There seriously is no good reason for a straight guy to pat another guy's behind. Yet, they do it. If I went around slapping other guy's butts, it would suddenly stir up litigious hullabaloo about flaunting my homosexual lifestyle. What a bunch of hypocritical shit! People were shit.

And in spite of that, I stood there in the corner of the room wishing for nothing more than to bump my chest against Ellis's. I was so pathetic. I hated him, but I wanted him so bad. He'd never want me. He flat-out told me sleeping together was a mistake.

I could puke.

Russell and Andre The Giant Junior walked up to me. "Cole, this is Geoff. He's the goalkeeper on the team." Russell introduced the new guy to me like I cared.

I lifted the corner of my mouth. "Hi." I didn't feel like talking, but I did offer my hand. He shook it. "What does a goalkeeper do?"

All eyes turned my way, telling me just how stupid my question was. It wasn't what I'd meant to ask, but my mind wasn't on soccer, it was on the soccer player who hated my guts.

"Let me rephrase the question. How long have you been goalkeeper?" That seemed much more logical to ask.

"This is my fourth year on the college varsity team."

"You must like it. Doesn't it get boring?" I couldn't see myself standing there the entire game while all the other players ran around kicking the ball around. Even if the one game I went to was a loss, I didn't remember seeing him in the goal.

"Sometimes," he said casually. "But I'd much rather block shots than take them. I'm not a go-ahead guy. Being aggressive enough to play striker just isn't me. Plus, I'm big. I make a perfect goalie because I don't have to run and I take up half the goal."

Understatement of the year! He was big. I mean, Rob was a big guy, but Geoff was a wall. He could be a linebacker! (I know because I have ogled my share of linebackers.) "Yeah, I guess so."

"Are you coming tonight? It's one of our last games before playoffs. It should be pretty rowdy."

Rowdy? Just my style. "I don't know. I have studying to do and—"

"Aww, come on Cole, you have to!" Rob whined, throwing a fake tantrum. He always picked the wrong moments to interrupt a good decline. "I missed you the other night at the pub. You gotta come tonight."

"I bet you did." I glared at him, but all he did was smile wider and jump up and down like a puppy surrounded by little children. I looked away from his merry mirth, thinking to myself, *No, Rob would probably be the little child who gets on the ground with all the puppies and lets every one of them lick his face.* Crap! I couldn't yank myself away from Rob's jubilation. It was like a black hole that sucked helpless cynics—like myself—inside. "Fine," I sneered, although no one but the new guy—Geoff—looked bothered by my tone. "Except I've got stuff to do first. Maybe I'll come for the second half."

I didn't know why I put myself in these situations. I was stupid, and pathetic. I didn't want to go, and yet I did. I felt this mysterious gravitational pull toward Ellis just as strongly as negative energy repelling me in the opposite direction.

Rob got right in my face. "You're not trying to get out of it, right? No forgetting to show up!" he asserted.

Leave it to Rob to call my bluff. I really planned to conveniently "forget." I shoved him away from me. "No, I'll come. Just not now. I need to wash my hair first." It worked for women, why not me?

At least Russell laughed, but I don't think he believed me.

TWENTY minutes later, they all headed out the door. It was the longest he and I had been in the same room since I didn't know when. It felt like forever. Ellis looked back at me as he left. His expression looked curiously like regret, but just before I could ask him why, he shut the door. The room was terribly silent. The entire time they were here, the air had felt oppressive. Sometimes people talked about having a huge elephant in the room, but no one wanted to talk about it; well, that was me and Ellis and the conversation we avoided like the plague.

We had sex and it ruined everything.

I felt like I lost my best friend. We hadn't laughed in so long my heart ached for the sound his chuckle made when it bounced off the living room walls. Almost like an echo across a canyon when the sound vibrates over every nook and fills the void with tangible resonance.

Ellis's laughter enveloped me in ways I couldn't describe and didn't understand until the apartment was without it. I needed him. And no matter how much it hurt to see him kiss that girl, if I was honest with myself, I wasn't mad at him—I was mad at myself for not precluding it! I should have known he wasn't ready! He was an eager beaver full of hormones and idealistic expectations, not sound judgment. If only I'd waited and allowed our friendship to solidify, I could have avoided all this resentment.

Without thinking, I meandered into his room and sat on his bed. I folded my body into his comforter and pillow like it belonged there. I adjusted my face and smelled the place where his mind entered the world of dreams. What did Ellis dream of? Soccer? Exams? Cute blond girls who giggled when he kissed them?

After fifteen minutes of torturing myself, I'd had enough and exited the danger zone. I shouldn't have violated Ellis's privacy, anyway, even if all I did was lie on his bed.

I heard the *dingle-dingle* prompt of a text message, and I retrieved my phone from my pocket. I figured it was from Jon. He might live in Texas, but we still texted often.

Yup, Jon.

Hey, buddy. Boyfriend still avoiding you?

"Hardy har, har!" I grumbled at his message. I should have never mentioned my crush on Ellis. I texted back, *Yes. It's as if I have leprosy.*

And you're sure he's straight? Kissing one girl doesn't prove that.

True, but why kiss her at all?

Fear? Confusion? Fucking friends doesn't always end well. Remember Alisha? We were friends for seven years until we slept together.

I remembered the day she slapped his face in the quad. They hadn't spoken for two years now. *You had to remind me. Shit! I don't want to lose Ellis like that. I want my friend back.*

Then the next time you see him, apologize. Say you're sorry and take all the blame.

Another text came through. Much to my shock it was from Ellis. *You don't have to watch me play.*

I texted Jon quickly, *Ellis is texting me.*

Then text him, *not me! Idiot! Tell him you're sorry. Talk to me later. Good luck.*

Did you hear me? Ellis repeated. Even through text, I could hear his voice getting agitated. *You don't need to come.*

"Be straight with me, Ellis!" I hollered at the phone. "You don't *want* me there!" Just when it was getting so easy to talk to him, I fucked it all up! I texted back, *Rob might strangle me, I have to show.* I wanted to type, "I'm sorry," but I felt I needed to work up to that.

Ellis responded right away. *Ignore Rob. Don't come. I know you hate me for what I said. I'll start looking for a place to stay after finals.*

"What?" I shrieked in the quiet room, piercing my own ears with my shrillness. This was not where I'd expected him to take the conversation! I texted as fast as my fingers would allow and before my nerve talked me out of it. *I don't hate you! I thought you hated me. Please don't move out! Can't we work past this somehow? Please?*

Did I sound desperate?

This was different than the first time I panicked. Before, all I could think about was getting a roommate worse than Ellis. Now, it was about losing Ellis. I held my breath until he texted back.

Hate you? I don't hate you. Relief chased the air back out of my lungs. *Look—I gotta go or Coach is gonna take my phone. We'll talk after the game. I don't hate you. I promise. I'm sorry.*

He didn't hate me! If I'd had some pixie dust, I could have flown. "He doesn't hate me," I reassured myself.

Okay, I'll be at the game. I'm sorry too. Kick some ass and break a leg! I hit send and then second-guessed my message. "Why did I say that? 'Break a leg' was for thespians, not jocks. Idiot."

I hurried to my room and changed my shirt. Ellis liked the "particle science" one. I was going to prove I was sorry. Things were going to improve!

I ARRIVED at the stadium just as the clock started. The bleachers were full for the "home" side, as well as "away." I scanned the players for number 11. There he was, running fast toward the opposing team's goal. I stopped and watched as he ripped a shot and hit the upper nineties for a goal thirty-seven seconds into the game!

(I know I act all ignorant at times, but I do know *some* sports talk.)

Ellis leaped and high-fived his wing, and the crowd erupted. Geoff, the goalie, had said it would be rowdy. "Rowdy" didn't cut it as far as adjectives go. This crowd was deafening. Who knew there were this many college soccer fans in the great state of Pennsylvania?

I got chills. It was awesome!

By halftime, I'd figured out at least four of the players' names just by listening to the chants and the parents in the stands, talking. Kevin was the wing, Ollie was a midfielder, Steve seemed to change positions randomly, and Marcus subbed for Kevin when he came out. I know there are like fifteen other players down there on the field, but could I really be bothered to remember all the names? I was focused on only one player—Ellis Montgomery. I watched Ellis nonstop. He was like a cheetah with a soccer ball—fast, fluid, and sleek. Beautiful.

I think this was the first time I was surrounded by jocks and their fans when the "jockness"—bulging muscles, sweat, and male aggression—didn't turn me on. I didn't give a hoot about all those built guys on the field. I only cared about one guy. No matter where the conversation went tonight, I was determined to do my darnedest to make things right.

I needed Ellis back in my life!

WHILE the players were getting their halftime pep talk, I stepped up to the snack shack and purchased a shriveled hotdog and bottled water. I thought of Russell as I laced it with mustard and relish, snickering to myself as I mused over what would happen if I waved it in front of him when I got back to my seat in the stands. *Tee-hee, I'm so sadistic sometimes.* I thought these things, but I never followed through. I was secretly sadistic, but outwardly passive. Call me boring.

I sat down and munched while Russell and Rob continued their discussion. Still! It was going on fifty minutes. They'd been arguing since before I sat down about who made the better starship captain: Jean-Luc Picard or James T. Kirk. I rolled my eyes and watched Ellis. The team was back on the field, shooting in the other direction. The score was 2-2. Soccer is normally a low-scoring sport because it's all about running the ball and shooting at a well-trained goalkeeper who blocks the shots. Of course my fingers were crossed for Ellis to crush the guy! He ran like rolling thunder. Powerful. His passes were precise and his setups remarkable. *Argh, that freaking goalie and his quick hands!* Ellis hadn't made a goal yet this half!

In the background, I heard Russell say that William Shatner hadn't played a convincing role, and Rob lost it. I shook my head as Rob bellowed, "William Shatner and James T. Kirk are not the same person! That's like saying Miley Cyrus is the same person as Hannah Montana, when clearly, they're not!"

Russell didn't hesitate to reply, "Yes, they are!"

"No… they're not!"

I smirked to myself. I loved how Rob paused in the middle of his sentences to calmly make his point. I thought it was funny. But seriously, whatever banter ping-ponged between them mattered not. My attention was on Ellis; crisp and clear, sharp-focused while the rest of the world blurred into the background. He said he didn't hate me, and that proclamation chipped a little more of my regret and self-loathing away every time I repeated it. *Ellis doesn't hate me.* It was a proclamation of emancipation of the Reid variety and I was chuffed. *Ellis doesn't hate me.*

Time flew on and the other team's defenders were making it tough on Ellis. It was like they knew he was the best one out there, therefore they never gave him a chance to get a clear shot. I had to give it to Geoff, though; he was doing a great job defending our goal too.

Only minutes left, and they were passing the ball and running it up the field. Kevin the wingman dropped a pass right at Ellis's feet. He looked to the goal and shot. Short and deflected by the defense, yet the ball got bounced around from head to chest to knee and it didn't really go anywhere. It was like free-for-all pinball, and the bodies in the box crowded each other to the point of losing the ball momentarily. It rolled within inches of the goal and Ellis reacted. He leaped to follow it in and finish. But another guy leapt too, so Ellis dropped his body and let his feet slide in. (Akin to a slide tackle without another player involved.)

The action was like slow motion. Ellis dropped to his back and slid. A defender careened over him and crashed into one of his own players. The goalie, seeing Ellis about to connect with the ball, dove. The goalie's body was parallel to the ground as he flew several feet toward Ellis and the ball. Ellis nudged it, and it rolled in just as the hovering goalie lost his battle with gravity and plummeted. He landed on Ellis's legs but couldn't stop the ball.

The whistle sounded three times. Our team won 3-2!

I jumped up and cheered with the hordes of students. I jumped. I pumped my arms. I screamed. I stopped pumping my arms. I went silent. I stared. A chill passed through me. Someone was helping Ellis to his feet, and he wasn't walking. They carried him off the field.

"El?" I heard Rob say behind me. "Come on," Rob urged, rapping my shoulder and then barreling his way down the bleachers in the blink of an eye. Russell and I followed as quick as we could.

"Give him some space," the coach said, stretching his arm out to stem the huddle.

The three of us didn't make it to his side because of the team crowding in, and I wasn't even sure Ellis knew we were there. Still, we were standing close enough to see the bulge on the inside of his ankle when the assistant coach removed his shin guard and sock.

"Eww." I cringed and turned away. Even before the coach told him his leg was broken, I could see it for myself. No bone stuck that far out and wasn't broken.

Another guy on the team came running up with a bag full of ice and some plastic wrap. (Thankfully for Ellis, his teammates act fast.) He took the ice and placed it over the wicked bulge in Ellis's ankle and proceeded to wrap the plastic around the leg to affix the ice in place. (Something I have never seen before!) "That should hold while you're on the way to the hospital," he said.

"I'll go get my car since it's parked close," said the coach. "We'd call an ambulance, but truthfully, they take longer. We know it's broken. I'll take you to the emergency room myself."

"Come on!" Rob said, gesturing for us to follow. He took off at a jog, and Russell and I beat feet to catch up. "No sense in us hanging around if he's going to the emergency room. We'll beat him there."

THERE was no traffic and the hospital was less than twenty minutes away. Rob parked and then we all headed in. Russell grabbed a wheelchair, and we went back outside to meet the coach when he pulled up.

"I gotta hit the head," Rob announced, oddly. "I'll be right back. Text me the room number if he gets here before I'm back."

Rob rushed off and Russell and I shrugged our shoulders at each other. Then Russell called Ellis's mom and discovered she was on her way because the coach already phoned.

Once they arrived, and Ellis was in a wheelchair, the coach filled out the necessary paperwork and waited until Ellis was wheeled back. Rob followed Ellis, and Russell told the coach he could go if he needed to because Ellis's mom and dad should be by soon. The coach agreed he couldn't do any more for Ellis and told Russell to call him with any questions.

Thankfully, the triage nurse let Russell and me join Rob in the room they'd assigned to Ellis. Normally it is only two guests per patient, but I guess I looked pathetic enough not to turn me down. I was only *one* more than the limit. Surely that wasn't too bad.

Anyhow, we were in the tiny room together and crowded to say the least.

They rolled Ellis's bed out to take an X-ray, leaving us to wait.

"Did somebody call his mom?" asked Rob.

Russell's eyes popped open like the little goo-filled squeezie-toys I used to play with as a kid. (The ones where the gooey eyes pop ooze out of their sockets when squished. That was Russell as he slapped his cheeks with both palms in utter distress.) "Oh no!" he exclaimed. A split second later, he took his hands away, smiling like an asswipe. "Just kidding. I called when you took a leak."

"Jerk."

"But you love me anyway," Russell replied confidently.

Before long, Ellis was wheeled back in. His face was very pale. He looked as though he was holding in the pain and trying to be tough about it. "Um, did anyone give him something for the pain?" It might sound stupid, but I didn't trust the nurses when his expression said the contrary. His ice was gone and his leg looked mutilated. It made my stomach churn.

"We gave him one milligram of morphine. The doctor should be in soon to look at the X-rays." The nurse smiled politely and left us alone again.

I peeked out into the hall. People were rushing everywhere. It was a busy place! I guess I should have been glad that they gave Ellis anything at all for the pain.

Ellis was lying still and hadn't opened his eyes since he returned to the room. I still wasn't sure he knew I was there. Would that comfort him? Upset him? I didn't want to be the cause of more suffering, yet if I left, then I would be the one to suffer. I couldn't help being selfish; I was staying, gosh darn it!

When the doctor came in, he examined Ellis's leg by taking hold of his foot and tilting it to the side. I swear, if Ellis weren't on morphine at all, he'd have leaped up and punched the guy. In fact, I was seriously close to doing it myself. Ellis screamed in agony at the slightest touch!

Seriously? You're gonna do that to the guy? I mean, why? The bone was all but sticking out of his leg! Sure, it didn't break the skin, but any moron could tell it was broken! Ellis's foot sort of flopped in his grasp, and Ellis gripped the bed until his veins exploded from his forearms.

"I know you're a soccer player and you probably don't want to hear this, but your leg is broken," the doctor commented casually.

"No shit, Sherlock," I grumbled. "Glad they pay you the big bucks to diagnose that one!" I glanced away from Ellis's clenching fist and up to find all eyes glued to me. "Oh, sorry," I apologized. "Verbal diarrhea. Won't happen again." I made a sign across my lips with my fingers to signify that they'd not hear another peep because my lips were zipped shut and locked with a key. I didn't regret my cynicism, given the doctor's colossal insensitivity, but I was thankful that they didn't ask me to leave. They could have!

Dr. Kevorkian told the nurse to give him more pain meds and left without another glance in my direction. *Jeez, if you can't take the heat, don't fucking commit the crime!* (Not that touching a patient was a crime, but I swear if he did it again just for laughs, I *would* tackle him!)

Literally two seconds after the nurse gave Ellis another dose, his face relaxed and his fingers unfurled. And, coincidentally, my shoulder blades weren't touching any longer. Hmm, imagine that! I watched as he opened his eyes and groggily took note of his audience. He saw Rob and smiled. "Rob," he whispered. Then he leaned his head my way and he mewled. "Cole." His attention lingered on me, but Russell cleared his throat and stole his attention. "Hey, Russ." His voice was woozy; the morphine was definitely taking away his pain, which made me feel so much better for him.

"Your parents should be here soon," Russell said.

"Mmm, good," he sighed again, turning his attention back to Rob.

Rob, who was on the opposite side of the bed, looked down at poor Ellis. He reached out and smoothed his hair off his forehead. I thought the gesture was endearing and wished I could be bold enough to touch him. "We're here, buddy. Not leaving you alone." After a few minutes of standing there silently, Rob suggested, "I think we should pray."

Rob's suggestion snapped me out of my daydream scenario where Dr. Killjoy had the broken leg and I was the one testing it. *Muahhahhaha!* I blinked. What did he say? *Pray?* I know he's religious and all, but I wasn't. I felt uncomfortable. Why was I sweating? Praying wasn't a big deal. Ellis would probably appreciate it. Was he religious too? I didn't know. For now, I could get over myself.

Rob reached across the bed for my hand and took Ellis's hand in his left. Russell reached for Ellis's other hand after taking mine. Ellis, a bemused expression on his overly serene face, slapped Russell's hand away. "I want to hold Cole's hand." He declared this openly, sounding partially intoxicated, while waving his hand through the air above his head as if in search of mine.

Russell lifted his brows and looked at me.

Rob squawked, "Don't keep the man waiting, Russ; switch spots!"

Russell jumped to it and pushed me closer to Ellis's side. Ellis took my hand and smiled contentedly. "Mmm," he sighed. "I like Cole's hands. They feel so nice."

Rob cleared his throat. "Alrighty, then! Shall we pray?"

Rob looked at me, I looked at Russell, Russell looked at Moonstruck Montgomery, and then we all bowed our heads. I was uncomfortable, but thankfully Rob kept his prayer short. Plus, I was holding Ellis's hand. I liked that part of it a whole lot!

"Dear Lord," said Rob quietly. "We ask that you would be with our friend Ellis. We ask that you would ease his pain and help the doctors to fix his broken leg. And we pray that he will be able to play soccer again soon. In your name we ask it, amen."

When Rob was done, I discovered that Ellis was not letting go. "Ah," I murmured. "He's, um, not letting go." I tugged to display my intent.

Rob waved his hand. "No worries. Let him hold your hand if it makes him feel better. He's got a broken leg, after all. Plus, he's so drugged up he probably doesn't know what's going on."

I was relieved in one sense because I really didn't want to let it go, but the other part of me was disappointed that he might not be aware of his actions. Oh well. Can't have everything, I guess.

"WE'RE going to do one more X-ray; the side view wasn't clear enough," the nurse said just before rolling his bed away (gurney, I guess it's called) and leaving me and the guys standing around twiddling our thumbs.

"I'm going to visit the little boy's room while he's out and see if his mom and dad are here yet," Russell said.

He left and I looked at Rob.

"And then there were two," he said in a funny voice. Possibly a movie reference, but who knew with Rob? He was leaning on the wall between a sanitary deposit for discarded needles and a supply cabinet, staring at me. *Why is he staring at me?* "So," he said with a glint in his eye. "You and Ellis, eh?"

If I had been drinking water at that moment, I would have spewed it from my nose. As it was, I choked and sputtered before I had the wherewithal to compose myself. "W-what?"

"You don't have to act all confused. I watch. I notice things. I see how he looks at you. And…." He leaned closer to whisper the rest. "I saw your right thumb sliding back and forth over his hand while we prayed."

"Hey! You were supposed to have your eyes closed!"

"That's not a rule, it's more like common courtesy."

"Still," I protested weakly. I didn't know where he was going with this. Was he going to rail at us? Was he going to call us Sodomites or whatever the Religious Right deemed the term for sinning against God's holy law? I had nothing to say, and for the life of me I couldn't line up any comebacks if he *did* judge me. He was Ellis's close friend. What would he have to say to him if I outed our relationship before we even had one?

"You don't have to back away from me. I'm not going to bite you."

I hadn't noticed I was moving until he said that and I thumped against the wall behind me. Then I hit my head as I moved in a different direction. *Shit!* "Ouch!" I grumbled, rubbing my lump.

"Careful, Gilligan. We might be in a hospital, but I don't want to have to come here and visit you and Ellis separately."

"Shut up, Rob."

"Hey, I told you I'm not going to bite. You don't need to be grouchy."

"I'm always grouchy."

"Not really. You've mellowed out. Except for the last couple weeks, after we all went camping. Did you and he…?"

No, no, no, he is not going there! I was about to have a full-out panic attack when the nurse brought Ellis back. Rob quieted down and stepped out of her way. When she left, he looked at me again with a weird expression.

He gestured toward Ellis, who was sleeping. "Go ahead. I won't say anything."

"Go ahead and do what?" I honestly didn't know what he was insinuating I do, and the mysterious mirth on his lips was creepy. Luckily, Russell came back with people I assumed were Ellis's parents, and I didn't have to entertain Rob's fantasies any longer.

His mother moved to his side immediately. When she touched his cheek, Ellis opened his eyes. "Mommy," he said, reaching for her hand. I was completely jealous, but more than that, I was disappointed that his parents had no idea who I was. I was a nameless face to them. If Ellis and I *were* dating, would he have told them?

"Ellis!" a girl squealed, pushing past Rob and collapsing over his chest, burying her face in his neck. My eyes went wide. I recognized this girl as the one from the pub. The world felt suddenly cold. Was he still dating her? Oh my God, I felt so stupid showing what little affection I displayed in public when it was clear he wasn't looking to advance anything with me. He was with this girl! Maybe he simply wanted to try to be friends again and I had jumped to romantic conclusions. *Oh God.*

The girl was crying as she looked at him. It was sickeningly obvious how much she loved him. She lifted his hand and kissed his palm, and he smiled. Just like that, I felt the door between us slam closed. I backed up slowly, trying to fade into nothingness. Ellis wasn't mine, and I knew I'd never see him again.

Chapter 11
The 'Rents

BRIAN and Meredith Montgomery had lived a comfortable life in northern Carroll County for nineteen years. After moving there from Baltimore when Benjamin was almost five, Brian Montgomery had known that it would be a better place to raise their three children once Meredith gave birth to their third. Ellis was only one at the time and didn't remember moving, but Benjamin remembered gunshots echoing down the street and was thankful his parents had moved someplace quieter.

After Sara was born, Meredith had her hands full and never found two minutes for herself until Ellis and Sara were both in elementary school. But just because her children were successfully occupied for more than eight hours a day, every day of the week, it still was not adequate to assume that Meredith had time to do the things she wanted. Her life was consumed with driving everywhere under the sun, and laundry, and food preparation, and oh, more dirty laundry! Perhaps she had an hour or two after the kids got on the bus, but how much could actually be done in an hour?

Meredith was an aspiring author. She tried to write about characters on other worlds, but no story ever had an ending. Her books started off well, but fizzled out when the plot lacked details and the antagonist's sinister dealings had no evidence of support. Plus, when on vacation one year in the Outer Banks, a random vacationer had asked what she was typing away at. She'd answered, "I'm writing a book." The person then commented, "Oh, just like every other housewife in America." Needless to say, Meredith felt discouraged and hadn't written a thing in years.

Nothing came to mind, anyway. How did one create a whole other world? She loved R. A. Salvatore and David Eddings, but she knew her writing was far below those amazing science fiction and fantasy authors. She needed inspiration, and until it happened along, Meredith decided to be the perfect stay-at-home mom. She tried her hand at selling Pampered Chef, but she wasn't ambitious enough to make it a lucrative endeavor. She was up every morning by five, so by eight thirty at night, Meredith was ready to hit the hay.

Life continued in a state of repetitive redundancy until Sara graduated from high school.

Sara was a life-giver in and of herself. She was perky and sweet, and Meredith treasured her daughter—and youngest child—with all her heart. Even after she came out to the family that she was in love with her best friend Lori, Meredith never loved her less. In fact, she found Sara's strength of conviction in the face of possible ridicule and condemnation admirable. Besides, Lori was a wonderful girl, and it was obvious that she loved Sara more than anything else on the planet.

Meredith could only wish all her children could be so happy.

Benjamin had married young due to his girlfriend's pregnancy. Rachel was sixteen and Ben was nineteen at the time, and Meredith was mostly glad no one had pressed charges or accused Ben of raping such a young girl. No one knew about the relationship, which had started in the workplace, until she was six months pregnant. It was a rocky beginning, but Benjamin had stood by Rachel even when things between them were not congenial. He refused to leave like so many other teenage fathers, and his perseverance had paid off. Now, after five years, going on six, Ben and Rachel had a pleasant life with their son Brice. They both worked, and Meredith looked after Brice whenever they asked. (More time taken away from her "free time," so to speak.)

And then there was Ellis!

Ellis Walter Montgomery. The middle child. He wasn't her "baby" because all that doting went to sweet little Sara. Ellis was also not her trying older son, who had so many challenges it boggled her mind how they survived them all. Ellis was the one stuck in between, who never got enough attention and had been pushed aside one hundred times too many. He was smart, she'd give him that, but he was also quiet, reserved, and often in his own little world. (Much like her.) Ellis was the conundrum. He was the one she felt was most like her, yet the one who never came to her with any sort of need. This was probably because she'd never had time for him when he was younger. (She deduced.) She'd pushed him aside so often that when he grew up, there was nothing between them to talk about.

She thought that once he was an English major, they would find things to chat about. But so far—no. She wasn't good with grammar. Her punctuation was random. And her vocabulary was severely lacking. What English major would want to talk about writing with her? Ellis also read all the time. She didn't. She heard a writer was supposed to read constantly in the genre of their chosen field. And although she'd loved sci-fi novels years ago, now they felt dry. Her love had dissolved with each passing year as a housewife and mother of three. One day she'd take it up again, but when?

Ellis wasn't around anymore.

He'd started college and made some really great friends. He spent all his time with Rob and Russell. Meredith felt like she didn't know her son at all. He was much more outgoing than she remembered. He was talkative and funny. She'd hoped that since he was unable, financially, to afford campus housing, he'd spend more time at home with his friends and she'd get to know Ellis vicariously through them. But it didn't happen that way. Ellis sold the car he'd spent four years saving for and paid for an apartment on campus.

Her usefulness as a mother was waning.

THEN one night she got that fateful call. The soccer coach said that Ellis had broken his leg playing soccer, and he needed her. Her son needed her! She packed up her cell phone and insurance cards, called her husband, texted Sara, and then off she went to the hospital.

Russell Davenport, Ellis's friend, was even kind enough to meet her outside. Brian arrived five minutes after her, but in that time, she was able to find the nurse and give her Ellis's insurance information and fill out his medical history. She had purpose.

"Are you sure he's going to be fine?" she asked Russell as they walked back to Ellis's room.

"Yes, Ms. M, the doctor said it's broken, but he's not going to die. Ellis is in pain and they gave him morphine, but I'm sure he'll feel much better when you get there."

Russell was such a nice boy. He was close to his mother and Meredith suspected it was *his* influence that encouraged Ellis to call her at least once a week. "I'm glad. Do you know if he'll be able to play soccer again?" She felt bad about the broken leg because she knew how much he enjoyed soccer.

"I think so, but we were just hanging out with Ellis; it's not like we were his parents. I'm sure the doc will fill you in on more details than he gave us. I mean, he was talking to Ellis, but I'm not sure he was giving him all the information. And he has a lame bedside manner, if you ask me. You should have seen the way he grabbed his ankle and moved it around; I was pretty sure Cole was going to punch him for being so insensitive."

"Oh dear," she said, feeling sorry for Ellis, covering her mouth with her hand.

"Who's Cole?" Brian Montgomery asked from behind the two of them.

"El's roommate," Russell answered, glancing back at him. "He's a nice guy, once you get to know him."

"Is he a soccer player too?" Sara asked, walking arm in arm with her dad.

"No," Russell replied. "He's like Bill Nye the Science Guy or something. Only with better hair."

"Oh," Sara said.

As soon as they entered the room, Ellis's eyes met Meredith's. Her heart fluttered.

"Mommy," he called to her weakly, reaching out like he did when he was eight. She took his hand and didn't bother to notice who else was in the room. She was with her boy, and he needed her.

WHEN they arrived home, she made sure to give him a spot in the living room to sleep so he wouldn't have to walk up the steps to his room. Luckily, Brian didn't protest and was very understanding. She gathered his favorite pillow and blanket, while Brian helped Ellis into the house. Sara was even kind enough to get the prescription filled on her way home. Everyone was working together, and Ellis was safely sleeping on the sofa in no time.

Rob and Russell hung out for a few hours, but left early enough to get some sleep before class the next morning.

"Good morning, sleepyhead," Meredith greeted her son as he opened his eyes for the first time. He'd slept for thirteen hours, and she was beginning to worry.

"Hi, Mom," he said quietly.

"Are you in pain?" she asked, kneeling down and feeling his forehead for a temperature. She couldn't always tell with a touch to the forehead, like other moms—Meredith often had to reach her hand down the back of her children's shirts to feel their skin to ascertain their temperature. Ellis was lying on his back and she didn't think he'd appreciate it if she reached up the front. He was twenty, after all, and she wasn't completely daft. He felt okay, so she let it go.

"Yes," he said with a nod.

"I'll go get you some Percocet. Are you hungry?"

"No."

"You need to eat something soon. You have to keep up your strength."

"Later," he whispered, closing his eyes again and tilting his head away from her voice.

Meredith adjusted the blankets up around his chin and hustled off to retrieve his pain meds. She also got a thermal bag and filled it with ice for his leg. The doctor had recommended keeping it iced, even through the soft cast, so that the swelling would go down faster. Ellis had to have surgery in a few days to fix the break, and until then he was to remain off the leg as much as possible and keep it iced.

Ellis opened his eyes and sat up only enough to take the pills with some water and then he went to sleep again. The phone rang.

"Hello?" she answered.

"Hey, Ms. M, it's Rob. How is Ellis doing?" Rob's chipper voice always made her smile.

"He's fine, Rob. Sleeping a lot." There wasn't much else to tell.

"Do you think I could come over?"

"There isn't much point. Ellis is asleep and the pain medicine should make him loopy when he's awake." She gave it to him straight. Meredith didn't want to give Rob hope of talking or playing Xbox as they normally would when Ellis would probably sleep the rest of the day.

"I don't mind if he's asleep. I just want to be there for him. I can bring my guitar and my homework to keep myself busy. Plus, I got some papers for you to sign so he can be excused from a few assignments while he's out."

Meredith smiled. These were the kinds of friends Ellis had! Rob would be willing to sit by his side even when he was sleeping? It made her happy. "Of course you can come by. Is Russ coming over too?" She asked because they were together often.

"Not tonight. Maybe tomorrow."

"Okay. As long as you explain to Russ not to get too loud."

"Gotcha, Ms. M. I'll be by in about forty minutes."

Rob came by and did as promised. He sat in the chair across the room and played soft music on his guitar. Ellis woke up for ten minutes and said hello, but was asleep again quickly.

"You think I could text him later?" Rob asked as he walked to the door.

"You can, but I took his phone," she said. "I think he needs his rest, and if I don't take the phone, he'll be playing those silly soccer games and commenting on Facebook. I think he'll live without it for a while."

Rob looked shocked but didn't question her further. Meredith liked the fact that he didn't challenge her authority in her own house.

ROB also came by the surgery center and waited in the room with her and Brian while Ellis was in surgery. He was the most faithful friend she'd ever seen and often envied the relationship they shared. Russell also visited just after they called Ellis's name to go in the back.

"Good luck, man!" Russell said, squeezing Ellis's hand and then thumping him on the back.

Rob added, "Yeah, El, see you when you get out."

"Is Cole coming?" Ellis asked, his countenance hopeful.

"Nah, man. Sorry. Cole is MIA lately," Russell answered.

A shadow passed over Ellis's face. One that left Meredith wondering what he was thinking. And who was Cole that Ellis should want him here so much? Her thoughts were fleeting, though, as the nurse prompted her to escort them into the surgical prep room.

It was nothing more than a gurney separated from others by a curtain. This was not a hospital, it was a surgical center, and the orthopedic surgeon did dozens of surgeries in a day. *They line them up like sheep*, she thought.

"Are you nervous, honey?" she asked her son.

"Of course he's not nervous, Mere. The boy's twenty years old."

"It's just a question, Brian."

"I'm fine, Mom." He smiled, but something about him wasn't right. He looked sad. "You didn't bring my phone, did you, Mom?"

"No, dear. I told you a few days without it wouldn't hurt. Give it a break. Your friends have come by every day. I'm not sure what else can be accomplished by having that phone in your hand."

"Just in case someone texts, Mom. Like Geoff or Kevin… or Cole."

"Your soccer buddies have all been by the house." The thought occurred to her that Ellis hadn't seemed encouraged by their company. Instead of laughing with them like usual, he pitifully stared out the window every time they visited.

"Cole doesn't play soccer, Mom," Ellis said with an edge to his voice.

"And who is Cole again?"

"Um, he's my… roommate. He was at the hospital when I broke my leg."

"Oh, I don't remember meeting him. I'm sure if he wanted to come he would have hitched a ride with Rob or Russ." Why not, right? They were all Ellis's friends.

"But what if he texted me, Mom, and didn't come because he thought I didn't want him here? All because you took my phone." Ellis was now agitated and Meredith found it disturbing.

"Ellis! You don't need to speak to me like that," she chastised him with a glare.

Ellis immediately backed down. "I'm sorry, Mom. I didn't mean to snap. I'm just tired. And my leg hurts."

"Okay."

"Ellis Montgomery?" the nurse asked as she popped around the corner of the curtain. "It's time to go back."

Meredith kissed her son's forehead. "I'll be right here when you get out."

"Thanks, Mom."

THE surgery went well and Ellis was released to go home later that day. His mother worried because before he could leave his blood pressure had to be stable, yet every time she walked over to his bedside, it shot up! Luckily it only took forty-five minutes to calm down and stay down, so he was able to leave the center.

The first few days repeated the same scenario as the day he broke it: lots of sleep. Rob and Russell stopped by, and so did Mike and Geoff and countless soccer players whose names she lost track of. They brought him presents and some schoolwork he'd missed. They were great friends, but so far she was sure no one named Cole had graced their house.

Ellis took less and less Percocet and eventually switched to ibuprofen to sleep comfortably. He wasn't eating. He wasn't reading. And he didn't seem to want to watch television. He slept sometimes, but more times than she could count, Meredith found him staring out the window over the back of the couch.

"Are you okay, honey? You haven't eaten anything. Can I make another batch of bread pudding?"

He smiled weakly. "No, Mom. Thanks. I'm good." And then he went back to looking out the window.

What was he hoping to see? It was cold and gray, and not even many birds visited the front yard. It seemed boring to look out there for hours on end without talking or anything.

"Sweetheart, do you want to talk about something?" she asked, hoping to get a favorable response.

Ellis shook his head. "No. I'm fine."

"You don't look fine. You look… down."

"I broke my leg, Mom. I've been cooped up on the couch for days. I just want to go back to school."

He didn't say it very kindly, but he wasn't mean about it either. Ellis seemed… *edgy.* "Oh. Well, I don't think it's a great idea."

"But, Mom… Rob can only bring me my work so often. If I was there on campus, he could bring it by my place every day. I could do it while I rested, and he could hand it back in right away." His eyes and voice pleaded this time.

"Hmm. I'll think about it."

"Can I have my phone back yet?" he asked as she was about to leave the room.

Meredith turned on her heel. "Ellis, I'll give it back in another day or two. I just want to make sure you've had enough rest and that you aren't playing on the phone the whole time."

"Mom, I'm not a kid!"

"No. But you are in my house, and you do need to rest, according to the doctor's orders. If I have your phone, at least I know you aren't staying up all night texting. If you want to talk to someone so bad, call them the old-fashioned way."

"Mooom," Ellis whined, punching the back of the couch. "I just want to check it! I don't know the numbers. I push speed-dial and text. Can't I just see it?"

Meredith hadn't seen him so distressed in years. He was normally passive and quiet. Something was going on with him and not having his phone was only a small part of it. She was tempted to turn it on and check to see who might be texting. Maybe it was a girl? He hadn't brought anyone around in high school or college, but that didn't mean there wasn't someone special. Ben hadn't brought Rachel by until she was pregnant. She hoped to God Ellis was smart enough not to get a girl pregnant! She was tempted to check the phone, but didn't. Ellis deserved his privacy. "Fine." She went upstairs to retrieve it.

On the way back down, she tripped over the corner of the area rug and the phone went flying from her grasp. It hit the wall and crashed to the floor.

"Mom!" Ellis yelled. He rolled off the couch and crawled over to his phone like it was a wounded animal. "You cracked the screen! Mom! What am I supposed to do now? I can't read it!"

She felt bad, really, but there was nothing to be done. "I can take it to the store in the morning. I'm sure they can fix the screen or transfer the content to a new one."

"But I wanted it now!" Ellis thumped his hand on the floor in anger and then threw the phone at the other wall.

"Ellis Walter Montgomery! You change that attitude right now, mister, or I won't allow your friends to see you the next time they visit!" She'd had enough. Meredith wasn't sure what was wrong with Ellis, but this aggression was going to end!

He sulked with his arms crossed over his chest. "Fine. I'm sorry."

He didn't sound sorry. "I'll talk to your father about getting you another phone, but you remember your manners or there won't *be* another phone."

"Yes, Mother," he grumbled with slightly less edge to his voice.

Meredith picked up his broken phone and left Ellis to calm down.

NOT too many days after Ellis threw a tizzy over not having his phone, there was a knock on the back door. Only friends used the back door. Meredith wondered who might be dropping by, and hoped it was someone she wanted to see. She had friends, but often they seemed vapid, and entertaining the thought of meaningless banter for the sake of appearances seemed empty. None of her friends really knew her. They driveled on about the PTA or ballet lessons their kids were in, but no one really wanted to know about *her* children.

Sara was a lesbian. Meredith thought that people were terribly quick to judge and afraid of something they didn't understand. If only they saw how happy Sara was! But no, they got stuck on the "L" word. And Ben was forever dubbed the "teenage dad," no matter how old he got! Sometimes they would ask about Ellis, but she had nothing to say since he didn't share his life with her.

Having friends was tiresome.

Thankfully, it was Rob and a friend. The friend looked familiar yet hung behind Rob, looking down at his feet. "Hello, Rob. It's nice to see you. Come in." She ushered them in by stepping aside in the doorway. "And you brought a friend, how nice."

"Yes. This is Cole Reid. He's Ellis's roommate."

"Oh. How nice to finally meet you. Ellis has mentioned you a few times. I guess college life is busy and that's why you haven't popped by before." It came out colder than she intended, but she wasn't about to rephrase it, even after his dark eyes darted away from her face and he bit his lip. Not socializing was affecting her personality. (And politeness.)

"Ah, yeah, I guess," Cole said, uncomfortably, pushing his glasses up the ridge of his nose.

"Can I get you boys some lemonade?" she chirped, feeling all hostess-like all of a sudden. It was fun to have guests to spoil. Maybe they would like some homemade chicken soup? She had some simmering in the Crock-Pot for Ellis.

"That would be great!" Rob said happily. "I'm just gonna show Cole into the living room and then I'll come back in here and help. Okay?"

"All right," she answered, watching him scoot out the door.

Wanting to know more about Ellis, and needing to figure out who Cole was, prompted her to listen by the door. Just this once. No one would know. She cracked it to get a clearer sound.

Ellis's surprised voice was hard to miss. "Cole! What are you doing here?"

"I came to see you," Cole answered, sounding as nervous as he'd looked when she was rude to him in the kitchen. *Did she make him that nervous, or was he nervous talking to Ellis?* Meredith couldn't tell from the sound. She wished she were in the room.

Rob cleared his throat and said, "Well, I'm just gonna… go. I'll see if your mom needs any help with that lemonade." *Why did he sound uncomfortable?*

Meredith jumped back from the door and hurriedly snatched the pitcher from the cabinet. She had the lemonade mix in hand as Rob entered the room. "Is Ellis happy to see you?" She asked as if nothing were amiss.

"Yeah."

"And Cole too? I wasn't aware of their friendship." She added the water to the pitcher.

Rob strolled over next to her. "Well… they're roommates."

"That doesn't mean they're friends. I roomed with a girl in college—the one year I went—and we couldn't stand each other," she pointed out.

"Yeah, I guess that happens. Cole and Ellis didn't exactly hit it off right away, but they're fine now. Cole is less cynical around him, I think, and Ellis smiles more."

"Oh? Is he funny, like a class clown or something? He looked kind of nerdy to me." *Why am I acting like this? Rob's going to think something crawled up my butt!* Meredith was feeling combative for some reason. Who was this "Cole" and why did Ellis smile more around him? Rob was the most pleasant friend Ellis had, so for Rob to say Ellis smiled more around Cole gave Meredith a queasy stomach.

"Cole's sarcastic but harmless. If you look past the 'dour' he's actually a great guy. He went camping with us in September, and even though it rained practically the entire time, I didn't hear him complain once!" Rob smiled and added the powdered lemonade mix to the water and kept talking. "And he's real smart too; a physics major."

"Wow." She was genuinely impressed. Ellis normally made friends with the jock crowd. It was truly unusual for him to bond with someone intellectual. Not that jocks weren't intellectual, but often times—in her experience—they had less brain and more brawn. Maybe college life was changing Ellis? Maybe he'd found he could make friends with anyone there? Maybe he would go back and forget her once she was not taking care of him? Maybe he would move away and never look back?

"Ms. M? Are you okay?" Rob looked serious.

Meredith shook her head to clear away the speculatory nonsense. "Uh, yeah. I'm fine," she said. But she wasn't, not really. It was hard not to imagine the worst case of abandonment scenarios when she'd dreaded the onset of "empty nest syndrome" for years. True, they hadn't all left the nest yet, but she knew it would be soon. Sara was with Lori, Ben was with Rachel, and Ellis... Ellis was with...? Hmm, she didn't know. Why worry about some random friendship? Ellis was still her boy.

"Can you get the tray from the cabinet over there?" she asked and directed him with a gesture. In a minute, the glasses and pitcher were arranged and they were walking back into the living room.

As soon as she entered the room, it felt different. Ellis's countenance was no longer glum but radiant. Why wasn't he radiant for *her*? It was difficult to ward off the jealous tendencies and remember he was older now. He wasn't a little kid who ran to Mommy when he scraped his knee. He was practically a grown-up, and his friends where a huge part of his life. It was their presence that buoyed him, not hers.

"Well, I see someone is looking happier today," Meredith said with a smile as she set the tray on the coffee table. Cole had moved out of the way and stood next to the couch near Ellis. Out of the corner of her eye, she could have sworn she saw Cole touch his hair, but as soon as she turned his way, his hand was at his side. *Curious.* She smiled, masking the awkward quiver in her stomach.

"Yeah." Ellis grinned uncomfortably and looked away.

Either he was lying or having her in the room was causing the silence to reproduce. No matter what, this was the first time in a long while that Meredith felt like she had a third eye or a growth on her back that no one wanted to mention in polite conversation. She was the third wheel in a room of four people and didn't belong among them. Ellis was sinking away from her and she was helpless to stop it. Just when things were growing impossibly tight, Rob coughed. It was obvious he was trying for a sound, any sound.

"Mom," Ellis said quietly, peering up at her with his sad blue eyes, "I really miss my friends."

"I know, honey." She tried to console him, patting his shoulder. "They can come by as much as they like." She turned to Rob. "Perhaps you could have a movie night? Invite some of Ellis's friends from school?" She turned to Cole, who looked about ready to hide behind the sofa. "You could come too, if you want." She meant for it to be sincere but worried it came off as flippant.

"That's not what I mean, Mom. I want to stay there."

She looked him in the eyes. They pleaded in inaudible ways that pained her. Why was he looking like that? Was her care really that horrible? "I don't know, dear. How will you get around?" She tried not to allow her quivers to sound in her voice.

"Rob can help me, and Cole. I can use my crutches to get to class and take the elevators to the lecture rooms. It will be fine, Mom. Really."

"And the doctor's appointments?" She was trying to think of all the reasons he should stay without asking what he'd do without *her*?

"Well... I could... take him," Cole muttered sheepishly.

Is he always so namby-pamby? Meredith thought. She could not see why he was here at all. First he hadn't come around for weeks, and then when he did he looked paralyzed by fear. Why would he dare to suggest he drive Ellis around? She paused. Her internal criticism against a person she'd just met opened her eyes to the truth. *He's afraid of me! Why?* This Cole person was afraid of what she'd say, of what she'd do, and perhaps that was the whole reason Ellis wasn't talking to her about the girlfriend he had on campus! She wasn't approachable. She'd walled him off for too many years, and she'd lost her chance! Ellis was gone already. She swallowed her tears. "I guess I could think about it," she said, straight-faced.

Ellis didn't let it go. He begged, "Can I please go back to living on campus? Pleeease, Mommy?"

He used the "Mommy" card. It got her every time.

SHE allowed him to go, not realizing it meant immediate evacuation. In twenty minutes, they were up and out of the house with all of his belongings and medication. The house felt like a graveyard. Meredith fell asleep on the couch, smelling his sweat on the pillow and pondering how her son's life had slipped through her fingers, and only then did she realize she didn't know him at all.

Chapter 12
Explain yourself

"I KNOW you're in there, Cole! You can't avoid me forever!"

Rob yelled through the door as I leaned against it from the other side. He'd tried this tactic now on seven other occasions, and I'd managed to fake him into believing I wasn't there. Only this time I think he spotted me sprinting past the theater building. I ducked behind the bushes, hoping to lose him, but he showed up at my door anyway. *Crap!*

"Cole! Open this freakin' door!" He pounded on it. "You have to help me! Cole, you infuriating pain in my rear, open this door and help me get Ellis back!"

I exhaled loudly and realized my mistake only after. I clamped my hand over my mouth, but it was too late.

"Cole?" he said in a softer voice. "Did I just hear you on the other side of the door? Cole, come on. Open the door and let me talk to you. You've been dodging me ever since Ellis broke his leg two weeks ago. Come on!"

Against my better judgment, I relented.

Rob barged inside as soon as I turned the knob. I'd never seen him so pushy. "You know," he said to me with a look angrier than I have ever seen on Rob, "you can be a total dickwad!"

I stepped back a pace in shock. Rob just cursed at me! "What did you call me?"

"A dickwad!" Oh my gosh, Rob was mad! Normally he altered Mike's favorite phrase from "dickwad" to "dipwad," so for him to say "dick" he seriously got my attention. (Rob never cursed.) "Your best friend is lying at home, being held prisoner by June Cleaver, and you sit here doing nothing! What the heck? And you don't call, you don't text, and I bet you even deleted my voice messages without even listening to them!"

He had me there! "First of all," I asserted, "I *did* text Ellis, three times, and he didn't respond."

Suddenly Rob backpedaled his high horse. "Oh... yeah... well... here's the thing.... His mom kind of took his phone away for a teeny-tiny bit." Rob rolled his eyes and flopped his wrist flamboyantly as he tried to make her actions sound silly. (Rob acted gayer than me sometimes!) "She said something about it distracting him from all the rest he is supposed to have."

I narrowed my eyes. "Then why are you giving me shit about it?"

He got red in the face and bellowed, "Because you didn't answer *my* calls! Mine! I thought we were friends too."

Talk about mood swings. Wow! "What if I didn't want to talk to you?" I yelled back at him.

Rob covered his heart. "Ow! That hurts." Resetting his jaw and fortifying his willpower, he looked me straight in the eye and said, "No. I don't accept that. You're such a pain in the ass and I'm not letting you get away with it!" *Oh my. He said "ass" that time.* Then he paused and took a deep breath. When he spoke again, his voice was controlled instead of on the verge of hysteria. "Look, I came here to get you to go with me to Ellis's house and help convince his mom he'd be better off on campus. I've done the best I can bringing his assignments to him, but it takes up all my free time driving back and forth. Plus, he's alert now, he's not on Percocet, and his mom has kissed his forehead twelve too many times. It's sickening. We have to get him out of there or he's going to die of sugar shock and get fat on homemade bread pudding."

"Have you ever thought that maybe he doesn't *want* me there?" Hadn't Rob seen the blond girl draping herself over his chest in the hospital? *Jeez!*

"Now why would you even think that?" Rob looked flabbergasted. *Really? Why?* I didn't know what was going on in Rob's head, but he had to know Ellis was dating that blond girl.

"Maybe because we haven't spoken two words to each other in weeks?" I replied. "He's been mad at me for a while now. We *almost* got a chance to clear the air, but then he broke his leg."

"Yeah! Nice of you to show up for his surgery, by the way!"

"Hey! I didn't know when the surgery was—it's not like his family even cared to inform me. They probably don't know I exist."

"That's why I called you, you asshole!" Rob reached out and swatted me on the side of the head. "He asked if you were coming, and I had to tell him you weren't answering my calls."

That made me feel ashamed. "Oh, I'm sorry. I didn't know. He really asked about me?"

"Of course, he did! Why wouldn't he? Ellis is in love with you, for crying out loud!"

Rob said it matter-of-factly, but the sudden squeeze in my gut left me speechless. "He l-lov...." Talking and me weren't together on this one; I stood, slack-jawed.

Rob, on the other hand, always seemed primed and ready for more. Perplexed by my silence, he continued, "Surely you knew that? Come on, Cole, with all the time you spend together? Stolen glances. Secret caresses. And then that hand-holding thing at the hospital?"

"You said it was drug-induced and he wouldn't remember!" I found my voice out of sheer desperation.

"I said that for Russ's sake." He blew it off with a wave of his hand. "I didn't know how he'd react. I wasn't going to share my theory about the two of you until I knew for sure."

"The two of *us*?" Rob was doing it again. He was assuming, yet overlooking one all-important factor—that girl! "Don't you mean Ellis and his *girlfriend*?"

"Girlfriend? What girlfriend? Ellis has a girlfriend? Since when? And why would he write a poem about *you* when he has a girlfriend?" He unshouldered the backpack he had on and unzipped it before pulling out a piece of paper. "Look," he said, handing it to me. "Read that and tell me I'm imagining things."

I glared. "You're imagining things!"

"You haven't read it!" he pointed out as I scoffed.

I didn't know what the hell was going to be so convincing that I'd believe Ellis was in love with me. Sure, he'd murmured he loved me, once, after sex, while he was falling asleep. He could have said anything. Halfheartedly, I looked at the paper in my grasp. It was a poem.

Of Love and Sadness

And what should I speak to you today,
Of paper flowers and skies of gray?
Or moon-lit nights, sitting alone,
Candles burning with no one home.
Pure sadness falls upon mine ear;
I hear it whisper, because you're not here.
My cold tears that fall, deafen the night
In ways that can't be found in light.
The shadows cry of a love so dear
That my heart won't beat without him near.
Cupid calls, "Fear not, my friend, for love is a fire;
Which kindles, ignites, and consumes the pyre."
Love is the flame that banishes dark,
And teaches a tune to the morning lark.
It's love that beats within my breast,
And love that gives each soul true rest.
So when my heart in sadness sighs,
I remember that love is in his brown eyes.

IT WAS nice but there was no evidence it was about me. So I had brown eyes. It didn't prove anything. I looked up. "It's not about me."

"Yes, it is. It has to be! You haven't seen him lately; he's a mess. Glum. Listless. Bored out of his mind! I'm telling you—he misses you."

I lowered my eyelids halfway. "Because I put the 'hoot' in hootenanny, and Ellis never knew fun before he met me." *Snide?* Not me.

"Cole, why do you have to do that? Not every situation is negative."

"Because people *don't* fall in love with me!" Oh God! I'd said it out loud, and my mouth kept confessing. "I'm unlikable, Rob, or haven't you figured that out? I'm prickly and derisive, and I'm not good for more than a fifteen-minute fuck before the guy's out the door. Why should Ellis treat me any different? He sure left in a hurry the morning after *we* fucked!"

Maybe I was too blunt? *Oops.* Rob certainly looked shocked as he held up his index finger. "Ah, let me just say, I didn't need that word picture." He reached out and grabbed the wall. He looked gaunt. *My bad.*

"I guess I shouldn't have blurted about me and Ellis—"

"Stop!" He threw up all five fingers to block the words from entering his personal space. "Let me just…." Rob carefully made his way to the couch and sat down.

"Can I get you some water?" I asked because he looked ill.

"Please."

I left and filled a glass for him. After he drank half of it, he motioned for me to join him, so I sat and waited. Maybe he was processing the information I'd let fly? I'd already acted like an ass by not returning his calls, so this time I waited until he was ready to talk to me.

"I knew he liked you," he said finally, quietly, breathing through his nose again instead of heaving gasps through his mouth. "Ellis changed as soon as he moved in, and I credited it to leaving his parents' house. But that morning, when we went to breakfast, I saw it in his eyes. He looked at you differently." Rob was looking at the table and then finally brought his eyes to meet mine. "I knew he loved you. The camping trip confirmed it."

"How?" I asked. Love at first sight never settled well with me. Romance movies and fairytale princesses falling in love at a single glance—that stuff wasn't real. Nobody could *know* without knowing a person. You could easily *lust* in one glance, but love? I doubted it.

"Have you ever walked onto the porch in the wee hours of the morning after it snowed the night before and watched the sun peeking through the snow-laden trees and breathed a deep lungful of cold, crisp air and felt more alive than you've ever felt before?"

I shrugged my shoulders. "Yeah, I guess I have. It's been a while."

"I remember a few winters ago walking outside just before sunrise. The freezing air filled my lungs and made my chest hurt with cold, but it warmed me, too, with the very nature of life. I felt connected to everything, even if only briefly." Rob smiled. "You're that lungful of winter air, Cole. I could see it in his eyes: at breakfast, and every time we were all together afterwards. You may not believe me, but I'm pretty intuitive that way."

I wanted to believe him, I did, but my memories looped a vision of him with that girl over and over. Rob had to be wrong. "But what about that girl?"

"What girl? You keep saying that, but I don't know what girl you're talking about."

"The blond at the pub! He kissed her right in front of me. And then she showed up at the hospital with his mom. He loves that girl, not me."

Rob smirked. Then he grabbed his mouth and snickered behind his hand. "That girl? The blond at the hospital. You're worried about *her*?"

"Yes!" If he didn't stop giggling I was about to….

"You mean Sara?"

"Yes, Sara! I don't care what her name is! She's the one he loves."

Rob nodded. "Yup, he does."

Now I felt sick. "I told you. Why did you have to go on and on if you knew he loved that girl?"

"Cole," he said, this time with more consideration than his giggling had conveyed. "He loves her because she is his sister. And his *lesbian* sister to boot."

Did I hear him correctly? "Sister?"

He nodded again. "Sister."

My skin grew hot. My mind was swimming. My eyes stung. "She's his…."

Rob reached out and gripped my shoulder. "Yup. Sister."

"He…." I didn't know what to do now. It was like the broken record that kept telling me Ellis was straight ground to a halt and snapped the needle. "She's his sister?"

"Yes, Cole. Sara is his sister."

"And he loves…?"

"You. He loves *you*."

As soon as I looked into Rob's eyes, I knew I was crying. I covered my face with my hands. "Oh God," I moaned. "You must think I'm a complete loser." I wiped my cheeks and rubbed the tears away, but they wouldn't stop. "Shit." I jumped up and awkwardly went to the bathroom. I blew my nose and washed my face, and then glanced up to find Rob watching me. "Aren't you going to tell me how stupid I am?"

"No."

"Aren't you going to condemn me or something? Doesn't your Bible say homosexuality is a sin?" (I don't know why I have to drag that into the conversation. It wasn't as if I didn't have enough to think about.)

"No."

"Are you going to chastise me for stealing his virginity?"

"La la la." Rob turned away from the bathroom doorway, shielding himself from my words again with a raised hand. "Okay, Cole, that's enough. What you and Ellis do together, I really don't want details."

I followed him into the living room. "But you don't approve," I said with deep curiosity.

"I have to admit I was repulsed to think about it, initially."

I could hear in his voice he wasn't finished. "But?"

"But... Ellis is my friend. One of my best friends. He's the only person besides Russ that I can honestly say I would die for. I've never known a homosexual before. I mean really *known* one. Gays were always 'over there' in that group, but not in mine. It's easy to bash or criticize something or someone you don't know. But I know Ellis. I love Ellis. He's like my brother. And yeah, I'm having a hard time with it. I don't understand how it fits into God's plan, but I'm trying. I want to understand. I love him, and I believe with all my heart that God does too. And if Ellis is in love with you, what kind of a friend would I be to hate him for loving someone?"

I had no verbal response for that. I reached up and squeezed his arm.

Rob went on to say, "I don't think sin is as black and white as people want it to be. I think sin comes in an array of colors, and one of them is so bright that it blinds us to our ability to love. And if I don't think I can love you just because you're gay, then Satan wins; because without love, the only color left is hate."

Well, damn! I was crying again! And as stupid as I felt for being so emotional, I caught a glimpse of a tear welling in Rob's eye and suddenly I didn't feel so dumb.

Rob hugged me and held me tightly to his barrel of a chest. I heard him snivel in my ear. "If you love him, please take care of him."

"I promise," I answered back. That was the closest I had come to admitting how I felt. My emotions were still an untidy heap in my brain. You know? I'd been jealous of "that girl," and I was hurt when he left the morning after, and then my mind swirled with thoughts after reading the poem; it was hard to sort all at once. Did I love him? I think I did. *I think I do.* But telling Rob didn't seem right. I needed to tell Ellis first.

Rob eased back and patted my shoulders. "Let's go get him."

"Yes, please."

As we headed to the door, Rob paused. "You were kissing in the tent that night, weren't you?"

I felt my face flush. "You heard that?"

"I heard something. I thought it was Russ making noise in his sleep, but now that this is out in the open, I had to ask."

"What about a word picture?"

He shrugged. "It was weird enough hearing you kiss, and it will probably be strange *seeing* you kiss. Break me in slowly, okay? I'm trying to understand and get used to you and Ellis, but if you *ever* tell me about the sex, I might have to strip you naked, smear your body with honey, and tie you up next to a fire-ant mound. No sex talk, and no groping in public."

"Okay. Got it! No sex talk." Which was fine by me. I understand guys talk about sex all the time, but it never felt right to me. What Ellis and I did together should stay between us, as far as I was concerned. Not talking about our sex life was a no-brainer. "But you're fine if I kiss him?"

He made a face. "I've never seen two guys kiss, and I'm kind of curious and kind of grossed out. Just warn me beforehand."

We walked out the door and down to his car. "I can do that."

"And don't tell Russ."

I got in and buckled the seat belt. "What? Why?"

"He might freak out. And since it made me sort of squeamish, I want to break my buddy in gently."

I shrugged. "Alright. I guess. Just don't wait for months or anything."

"I won't."

I THINK Rob was done, as far as the talking went. He was a huge talker by nature, but I think our convo in the apartment was good for a while. Once we drove off, the entire ride was filled with silence and it wasn't uncomfortable at all.

The drive was nice. Ellis lived in a nice, spacious neighborhood. Lots were probably two to three acres each, if I had to guess. Some wooded, some not, but all the properties had lovely single-family, two-story colonials adorned with professional landscaping and matching luxury cars. I spotted several driveways sporting a Lexus or a Hummer.

AFTER we met his mom at the kitchen door (a rather "familiar" and casual entrance, if you ask me), Rob walked in, in front of me, and spoke to Ellis first. Ellis was on the couch, facing the other direction, so he couldn't see me anyway. "Hey, buddy," Rob said. I hung back, waiting. "How you doing?"

Ellis looked like he shrugged, but he was lying on the couch, so his shrug was more of a wiggle.

"Okay, I guess." He sounded awful.

"Anything I can do?"

Another shrug/wiggle. He wasn't talking. If I knew Ellis, I bet his face was gray and his eyes were gaunt. Just the lack of expression in his voice told me that.

Rob waved me over. "I brought someone to see you."

"Aww, Rob, why?" he whined. At the sound of his protest, I stopped three feet behind him. "Unless it's Russ, I don't want to talk. I'm tired, and I stink. Did you know my mom won't let me take a shower by myself?"

"Dang, that sucks."

"Tell me about it. I haven't showered since my brother visited six days ago."

"That's why it smells so bad in here! Peehew." Rob pinched his nose, and I choked back a laugh.

"Shut up. So who'd you bring?" Ellis asked.

"Me." I stepped into his field of vision. I offered the answer, but took care to read his expression *before* breaking out in a romantic aria of my undying love. I had an inkling he loved me, but he didn't know I knew. We were still wading through the relationship quagmire as far as he was concerned. Plus, I wanted to hear him say it!

"Cole!" Immediately he struggled to sit up. His hair was a mess—it stuck out on all sides and the back of his head was as flat as the pillow he rested upon. And as I drew nearer, I could smell him. Normally I didn't mind his sweaty smell, but I did now. "What are you doing here?" he asked, surprised.

"I came to see you." I shoved my hands in my pockets and inched my way into his presence. I had to be sure I was welcome.

He stared at me as if lost for words.

Rob caught on to the awkwardness and coughed. "Well, I'm just gonna… go. I'll see if your mom needs any help with that lemonade."

He backed out of the room, leaving us to fill up the space with silence. Why did this have to be so hard? Rob had blurted it out quickly, like ripping off a bandage. Maybe I should do the same. "I, um, Ellis…." I stepped closer as I searched for the right words. I guess Ellis could see I was floundering because he grabbed my arm and held it securely.

When I looked at him, he said, "Cole, I'm sorry."

"What for?" I asked, but the question was superfluous. We both had things to be sorry for; he'd simply beat me to an apology.

"For avoiding you and treating you so callously." He looked very pathetic, and I couldn't hold onto my detached expression for long. Ellis continued, "I shouldn't have acted like that the day after we…." He paused and looked at the doorway. "You know… after. I should've been more mature and talked it out instead of pretending like it didn't happen. So… I'm sorry."

I hated that Rob had churned my emotions earlier, because now they threatened to break loose again. I didn't want to cry in front of Ellis, not yet, but I was one second from it and I knew my quivering lip would give me away. I took my hand out of my pocket, and Ellis moved his hand—the one that held my arm—down my skin until he was clasping my fingers. I shut my eyes and felt my body shiver. When he let go, I wanted to reach out but didn't.

"I've missed you, Cole." Such a simple statement, but one that summed up my feelings exactly.

"Me too." He looked at the door one more time. He was nervous, and it wasn't right for me to expect him to spill his guts in his parents' living room. I needed to get him out of here and back to our place, where he felt comfortable.

"I just… there's so much… I don't know what to say, Cole. I'm not an articulate genius. I don't talk about my feelings, and now that I have them, I don't know where to begin." He looked down as if embarrassed. Why? Feelings weren't at the top of any guy's conversational repertoire. Cars, belching, video games, farting, sports, or in my case the occasional conversation about Newton's laws of gravitational forces, but the point is, guys didn't talk about feelings often. Ellis had no need to beat himself up over it.

It seemed like the perfect opportunity to reveal Rob's interference in his love life. (Rob might get in trouble for that, but oh well.) I wanted to suggest he leave with me and Rob first, but I had to know if the poem was indeed about me.

I reached into my pocket and pulled out the folded paper. "Ellis," I said. "Did you write this about me?"

He looked slightly scared when he saw what I had. "Where did you get that?"

"Rob."

"Oh," he groaned.

"Did you write it about me?"

"You weren't supposed to see that. It was part of our poetry midterm."

"Ellis?"

He nodded slightly, putting his face in his hands as if trying to hide from my rejection. Only, I wasn't going to reject him. I squeezed next to him on the three inches of sofa cushion and pulled his hands away from his face. "Ellis." When he looked at me, I tried to give him strength. I didn't want him to be afraid to tell me what he was thinking. I held his hands tightly in mine and fell into the blue depths of his eyes. He was scared, and I had to take the chance for us. I whispered, "I love you."

Faint shock washed over his face, and then a smile materialized replacing his worry. "You do?"

"Why do you look surprised? Surely you know how easy it is to love you."

He blushed—how adorable. "I don't know. I've never felt…. You're the first person I…." Ellis struggled to find the right words and looked exasperated. He kept turning his head to look at the doorway behind him as if expecting Rob or his mom to walk in. And his hands were shaking. "Please get me out of here."

"I will." I stood and stepped toward the other room, but Ellis still held my hand fast. "What's wrong?" I asked.

He searched my eyes, finally whispering, "I love you too, Cole."

I smiled proudly. Hearing those words made me tingle. I needed to get him home! I leaned in and kissed him, which of course made *him* smile. "You don't need to be an articulate genius, only honest in however little you say."

"I'll try."

As soon as he let go of my hand, his mom walked in with lemonade.

Chapter 13
Back Where You Belong

I GAVE Ellis as much space as he needed. The transition from his parents' couch to mine wasn't hard, but simply having him home didn't transform him into Chatty Cathy. He slept a lot when he wasn't doing schoolwork, and when he was awake he smiled at me more than anything. (Still no deep discussions.) I longed to return to our much-needed conversation, but there were moments of flirtatious glances and soft touches that gave me hope. So I waited.

Russell and Rob brought his assignments by daily, and also dropped the completed work off with his instructors. They were great! Ellis had already made up the work he'd missed and read constantly to keep ahead. And on a few occasions, Mike even used FaceTime to let Ellis watch the lecture live! (Ellis has some pretty awesome friends.)

I WALKED into the living room one afternoon to find him scratching his leg inside the cast with a pencil. "You know you're not supposed to do that," I pointed out. "What if you cut yourself or get lead jammed under the skin? You could develop gangrene and then they'd have to amputate."

Ellis glared, although not in a menacing way.

"Do you want something to eat?" I asked.

Ellis shook his head.

"I think you should eat. You look like you've lost weight and I wouldn't want you wasting away to nothing."

"I'm fine."

I sat on the edge of the coffee table and waited. I was trying to give him time to work through his issues, but whatever personal problems he had were taking too long to surface, in my opinion. Avoidance didn't solve anything; it only prolonged the distance between us. I didn't like distance. We'd confessed our love, shouldn't there be lots of kissing and handholding and more kissing? I wasn't expecting sex, especially while he was in a cast, but some kissing would be nice. I'd even like to lie next to him and feel him holding me.

I watched him and he watched me. Our eyes were not afraid to linger, but I was still unable to read the unspoken thoughts. I gave him a smile and was rewarded with one in return. I took a chance and moved my body closer so I was able to touch his arm. Ellis took my hand and held it, caressing each finger and studying the contour of every joint. I felt so treasured. He kissed my fingertips, and I closed my eyes. I felt him rub his cheek against the back of my hand and the hair on his face scratched, but in an enjoyable way. I liked his scruffy look and was glad he hadn't shaved in days.

Another tender kiss, and then he asked, "Can you make me a grilled cheese sandwich?"

Talk about a non sequitur? That was so random! "What? Sure." I reluctantly pulled away and absently served him. Should I be angry? I guess not. He wasn't being mean.

ANOTHER day or two slipped by, and I was on the verge of banging my head against the wall. Lingering to the point of stagnation was our current state of affairs. I am aware that guys in general, as a collective whole, are not notorious for sharing emotions readily— not usually—but this was getting ridiculous. I did my share of bottling things up and hiding how I felt, but this was different. I sensed that he and I were on the brink of something amazing, and if I allowed it to drag on too long, maybe that "something" would disappear. I had to act. Rob had told me Ellis was shy, so maybe I could get him to talk if I gave him a nudge in the right direction.

He changed positions this morning and currently had his leg propped on a pillow on the coffee table so he could play Xbox.

Only… he wasn't playing FIFA, and the couple times I peeked into the living room earlier, Ellis was just sitting there, staring at nothing. The amount of curiosity I had was enough to kill *eight* cats.

I walked over to him and sat down on the sofa. "I'm sorry," I said, taking all the blame on myself. "I don't know exactly what I did, but if I made you feel like you couldn't talk to me about what is going on between us, then I'm sorry."

He lifted his heartbreaking expression in my direction. "It's not you, it's me."

Yeah, how many times have you heard that phrase and suddenly felt better? I wasn't buying it. "Ellis, talk to me." I paused and waited, but he remained quiet and contemplative. "You know I love you. And you told me you loved me too. I want to be here for you, but unless I turn into Edward Cullen in the next few minutes—"

He chuckled. "Please don't."

"—I don't have the gift of reading minds. You have to give me a clue or something."

More silence. God, this was like watching paint dry. (Which, by the way, sounds like a terribly boring job. Does anyone really do that?) "I know you were about to tell me something the night you broke your leg and therefore never got the chance, but since you've been home, you've slipped into this nonconfrontational demonstration of silence as a superpower. Ellis," I said softly, trying to sooth his tension, "please, whatever it is, it can't be that bad. Talk to me."

"I'm afraid," he admitted without looking at me.

Afraid? Okay. When silence continued and he didn't expound on his confessed fear I felt compelled to fill in the blank. "Is it a fear of… *bees?*"

Ellis snorted. "Apiphobia? No." He smirked and glanced sideways at me.

Oh, how I love that smirk! "How about ataxophobia?" I jested.

Ellis laughed and smiled at me. "No, I think that's all you!"

I smiled back. It delighted me to no end that he knew ataxophobia was the fear of disorder and untidiness. It was also very pleasant to hear him laugh—my skin was buzzing. I turned my body and tucked one leg under the other so I could face him as we talked. I also extended my arm and positioned it behind his shoulder so I could finger his hair. "Is it felinophobia?"

Ellis shook his head. "No, I don't mind cats."

"It's definitely not bibliophobia. How about blennophobia?"

Ellis furrowed his brow.

"Fear of slime," I answered.

He chuckled. "No."

"Katsaridaphobia? Decidophobia?"

Ellis shook his head and grinned as he reached over and took my right hand.

"Medomalacuphobia?"

"Nope."

"Laliophobia?" I had to take a stab at that.

"No. I'm not afraid of talking, only afraid of saying the wrong thing."

I squeezed his hand. "You realize we're having a conversation Rob and Russ would be proud of."

"Yeah. Probably."

"So," I mused, leisurely enjoying the softness of his hair and the mirth on his lips, "if you're not afraid of disorder, cats, books, *or* slime, and you don't fear cockroaches, making decisions, or losing an erection; *and* we ruled out a fear of speaking in general, then tell me, Mr. Montgomery, what phobia has you sitting on our couch for days unable to voice the reason you avoided me the day after we made love? That's when this all started, correct?" I had a feeling of what might be going through his mind, but unless I ruled that out too, I'd be haunted by the possibility.

"You said *our* couch."

"You're avoiding the question."

He looked down. "Genophobia."

Quickly I ran through the list of phobias I'd memorized. There were hundreds and certainly I couldn't remember them all—that's why I saved the phobia list under my "favorites" on my computer. Genophobia was.... "Fear of sex?" I asked with trepidation. It was the first time I didn't want to be right.

Ellis nodded. "At first I thought maybe I was confused, like I really wasn't gay."

"I was wondering the same thing, actually," I confessed.

"But no matter what I did, I couldn't stop thinking about you."

"Good thoughts, I hope."

He looked intently into my eyes. "Sexual thoughts," he said with a rasp that bordered on lust.

My groin pulsed. "Oh? Then why…?"

"Genophobia? It's my only logical conclusion. That morning," he explained, "when I woke up with you in my arms, I felt so happy."

"You did?" I wanted to believe him, but it juxtaposed the actual events that followed. "I guess I missed that part when I woke up alone."

"I *was* happy. It felt so good to be with you and kiss you and touch you, but when I moved…." Ellis stopped and looked away.

"Ellis, if the chemistry isn't right between us," I speculated, "that's fine. You just need to be honest with me. I'd rather keep you as a platonic best friend than lose what we have trying to force it to be more."

"That's not it, Cole!" Ellis snapped, and I jumped, not expecting such an outburst. Ellis gripped his fists like he was trying to will his sudden anger away. "I'm sorry," he said in a more controlled tone. "I didn't mean to yell."

"It's okay."

"No, it's not! I don't want to yell at you, I want to yell at *me*. It's all to do with *me*. I just don't understand why I feel like this."

"Then tell me how you feel. I don't understand what's going on, and I don't know how to help you if you don't talk about it."

Ellis rubbed his face and groaned. "I know. I'm sorry. I've never had to explain my actions before. I've never loved anyone. It's like I know in theory I should tell you what's going on, but in practice I'm still the only one in the room." Ellis looked painfully frustrated. "I've never had to think so hard in my life. It's not that I don't want to be with you—I *do*! I want way more than friendship." He swallowed visibly and seemed to be struggling with what he wanted to say. "I—Oh God, Cole, why does this have to be so fucking hard?"

I moved closer. I had my folded leg practically in his lap and my arm completely around his shoulders. "Hey, look at me," I urged, cupping his cheek. When he looked into my eyes, I could see oceans of affection. "It doesn't have to be hard. Just say it."

After a couple minutes waffling between bolting out the door and spilling his guts—assuming those were the choices behind his darting eyes and jittering hands—Ellis spoke. "After we… you know…."

"If you can't say it, we shouldn't be doing it." As soon as I said it, I knew I should have kept my mouth shut. I wasn't helping the situation. "Sorry," I quickly said. "Shutting up."

Ellis thankfully continued. "After we… *made love*… I woke up expecting to feel elated and relaxed and ready for more, but when I moved, all I felt was fear."

"What do you mean 'when you moved'?" He looked reluctant to explain. *Why?*

"I could feel you, still, inside of me, and it reminded me what we did. I felt trapped and violated and vulnerable. I wanted to touch you, but as I reached out I panicked. I felt ashamed, so I left." He sniffled. "I'm sorry. No matter how incredible it felt while we did it, that was nothing compared to the terror I felt when I considered we might do it again. I don't want to feel like that—degraded, or something… I don't know."

Ellis started crying. The depth of turmoil that had weighed heavy on his heart for so long burst forth. I guided him into a hug, and he leaned into me, burying his face in my neck. I was glad he wasn't afraid to touch me. In this moment of honesty, I felt I needed to share some things too. "You know, you're not the only one who felt out of sorts that morning."

"Really?" he asked, snuggling into my neck and holding me around my waist.

"No," I confirmed. "I wasn't comfortable with everything we did either. At the time it felt good, but in the morning...." I left the possible reasons open-ended.

Ellis pulled back. "Why? I mean—you've done it before, was I that bad?"

"Gosh no!" *I can't believe he just jumped to that conclusion!* I shook my head fervently. "Ellis, it wasn't you. Let me try to explain it in a way you understand." I took a deep breath and hoped he got what I was about to say, because I couldn't think of any other explanation. "You're a pitcher. I'm a catcher."

"Huh?" He gave me that "WTF" expression and I knew I'd lost him. *Damn*!

I tried again. "Soccer! You know soccer."

"Ah, yeah... so?"

"Okay, I'm a goalkeeper. You're a striker."

"Sometimes I play midfield—"

"Stop! I'm trying to use a metaphor here."

"Oh, sorry. Please continue."

"You're a striker. You like to score."

When I paused, he saw that I was waiting for an answer so he gave one. "Yeah, I love scoring."

"Why?" I asked, hoping he would give me right what I was hoping for.

"Because I like to be in the spotlight. I like taking charge and feeling in control. I run the ball, pass to the open wings, and wait for the open shot to rip it."

Perfect! I thought. Talking about soccer had relaxed his body language. I was on to something! "But you don't like to play defense or goalkeeper?" I asked with an ulterior motive.

"No," he said, shaking his head.

"Why?"

"Because I don't like waiting for the ball to come to me. I like going after it! I respect the keeper because he has to defend the goal against some hard-angled shots, but I would much rather run the ball down the other end and take shot after shot against the other goal!"

"Exactly!" I said proudly.

"Exactly what?"

"You're not the goalkeeper, I am."

"Huh?"

Ellis didn't get it. Crap! I guess I couldn't explain it; I was just going to have to demonstrate. But how would I get him to go for the goal without looking like I was taking control of the field? Let's see, more directness. Yeah. Ellis responded well to direct questions.

"Ellis," I asked. "Do you love me?"

He scrunched his eyes again. If he didn't stop doing that, I swear they'd stay in that position permanently. "I already told you that I do."

"Don't get huffy, just go with the question."

"Yes, I love you, Cole. I love you a whole lot. You're all I think about." Ellis moved his hand and proceeded to stroke my thigh, which made me all fluttery, and I almost forgot what I was talking about.

"But you don't want to…." I lifted my eyebrows suggestively.

"No." He shook his head and looked down. "Maybe… I don't know." I hated the frustration that hung between us. I knew things would work out, but I needed him to see his desire to try.

I let him sit and think as I rubbed the back of his neck.

My patience rewarded me when he looked up and started speaking again. "That night, in the tent, when I kissed you... I never thought it could feel like that. I avoided kissing girls for years because it felt weird to consider it. I didn't want to do it just because everyone else was. Girls were pretty, but I didn't want to do stuff with 'em. I wanted it to be special. I know that sounds dumb, but it's how I felt at the time. And then I met you." I could see desire creeping its way back into his expression—heady eyes, heavy breath. "Kissing you became this fantasy of mine. Every time I saw you biting your lip and playing with your mustache, I wanted to kiss you."

"I do that?" I had to ask because playing with my mustache made me sound like a sixteen-year-old growing facial hair for the first time.

Ellis nodded. "Yeah, and I think it's adorable. For weeks I watched you. I'd close my eyes and pretend to run my thumb over the hair on your lips and chin." He reached up and touched me just as he described. Lightly. Delicately. His fingers tracing my lips made me salivate. I suddenly had the urge to suck on his fingers. "Then I kissed you and it was intoxicating. The whole time we kissed I wanted to fuck you so bad it about killed me holding back."

"Why hold back?" I whispered, feeling my own desires churning.

"The guys were there. And then we came home to the apartment and I felt weird. Awkward. I didn't know what to do."

"But you didn't try."

"I was worried I'd do it wrong. I knew you'd done it with other guys before, and you knew, because of Rob, that I *hadn't*. I didn't want to disappoint you."

I smiled. He was so sweet to want to please me. "I think I can almost guarantee that I won't be disappointed."

"How do you know?"

"I just do. But I think you need to stop worrying about it and go with what you feel. Do it, act on instinct. No second-guessing."

"But—"

"No buts. Do you trust me?"

"Yes."

"Then kiss me again and see where it leads you. I guarantee it won't feel the same as last time."

"What if it leads me straight out that door?" He tilted his head toward the apartment door.

"And what if I'm right? Just kiss me."

Ellis paused and licked his lips. He looked at me like he was scared to try yet also scared not to. One touch of his lips prompted more. Tiny kiss after tiny kiss evolved into harder rougher kisses laden with sloppy tongues and nipping teeth. I felt him slip his hands under my shirt and grip my ribs.

I moved to find a better position. I was peripherally aware of his leg and the cast and his inability to maneuver, so I maneuvered around him. I turned my hips and leaned back in his arms until my body lay across his lap and my head rested on the arm of the couch. Ellis put both arms around me and kissed me deeply. In seconds, he slipped his hand under my shirt again and explored my stomach. Then he moved his hand lower and groped me through my pajama bottoms. I moaned into his mouth, and Ellis slipped his hand inside my pants.

He wasn't shy about touching me. He knew what felt good, and he wasn't holding back. He gripped my length and tugged perfectly. I tilted my hips and whimpered. But no matter how wonderful it was to be in this position, this wasn't the goal. Me getting off was not the plan. I wanted Ellis to feel *his* need to get off! I wanted Ellis to take hold of his desires and realize he wasn't afraid of sex, only of *penetration*. Reluctantly I reached down and grabbed his hand.

Wordlessly, I slipped out of my pants and removed my shirt. Ellis quickly removed his own shirt and pulled me into another kiss. I worked my way into his lap again, this time straddling his hips. I kissed him and rocked myself against him. "Fuck me, please," I rasped between kisses. "I want to ride you." More kisses. "Let me ride you?"

Ellis's hands squeezed my ass on both cheeks. "Are you sure?" he asked, tilting his hips to meet mine.

"Yes, Ellis. I want to feel you inside of me." I leaned back and searched his face for any sign of fear. When none came, I carefully got off his lap and went to retrieve my lube and a condom. When I returned, he'd already removed his shorts and presently stroked his notably engorged cock.

I *sooo* wanted to suck it down, taste him and make him lose his mind, but I had to remind myself of the mission at hand—he needed to feel good about *fucking me!*

As soon as I got near enough to touch, Ellis mapped out my skin with his hands. He pulled me close and kissed my mouth and chin and neck while he massaged my hips and ass and thighs. He groaned, reached behind me, and ghosted over my entrance.

I tore the condom packet and reached for his penis. He stopped my hand.

I questioned him with my eyes. He didn't look afraid; in fact, he appeared primed to ready. Ellis then removed the condom from my grasp and dropped it over the side of the couch. *Does he realize what he's saying?* He stared at me with a heady intensity that accelerated my already racing heart. He *did* know what he was doing, and I moved over his hips as his hands guided me. Ellis grabbed the lube and slathered himself liberally.

I was nervous. I hadn't been fucked in a long time. I knew it would feel impossibly tight, and probably hurt, but it was the price I'd pay for Ellis's education. He needed this more than I did. I positioned myself over him and sank onto him as slowly as I could. Ellis threw his head back as my body enveloped him.

"Ohhh!" His chest heaved a grand sigh of pleasure. He gripped my hips and dug his short nails into my flesh. "Cooole."

My ass hurt. It burned and my lower body felt impossibly full. The term "impaled" came to mind, but I knew from experience that soon the pain would subside and pleasure would replace it, I only needed to relax. I knew that in theory, but God, was he big! Thicker than me and longer than any guy I'd been with before, Ellis had no idea how many guys would line up to get fucked by such a beautiful cock! And this cock, the one that bore no barriers between its flesh and mine, declared exclusivity as soon as it sank into my core.

No condoms = no other partners.

Ellis had silently told me he was mine.

I panted, trying to will away my discomfort enough to move.

"You okay?" Ellis asked, touching my face tenderly.

Was I *okay?* He had no idea how "okay" I was to be joined like this with the man I loved. I nodded. "Just give me a second." After that second and a few more seconds, I lifted my hips and then came back down. The motion awarded me with those little electric shocks I craved so much. Again I slid up and then came down, up and down; undulating like ripples on a lake and picking up the pace with every wave of pleasure. As I tilted my hips forward, I felt his head graze over my prostate, and I hitched my breath. The internal explosion of endorphins that followed each downward thrust spurned me on to wilder and faster heights of gratification. Even the burning in my thighs would not slow me down.

Ellis was howling as I rode him. He grunted and clenched his teeth, breathing hard as he watched my every move. "I'm gonna… come… ahhh, Cooole!" he warned me. Ellis met my downward thrust with an upward tilt just as I started spurting all over his chest. I milked the jets of semen from myself as Ellis held my hips firmly, jutting upward in quick movements until his ejaculation was complete.

I sagged against him, threw my arms around his neck, and tucked my face against his hair. There wasn't an inch of me that wasn't teeming with adrenaline. I felt so alive and yet so vulnerable. I'd never felt so close to another person in my life. Even the first time he and I made love, it hadn't ended like this because it went against my nature to take charge as I had before.

This—right here, right now—was where I wanted to be. Not there. I needed Ellis to be inside of me, always, and as we sat on the couch, still connected, I felt scared that he might not feel the same. He held me tight, and I felt him gliding his hand up and down my bare back.

"I love you," he whispered.

"I love you too," I answered back, kissing his ear and neck.

"Are you crying?" he asked.

"No." *Why would I cry? That would be stupid.*

"Then why is my shoulder wet?"

I sniffled and leaned back. Yup, his shoulder was wet with fresh tears. I *was* crying and had no idea why. "Sorry. I don't know what came over me." I wiped my eyes hastily.

"I do," Ellis replied with a kiss. He looked at me with the most loving expression I'd ever seen on anybody. He caressed my cheek and coaxed me back into his embrace. He held me against him for the longest time.

Before long, I realized how sticky I felt and how much my thighs were killing me. I had to change positions no matter how much I wanted to remain where I was, interlocked with Ellis. "I think I need to move," I said.

Ellis loosened his hold around me. "Yeah. I know."

His softened appendage, which slipped from my body, left me wanting. "Oh man, my legs hurt!" I complained as I crumpled onto the cushions next to Ellis. "I don't think I can make it to the bathroom for a towel."

Ellis giggled. "I'll go." He was up before I could protest, hopping across the floor. It amazed me how steady and coordinated he was on one leg. In fact, I think he hopped with more balance on one foot, than I had *standing* on two. I watched him hop back into the room with a come-free chest and a damp towel. "Here. I know what Jonathan said about your 'no sex on the couch' rule."

"Jonathan." I shook my head. I took the offered towel and grinned. "Thanks." I wiped my sticky chest and groin, but the rest of the splooge would probably come out as I showered. *Oooh, shower!* "Ellis, do you want to shower with me?" I asked, looking up at him as he watched me wiping off.

Carefully he bent down until he was kneeling on one knee, keeping his weight off the other. He kissed my forehead. "I thought you'd never ask." He winked.

"Ellis?"

"Yeah?"

I stood up and followed his hopping self to the bathroom. I needed to know something first. "Was I right?"

He hopped closer and caressed my shoulder, and then he kissed me and smiled, saying, "You were right."

It made me happy to hear. Although I liked being correct, in reality I was only right 80 percent of the time. I'd banked on this occasion falling in the larger ratio.

He turned on the water and faced me as I brought in a plastic bag and some tape for his cast. (Rob and I had figured out how to get him showered with a bag over his cast the day we got him home.) Ellis continued his thought. "In fact, that felt so damn good, I think I'm going to have to fuck you again, just to make sure I wasn't dreaming. You up for it?"

I chuckled in response.

ELLIS was so different in the days that followed.

I'd expected to sleep alone that night and possibly for days or weeks until his cast was off; what I didn't expect was the complete romantic sap that greeted me the next morning and many other mornings. I was standing at the sink, filling the coffeepot, when I felt Ellis slide his arms around my waist. He pressed his chest against my back and kissed my neck, sighing in my ear, "Good morning."

"Yeah. I guess it is." I set the pot on the counter and turned off the water.

Ellis rocked me gently in his arms as he continued to kiss my neck. He nipped me and made his way up to my ear. He sounded hungry, and the hard object pressed against my backside made me wonder if he had more than breakfast in mind.

"Is that a hammer in your pocket, or are you just glad to see me?" I asked.

Ellis chuckled deep in his throat and turned me around. The look in his eyes was downright licentious. He dipped his head and tongued my Adam's apple, nipping my throat and making me whimper in the most helpless of ways. I'd never felt so powerless to pull away from anyone in my life. By the time he kissed my mouth, I was nothing but Jell-O wearing sweatpants, seconds from melting onto the floor. He kissed me deep and long and had me making all kinds of desperate needy sounds.

I could barely see when he leaned back, smiling, ever so pleased with himself.

"You're beautiful, you know that?" he asked, looking into my eyes with wonder and contentment written on his face.

"Oh," I replied in my stupor. I was finding it extremely difficult to think clearly.

Ellis rubbed my back and touched my face. "Yeah." He kissed me again and then pulled away. He took the coffeepot and poured the contents into the machine. "I wish I didn't have class," he lamented. "I'd love to lay around the apartment all day, kissing you and hearing all those little whimpers you make."

"Class?" My fog was dissipating. "Crap, I have class too. Can't we skip class?" It sounded logical to me. I didn't want him to do anything else either, unless it involved lube and Ellis moaning my name. "It takes you so long to get to class on crutches. Can't they make another exception?"

He smiled and shook his head. "No. Class. My professors have been very lenient already. Plus, my mom would kill me if my grades dropped and she found out it was over a guy."

"Oh, your parents don't know you're gay, do they." It was something I suspected but not a topic we discussed.

"No. But that's not the issue I'm getting at. My mom would get mad if my grades dropped because of a *boyfriend*. It's not the gay part, as much as not letting myself get distracted by a relationship. My sister's gay. And although they don't know about me, I'm sure they'll be cool about it. Who knows, my mom probably suspects anyway. I haven't had a girlfriend. And the way I practically begged to come back and stay with you while my leg is broken probably gave away my orientation."

I put some bread in the toaster. "Probably. You were pretty obvious about it."

"I know. I'll tell them after finals are over. Right now, I gotta get out of here." He leaned in and kissed me again. "See you later?"

"Yeah."

ELLIS was like this "affection monster" who got switched on one day and never looked back. He touched me every time he walked— hopped—by me; a caress here, a kiss there, and sometimes a light pat or squeeze on my butt. I never would have expected it, but I was certainly not complaining. He used to be so "contained," but now that restraint wasn't necessary, he just… *didn't*. I'd never seen him so relaxed. And you know? I'd never seen *me* so relaxed. His gentleness and genuine joy at being around me rubbed off in the most surprising of ways. I felt giddy.

He kissed me often, but so far we'd only had sex twice. The shower was not a particularly intelligent choice since it's wet and slippery and he only had one good leg to stand on. We tried, but gave up for fear of breaking the other leg. I helped him shower and promised to control myself as I washed him, and it wasn't as hard as I thought it would be. The key was to tease enough to make it fun but not to the point of full-on arousal.

JUST before Thanksgiving break, I came home to find a stimulating surprise: Ellis had cleaned the apartment for the second time! The smell of disinfectant filled the air and I felt my groin pulse in response. I looked around. The carpet was vacuumed, the television was shiny, the bookshelf was straightened, and ceiling fan was dusted. And it wasn't even my birthday! I suppose I could be seen as a complete loser by getting an erection from a clean apartment, but I did. And the best part was that Ellis knew I would.

I walked into the kitchen and dinner was ready for me— candlelight and everything! I could have cried.

"I wanted to make it special since we won't be together over Thanksgiving," I heard him say behind me.

I turned and there he stood, leaning on one crutch. He had on my favorite science T-shirt and his red basketball shorts. (Basketball shorts were the easiest to change over the cast, and my "What is the speed of dark?" T-shirt never ended up in my drawer after I washed it. Curious.)

"Everything looks great. And the place smells wonderful."

"I wanted it to be perfect."

"It is," I said, stepping up and then wrapping my arms around him. I kissed his lips and pressed my body into his. Since this was a "special occasion" and classes were done until Monday, and because I wouldn't see him for a few days, I was hoping tonight we could try a little of what ZZ Top called "The Tube Snake Boogie." Sex wasn't the main concern in a relationship. If you asked any housewife from here to California, communication and conversation were key, but in a man-on-man relationship, as far as I was concerned, sex *was* communication!

I had never had the prospect of recurrent sexual satisfaction before, and now that it was on the horizon, I wasn't backing away. I held myself in check purely out of concern for his broken leg and the cast that always seemed to be in the way. Once that puppy was off, look out, Ellis! Here comes your willing sex slave. (Of course he had no idea how far I'd go to please him! I'm not even sure I did.)

Ellis groaned, pawing my rear end. "Later, sugar. Let's eat first while it's still warm."

He hopped into the kitchen, and I questioned with an arched eyebrow, "Sugar?"

Ellis leaned the crutch on the counter and bent to open the oven door. "You don't like it?" He took out a roast turkey, balancing on one leg. Of course he'd never ask for help!

"No. Makes me think you're from the south, which you're not. Can't you just call me Cole?"

"I could, but where's the fun in that? Honey." He winked at me while stirring what I presumed was gravy.

"Honey? Um, no. I'm not voting for a nickname that reminds me of Winnie the Pooh."

"Sweetie?"

"Exercising my right of veto."

"Darling?"

"As in Wendy Darling? I'm not Peter Pan."

"Is there any endearment that you can't ascribe to a movie or children's character?"

"Cole."

"Cole is not an endearment. Cole is the person my endearment describes." He slapped his hands together with excitement. "How about Napoleon or Hitler?"

I tilted my head and scowled. "You want to nickname me after dictators?"

"You *are* a dictator. You like to control things, *and* you enjoy manipulating people to get what you want. "

"I like Cole. It's my name. It's short and easy to remember."

"And I'm still going to call you something… how about *lover* or *sex kitten*?" He smiled in a way that told me I wouldn't win. I pinched my lips shut before the choices got worse. I'd have to endure whatever he chose anyway. (I really hoped it wasn't "honey" or "darling." They seemed so girlish.) Ellis pointed to the table set for two. "Wash your hands and have a seat."

I did so, and a splendid repast was set before me: mashed potatoes, green beans, turkey, gravy, stuffing; everything my mom made but in smaller portions. He'd even made me a salad although he never ate them. I felt so spoiled.

Ellis hopped back in the kitchen to grab another spoon, and I reached for the salad dressing. As he hopped back in, he commented about fetching a pillow for his leg, and I jumped up. "Let me," I said. "You've done so much already!"

When I returned, and he had sufficiently arranged his limb on an adjacent chair, I reached for my fork. Ellis, to my surprise, scooped salad onto his plate. "Feeling adventurous?" I asked.

"Feeling guilty," he answered. "Mom keeps telling me I need to eat more green vegetables."

"I'm not sure iceberg lettuce even counts as a vegetable. I think it's 99 percent water."

Ellis reached across the table for the same dressing I'd used. I didn't realize what he was about to do until he proceeded to shake it. "The lid's not—!" I held up an urgent hand but stopped midsentence as the lid to the bottle went flying and French dressing painted my ceiling. I gasped.

Ellis lifted his eyes and surveyed the splatter that had sufficiently spread its fingers across wall, ceiling, and shirt alike. When his gaze returned to mine, he smirked and said, "Oops."

Aghast by his negligence and even more so by his flippancy, I found myself at a loss for words. "You.... I.... The lid...." My mouth hung open, but I couldn't form a proper sentence. It should not surprise me when things like this occurred in Ellis's presence, yet it did. Then a generous glop dripped from the ceiling and landed right in the middle of the mashed potatoes. "Oh!" I cried.

"It can all be cleaned up," Ellis reasoned calmly.

"But my house...." I interjected in a shrill voice. My hysteria was on the verge of epic proportions, but just as I attempted to finish my thought and chastise Ellis for his folly, he scooped the dressing-covered potatoes from the bowl with his fingers and flung them at me. "Ah!" I shrieked, more astonished than ever.

Ellis looked way too pleased as he grinned at me. He reached out and flicked another dollop in my direction.

"Stop!"

Ellis laughed and repeated his action. The potatoes were followed by a generous amount of roughage from his plate.

My heart seized and leaped into my throat. This could not be real. Ellis was *not* throwing food at me!

"Come on, fight back." Ellis egged me on by adding turkey bits and stuffing chunks to his ammo selection. "You know you want to. It's fun. Try it." More turkey, more lettuce. "Just once." Potatoes hit me in the eye, covering one lens of my glasses and slowly sliding off to my cheek.

That was it! I'd hit my limit of tolerance. I stood, seething under the potato mask that Ellis had kindly decorated me with, and pounded my fists on the table. "That's enough!" I bellowed right before another scoop landed in my mouth. Then gravy followed.

Ellis was snickering, proud as a peacock.

I removed my glasses and scraped the mush from my eye as I chewed on the potatoes in my mouth—they were good, by the way—and glared at him. He was so smug. He laughed at my dismay and threw it back in my face. But still, he was awfully cute as he sat there. His eyes glinted mischievously, as they often did, especially around his friends. His laugh was pleasing to my ears, as was normally the case, even if I didn't enjoy the circumstances for it. As I stared, his laughter quieted and his eyes grew more shameless and less mirthful. His smirk transformed into an amused challenge of retaliation. Would I return fire? Or would I simply leave the table and retrieve my cherished mop and bucket?

I held his gaze as I reached out and scooped up a copious amount of potatoes. Ellis didn't even duck as I threw them! In fact, as the potatoes hit his chin and neck, his mouth hung open in shock. A spilt second later, he was reaching for something else to fling and I was doing the same. The richly laden table became a free-for-all of edible ammunition. I didn't know what I was grabbing as I flung handfuls of comestibles to defend myself. Ellis was faster with his hands, but I was quicker on my feet as we stood on opposite sides, dancing around the edges of the small table, splattering each other with our dinner.

Never in my wildest imagination would I have considered this type of juvenile behavior fun! But it was. To my chagrin and my astonishment, my heart was racing with cheerful exhilaration. Ellis was laughing heartily and I along with him. Flinging and tossing and lobbing whatever I could in his direction, I made my way around the table. Ellis, who didn't attempt to flee, grabbed my waist as soon as

I stood near enough, hauled me in, and forcefully claimed my mouth with a commanding kiss.

I tasted Thanksgiving dinner on his lips and tongue as we groped each other and sank clumsily to the food-covered floor.

Unlike before, in our other attempts to make love in a planned-out and meticulous manner, this was primal and impromptu. Ellis pressed his body against mine and groaned as he roamed his hands all over me. "You have too many clothes on," he mentioned as he lifted the hem of my shirt and shoved it over my head. He rolled off me only to strip, careful to work the shorts over his cast yet less mindful of his leg than before. It seemed sex was more urgent.

I slipped out of my jeans and waited for his next move.

Ellis came back over me, pulling my leg over one shoulder as he rocked into me. With one knee on the floor and the other lifted slightly, Ellis leaned his weight to one side. He didn't bother to guard his cast or leg from injury, but I made sure not to add to that potential by wrapping my other leg over his hip, safely out of the way.

He explored me with his hands and practically devoured me with his mouth. He bit my neck and pinched my nipples. I felt him cup my balls and then he slid his finger into my crack. He only paused to suck on his finger before pressing it inside me, much like I had done to him. I moaned and mewled, happier than I had ever been before. He pumped my ass with his fingers and once or twice ghosted over that spot inside, making me beg for him to do it again. That knot of nerves hadn't been stimulated in more than a week, and I hungered for it even more than the food that littered the floor around us. But his fingers weren't enough. I needed more. Much more.

"Ellis, please," I begged. "I need you. Please fuck me."

He growled and chuckled deep in his throat, and I felt the vibrations of it through his chest into mine. It wasn't "ha ha" funny laughter, either; it was that of enjoyment and satisfaction. I could tell he got off on making me beg.

I eagerly complied. "Please. Ellis. Pleeease. I want you. I need you. Please."

He leaned back and positioned himself. He looked me in the eyes and pushed in. I swear debaucherous lust, laced with fire, radiated from his gaze and enveloped me as he sank in completely, claiming another scorching kiss as we joined. I surrendered everything to him. Ellis was indeed the master, and I would willingly submit to anything he desired.

On our kitchen floor, he conquered me.

Not that he set out initially to prove his dominance, but I think he discovered it in those first few thrusts. He didn't take it slow, and he didn't hesitate but for a few seconds. Ellis exploded in a sexually propelled rapture that consumed his being and drove his ambition, and I was the catalyst. He thrust into me deeper and harder, until I thought I'd split apart from his dynamic force. He practically snarled in my ear like a wild beast, and I could tell he was close to climax. He grabbed my knee and roughly pushed it higher, opening me wider as he let out an inhuman roar.

This was unlike anything I had ever experienced in the past. I struggled for breath as I held onto him in our throes of passion. The friction between our bellies was enough to tip me over the edge and I erupted like Vesuvius. And while the rush of semen shot ribbons over my chest, I helplessly rode out Ellis's newfound primal inclinations with loud exclamations. "Oh fuck! Ellis! Fuck!" He pushed me over the edge and kept me there longer than anyone had.

Ellis, too, shouted his triumph robustly as he collapsed over me in the end, panting in my ear.

I hugged him tightly as I huffed and puffed, attempting to regain my composure. I felt him slip from inside me, and again felt disappointment. I wanted that connection. I needed that connection. Ellis was the one. I knew that he was, and it scared me.

Ellis repositioned himself next to me and searched my face with his eyes. He touched my cheek and jaw tenderly, as if seeing me for the first time. I could feel him trembling against me. "Marry me."

I blinked in response. "What?" Surely I'd misheard him.

"Will you marry me?" he asked again, soft yet sure, caressing my cheek and brushing his fingers over the hairs of my mustache. "I love you, Cole. There's nothing about you that doesn't make me tingle all over every time you're in the room. Even your infuriating quirks make me buzz with anticipation because when you yell or grumble or protest something or other I've done, all I envision is ripping your clothes off and fucking you blind, like I did just now. Every inch of me wants nothing more than to be with you. Always. Every day, and everywhere. So… marry me."

I swallowed hard. He'd rendered me speechless once again. His words were unexpected, yet inspired. Yes, he was being irrational and impetuous, but he was also romantic and sentimental. *Ellis*, I thought as I gazed lovingly into his eyes, *God brought me this beautiful man—my soccer-playing English major—and he asked me to marry him!* I could not thank God enough. Insane or not, I said, "Yes. Yes, I'll marry you. But you do realize it's not legalized in PA, right?"

He smiled and shook his head, tolerating my negativity. "You're impossible." He leaned in, kissing me with sloppy, slurping sounds that made me giggle. Seconds later he pulled back and asked very seriously, "You know what?"

"What?"

"My leg fucking hurts! I gotta get off this floor." He sat up and grabbed for the table's edge. "Help me up?"

I did. And then I surveyed our mess. "Oh," I whimpered in that sad way little kids do when their favorite toy gets broken. I wanted to cry.

Then Ellis rubbed my stomach. "I'll clean it, Cole."

My blurry eyes found his.

"I'll clean it up, I promise. Just let me grab a shower and take some ibuprofen. Okay?"

His expression was so comforting. "Okay," I said weakly.

Ellis carefully leaned over and picked up his shorts from the floor, and that was when I heard the front door close.

"Culinary catastrophes, Batman, what happened in here?" Rob exclaimed, surveying the walls, floor, and table. "Did Linda Blair visit, and not like the menu?"

I looked at Rob. He looked at Ellis. Then he looked at me, and his expression immediately changed from bemused observance to shocked revelation. "My eyes, my eyes!" he exclaimed as he looked away, holding one hand over his face and the other out in front of him.

Ellis, who found humor in this, calmly rationalized, "I guess you won't use the key I gave you without knocking first. Will ya?"

For some reason, I always had to point out holes in people's reasoning. "In Rob's defense, you *did* say, 'Feel free to walk right in so I don't need to get off the couch.'" (I even reminded him with a mocking tone of his voice. Don't judge—Rob would have done the same.)

Ellis didn't comment but his glower sufficed. I grinned unapologetically.

The banter between us didn't matter once Rob pronounced loudly, "You're naked!" He was still covering his eyes and extending his other arm as if to keep us at bay. I wish I had a camera.

Ellis, unfazed, didn't overreact to his behavior. Instead he said, "You've seen me naked before, Rob. It's only been a couple of weeks since you helped me take a shower. Plus, remember last year, when Russ's little brother threw up his pizza and orange juice all over my lap?"

Rob tentatively lowered his hand. I could see the gears churning behind his expression, and then slowly a grin appeared on his lips. "Oh yeah." He chuckled quietly. "That was really funny. The orange juice made it all slimy and it soaked through to your underwear." He laughed some more and slapped a hand against his stomach and tilted his head back.

Ellis chuckled and added, "And Russ said I could borrow his clothes."

Rob pointed his finger at Ellis, laughing even harder. "And he tried to get you to wear his Spiderman underwear, but you protested, saying—"

Rob and Ellis said in unison, "Nothing but Batman will do." They both laughed, and Rob seemed to relax. That is, until his eyes caught *me* again.

"Ah, man!" He cringed, looking away. "I know I've seen you naked, El, but that was before... before you and Cole... I just can't look."

"It's not like I have different parts, Rob. I look exactly the same," Ellis tried, but Rob still slipped into the other room.

"Ellis, I can't," he said, heading toward the door. "It's weird."

"Wait," Ellis interjected, hopping like the Easter Bunny after him. When Rob stopped walking, Ellis sat on the chair and wrestled his shorts on over the cast. He gesticulated for me to do the same. And although the notion seemed futile given the fact I was covered in drying food particles, I did as asked and pulled my jeans on. It felt yucky. Ellis hastily hopped over to the door before Rob ran out of patience. "How about now?" Ellis asked. "Stay?"

Rob slowly turned a skeptical eye in his direction and then conceded with a half grin, "Okay. I guess that's fine. I'll stay."

"So... you knew about me and Cole?" Ellis liked to ask those obvious questions, either out of sheer ignorance or simply to make sure he wasn't incorrect in his assumptions.

"Yeah, El. Besides the poem, it was evident the first time you brought him to breakfast. You know how I sense things."

Ellis smirked. "Please, no Jedi mind tricks."

"Promise."

I had this sadistic notion to add my two cents. So as I strolled over to join them by the door, I said, "Besides the fact he heard us kissing in the tent."

"What?" The shock on Ellis's face was priceless.

Rob's also did not disappoint. He looked at me and sighed. "You know, Cole, sometimes it's okay *not* to share everything we talk about."

"I know," I said, amused. "But it's more fun this way."

"Argh," he grunted with a gust of aggravation, but I could tell he was exaggerating.

Ellis was stunned but recovered quickly. "So, does it bother you?" I could see he was hoping for a "no" on that one. Plus, his voice went up an octave on the end of his question.

Rob gestured halfheartedly. "I don't know. I'm still trying to grasp the concept that you're *gay*. I don't know how I feel about it. All I know is that you love that guy." Rob tipped his head in my direction.

"I do." Ellis looked at me. I swear if he looked at me one more time with that much affection, I *would* melt. My knees went weak with his slight glance.

Rob pursed his mouth on one side. "Then I guess I have to accept that. You're like a brother, Ellis. I'm not forsaking my brother because he's in love with a dude. I just don't want to see the two dudes naked, covered in turkey and mashed potatoes. What is up with that?" Rob asked as if completely baffled. "You guys are downright weird!"

Ellis smiled and I joined in. "I love you, Rob," Ellis said.

"I love you too, man. Only… let's never speak of this again. I'm not sure I want Russ to know I walked in on you guys naked. He'll ask too many inane questions."

"Got it."

Rob looked to me and pointed. "And you, my friend, should use gravy as a hair product more often. The spiked look suits you!" I knew he was poking fun at me.

"Oh God." I reached up and felt my hair. It *was* spiked as well as sticky, and I distinctly felt lumps of mashed potato in it.

"Hey, Rob, I was about to take a shower. Will you stay long enough for me to get cleaned off and then maybe help me clean up the kitchen?" Ellis gave him his pathetic expression. "Please? I promised my Cole I wouldn't leave it for him to do."

Rob heaved a sigh. "Fine. I'll stay and help. But don't fill in the details on what happened in there. I don't need to know."

Ellis grinned and slapped him on the back. "Agreed."

Rob started for the kitchen. "And don't whine at me with lines like, 'I can't clean 'cause my leg hurts,' or I'll seriously kick your tushy when that cast comes off on the third!"

Rob altered his pitch as he mocked Ellis, and I just about fell on the floor laughing! I think he enjoyed my laughter at Ellis's expense because he did it some more. "I can't sweep, Rob. My leg. My leg," he chirped, sounding more like Sara than Ellis. I was dying. "Oh, I gotta lie down. You'll do it all for me, won't you, Rob? You're my best pal!"

Ellis, although laughing too, hopped up behind him and gave him a shove. "Shut up! I don't sound like that!"

"Oh, Rob. I'm in so much pain. Please do this for me."

"Shut up!"

"Dude, you totally sound like that," I added, holding my sides and then wiping the tears from my eyes. (I think I really like Rob.) My mirth was silenced by another scoop of mashed potatoes.

Rob howled with laughter.

THE "Boy Wonder" helped Ellis clean up and then we ordered a pizza. (It was a joke to call him that, but he really did appear to be Ellis's sidekick.) After Xbox and hours of laughing, Rob left and it was time for bed. I walked into my room and found my bed stripped of linens. *When did that happen?* "Ellis," I called as I meandered back into the living room, "what'd you do with my...."

The answer to my question was set up on the living room floor. He must have made haste while I brushed my teeth because my blankcts and pillow were arranged on the floor next to his.

"Sleep with me?" he asked.

How could I turn that down? I sank to my knees and crawled over to him. Ellis kissed me, and then we curled up together on the floor. He leaned over me and dreamily said, "You're the best thing that's ever happened in my life."

Chapter 14
Sticks and Stones

THANKSGIVING weekend totally blew. Mike was stuck in the house with his alcoholic parents and emo sister, eating turkey and listening to the relatives argue about why they decided to come to the Foster residence this year? It was the same every year. The family argued and the next year they came to Mike's parents' house anyway. Even Mike himself wasn't sure why he bothered to show up except that his gran was going to be there too, and he wouldn't miss the chance to see her. She was ninety-two; how much longer would she be around, anyway?

When classes started up again the following Monday, he jumped for joy.

He hadn't seen anybody yet, and he was dying for some action. There had to be a party going on somewhere, right? Brent, Dalton, or maybe Frank had to have plans in the works. Nobody, after spending the weekend with his or her folks, could go long without throwing a kegger; Mike just had to scope it out. His *last* resort would be the local adult beverage dispensary, since he'd have to spend his own money. He'd rather drink on someone else's bill.

Mike Foster was a deadbeat. He knew it. He only went to college because his grandmother had offered to pay so he'd "get an education and stay out of trouble." And really, the last few years hadn't been so bad. Rob went here. He and his Siamese twin, Russell, had been decent enough to him over the years, despite Mike's crude remarks about Rob's church. Russell lived in the same neighborhood, and his mom continually brought over casseroles or pot roast as a "kind, neighborly gesture" for his mother. Mrs. Davenport was overly generous, and Mike doubted that his mom would ever return the kindness. She was normally too high to remember where the meal had come from, let alone cook one in return. *Stupid woman.*

Mike was glad for the nice neighbors, but at the same time he felt a twinge of jealousy. Why couldn't he have a great family like that? Life wasn't fair. So, because life dealt out unpleasant hands to the helpless human race, Mike often felt compelled to join in. Not horrible things, only little ones. He was only arrested twice—without conviction. No one could prove who egged Mr. Flannery's house. Mike knew how to cover his tracks. It served that man right, anyway, for marrying a black woman. *Mixed couples are disgusting!* Mike thought.

Mike wasn't racist. No. He simply thought that blacks should be segregated, like in the olden days. And intermarrying with them was unnecessary.

Mike stuffed his hands deeper into his pockets as he rounded the corner of the English department. He was fucking freezing. He couldn't wait for the end of this semester. At his dad's suggestion, he'd learned some management skills and taken some accounting classes, and had surprised everyone with a three-point-five GPA. Mike had the feeling his dad was gearing him up to take over the family tire business. Maybe. He could. Perhaps he'd end up making something of himself after all.

But not today.

He was on a three-hour break between classes—after his economics class, which ended at nine thirty in the morning—and hoped to catch Dalton before he stepped into Earth Science. Brent had texted ten minutes ago, asking him over to do a couple lines before his next class, so he was stoked. He thought Dalton would appreciate an invite. Mike strolled down the steps near the science department with a little skip in his step and a hum in the back of his throat. The thought of doing a little coke after a dry spell over the weekend was exhilarating.

Then his foot faltered.

Ahead of him, leaning on a brick wall that served as the backdrop for a flower garden on the other side, was a couple of male college students. One, smaller and thin, and obscured by the other guy's body, had his arms around the bigger guy. Their faces were way too close together to be having a conversation, and Mike was sickened by the thought of what he'd observed. They were kissing.

Seriously kissing. Mike tentatively approached, fixated by the repulsive act before him. *They're faggots.*

Still, as if witnessing a train wreck, he couldn't look away.

To make matters worse, one of them was making sounds like a dove, and mewling shamelessly in public.

Mike stepped closer.

One guy had a cast on his leg. Maybe Mike could sneak up and shove real hard, knocking them over the garden wall into the flowerbed. That would be hilarious.

As he edged closer, he heard a gasp behind him, so he turned. It was Russell. He was clamping his hand over his mouth and his eyes were as wide as saucers. "Ellis?" Russell asked weakly.

Only then did Mike's brain register who he had been watching. The whole time he was sickened and intrigued and then sickened some more, it had been Ellis Montgomery who was macking on the other dude. And as soon as Ellis turned his head, both Russell and Mike were able to see that Cole Reid was the other party.

"Oh fuck!" Mike recoiled with an exclamation.

"Mike, Russ, I…," Ellis floundered. "We…. Cole and I were just…."

"Save it, Monty! Save it!" Mike spat. "I've been here long enough to know what the hell you were doing, only I didn't know it was you until *Russell* showed up."

"Mike, I—" Ellis started again.

Mike cut him off. "And with a four-eyed physics freak like Reid? Way to pick a loser."

"Is this real?" Russell asked, bewildered. "I don't believe it. You're… *gay?*" He stumbled forward in a stupor that caused Mike to throw out a hand to ensure he didn't fall down the steps. Mike knew Russell wasn't drunk, but he understood his dazed appearance all too well. Mike would probably fall on his face, too, if he'd just come across his best bud making out with another guy.

"Is this why I haven't seen you at any of Dalton's parties?" Mike growled, challenging Ellis with his tone not to even think of refuting the facts. "You've been going at it with Reid? What the fuck? I didn't know you were a fuckin' queer. God hates queers, ya know. Tell him, Russ."

When Russell didn't say anything, Mike turned to look at him, only to find him backing away in silence. He was in shock, or maybe he was scared, or maybe he felt betrayed to find out one of his inner circle was a perverted homosexual. Either way, Mike figured he could stand up to Ellis by himself.

"Go ahead, say something," Mike urged with his chest puffed out, shoulders cocked back.

Ellis hung his head. "I'm sorry."

"Sorry for what? Being a freak?" Mike sneered.

"Sorry I wasn't honest with you," Ellis replied quietly, looking at the ground at Mike's feet. "All those times you made fun of me for not having the nerve to make it with a girl, I knew it was because I was attracted to guys, and I didn't have the gumption to tell you. So, I'm sorry. I never meant for you to find out this way."

"I told you it was a mistake to kiss on campus," whispered Cole, apparently trying to keep Mike from hearing, yet Mike was too close to miss his words. Cole even had the gall to hold Ellis's hand.

Gross! "You're a fucking genius," Mike ridiculed.

Ellis stiffened his arm across Cole's body and squared around to face Mike, leaning his weight on one crutch. "Say what you want about me, but if you talk to Cole like that again, I will beat the hell out of you with this crutch, I guarantee it!" (Only then did Mike notice the other crutch was leaning on the stone wall, which was partially why he hadn't known it was Ellis right away. He'd been fixated on the kissing and hadn't thought about the cast.)

"Whatever, Montgomery. You're still a faggot. I can take you on any day." He puffed his chest out again, even if he was shaking on the inside.

He knew Ellis was strong. They'd worked out together on several occasions, and Ellis always out-lifted him. His only real advantage was that cast! (The cast that would come off in another week.) If he was going to make a move, it would have to be before then. Slowly, he backed up and headed away from the pathetic losers and off to find Dalton. He knew between the two of them they could come up with an appropriate deed that would put the queers in their place.

DALTON suggested a number of things. "Egging" had been done before. "Toilet papering their apartment" seemed blasé. And leaving "flaming bags of dog poop" was just too juvenile. Mike needed something more significant to send a message that what Ellis was doing was wrong. It was wrong, and would not be tolerated.

At two in the morning, Mike, Dalton, and Brent snuck down the street to find Cole's Mercury sedan parked just far enough away to get the job done. Brent pulled out his spray paint and nodded. This was going to be fun!

IN THE morning, Mike hid behind the bushes, waiting for Cole and Ellis to descend. They were together every morning. Why Mike hadn't suspected something sooner just proved how stupid and trusting he was. He thought they were merely good friends. Like Rob and Russell. It never occurred to him they were fuck buddies. *Eww.* His stomach churned suddenly, and a loud eruption echoed behind him, relieving his intestines of the pressure of mounting gas.

"You're a pig, you know that?"

Mike jerked around to find Russell behind him. "What are you doing here?"

Russell made a gesture, glancing down briefly and then sweeping his hands down his attire. "Duh!"

Russell was sweaty, wearing sweatpants and a T-shirt in winter. "Oh yeah, jogging. I forgot you do that."

Russell gave him a weird look and then peered around. "Why are *you* here? You aren't up this early unless there's beer involved. What are you doing?"

Mike was about to answer when he heard voices across the street. "I… shh. Wait." He put his finger to his lips and signaled Russell to crouch down with him behind the bush. He pointed and Russell's eyes followed his signal. Then they were both watching as Ellis and Cole rounded the corner and approached Cole's car.

It was beautiful. Cole put his hand to his mouth as he surveyed what was left of his hunk-of-junk. Mike could not be more proud of how thoroughly they had busted out each headlight, broken off his mirrors, and smashed the windshield. Brent had added the perfect touch of "faggot" painted in neon pink across both sides of the car. And Dalton had thought to stab each tire with his pocketknife. "Perfect," Mike whispered.

Ellis hobbled up next to Cole and seemed to say something.

"What did you do?" Russell hissed behind him.

"Retribution."

Mike felt champagne bubbles bursting inside him, effervescent and tingly. Cole walked forward and touched his car, and then he yelled something and pounded his fist on the dented hood. Ellis limped up beside him, and Cole shoved him away causing him to teeter on his crutches. When Cole immediately changed his behavior and grabbed Ellis, obviously so he wouldn't fall, Mike grunted in disgust.

"If you're mad at Ellis, why take it out on Cole?"

"Same difference," he sneered. "Ellis still feels my wrath. See?" he said as he pointed to Ellis, who was holding Cole as if to console him. Cole had his face buried against his chest and Ellis was rubbing his back. Ellis's face was ashen. "Besides, if Ellis can't stand his weepy ass, maybe they'll break up and it will be like a bonus." He chuckled, proud of himself for that one. "Ellis is the fucking idiot who sold his car. It's not my fault they have nothing else to trash."

"You realize this is illegal, don't you?" Russell pointed out. "And flat-out mean!"

Mike had momentarily forgotten the guy was there because he'd been so quiet. He turned and shrugged. "So?" He was surprised that Russell would act as if that were a bad thing. "He's a queer. I thought you, of all people, would appreciate the beauty of this message." He pointed to the mangled car and the two pathetic losers hugging on the street next to it.

Russell looked irritated instead. *Why?*

"Mike Foster," Russell said, "don't you know that malicious destruction of someone's property is considered vandalism, and that premeditated vandalism on the basis of a person's race, gender, religious conviction, or sexuality is considered a hate crime?"

Mike, again, was confused by Russell's apparent sympathy toward Ellis. "Russ, Ellis is a queer. Don't you get that? Ellis Montgomery, my former friend and yours, has been taking it up the ass this whole time and making a mockery of God's intended design. Isn't that what the Bible says?"

Russell narrowed his eyes. "Foster, don't bring God into this. You don't go to church. Your dad is a professed atheist and your mother does drugs at the kitchen table. You don't get to use the Bible in your defense when you don't believe in it to begin with."

Mike squared his shoulders. "What about you, Davenport? Aren't you being hypocritical if you say you believe in the Bible, yet you're going to simply stand by and allow them to pervert all that's holy and true?" He thought his response sounded very logical and pious. How clever. "It doesn't sound very righteous to me."

"It's not my place to judge, Mike. And at the very least, it isn't my place to exact punishment upon another human being for what he chooses to do with his private life. Ellis and Cole are our friends."

"Were!" Mike quickly interjected.

"Are!" Russell emphasized. "Why would you do that to a friend? You totally busted up Cole's car because they're gay? Aren't you the least bit sorry that you did that?"

For a fleeting second, Mike felt a twinge of regret. *Maybe I shouldn't have gone this far?* But just as quickly as the feeling came, he dashed it aside. "No!" he snarled. "Queers deserve to be punished. I only wish I'd done more."

In the distance, he heard a siren. He looked around. When Russell made no move and looked suspiciously calm, Mike demanded, "What did you do?"

Russell took his hand out of his pocket. He was holding a cell phone. "I called Mr. George." He shook his head sympathetically. "You'll never learn, Mike. My dad's best friend is a cop. How many times has he been to your house to break up the parties when they've gotten too loud? How many times has he warned you to keep your nose clean? You were lucky when you didn't do time for the Flannery stunt, or the girl in the wheelchair, but this...." Russell held out his hand toward Cole's car. "I couldn't let you get away with it."

Mike's survival instinct told him to run. He rounded the bush and took off, but a cop car sat in his path. He changed his direction again and ran down another street. Blocked. He turned again and bolted for the buildings that led away from campus. Another car, and several officers walked in his direction; he felt trapped. His escape routes were systematically getting cut off. He'd talked too long to Russell.

He had one more shot, past the apartments and through the middle of campus. He turned and saw Ellis and Cole watching him. He could feel them laughing, taunting him with their perverse lifestyle. "What are you looking at, faggots?" he screamed, rushing at them in a fit of rage.

Pathetically, they clung to one another as he swiftly approached. Ellis even lifted a crutch as if to ward him off with his makeshift weapon. Mike shoved it aside easily and kicked at Ellis's one good leg. He howled in pain and stumbled, and Cole ineffectively attempted to stop his fall. Mike took that moment to shove Cole hard in the chest. He laughed in triumph as Cole yelped on his way down to the pavement, and then fled down the sidewalk. He collided with an officer as soon as he got ten feet past Cole.

As he struggled against the handcuffs and stumbled down the path the officer took him, Mike hatefully shouted in Ellis and Cole's direction. "I thought your Bible said homosexuality was an abomination? I guess you'll be joining me in hell!"

Russell, who now stood next to his friends, responded, "It also says love covers a multitude of sins. Hate begets hate, Mike. You gotta learn what it means to love!" He put his arm over Ellis's shoulder as if to throw heaping coals onto the flames that rose up Mike's back.

Bile burned the back of his throat as he was guided into the backseat of a county sheriff's car. No matter what Russell said, he still didn't regret what he'd done to Cole's car. "He deserved it!" Mike grumbled as the car drove off.

Chapter 15

Hate Crimes

I SOBBED against Ellis's chest, unable to pull myself away from the fragment of security I found there. I heard Russell rebuking Mike for his actions, but I was too upset to look up. It was Mike... Mike.... Someone I knew.... One of Ellis's friends.... *He trashed my car because I'm gay.... Because Ellis is gay.*

For some reason, high school memories painfully flooded my mind. Josh Green, punching me and calling me faggot. Jeremy Sterner spray-painting my locker with the same cutting words. And Brad Foley, the most hurtful part of it all; he stopped talking to me. Brad was my friend before he *knew*. Brad had treated me compassionately on the baseball team and in the hallways at school up until that day in the locker room. That day was the day I lost my dignity and the day I lost all my friends.

I blamed it on my lack of self-control, but that wasn't it. I tried to blame myself and thought I could outwit people's hatred if I just suppressed my emotions and precluded judgment by never letting anyone in. If I never made friends, if I built strong walls, if nothing mattered, then their hatred over *my* choices, and *my* sexuality, wouldn't matter. I could keep myself safe and someone like Josh could never harm me again.

I was so wrong. I should have never allowed myself to feel.

I backed out of Ellis's arms when the blunt truth of my stupidity sucked me dry of my last drop of faith. The world was a horrible place. Why did I even bother going on?

"Cole, I'm sorry." Russell offered a feeble apology, which wormed its way into my fried synapses and sparked enough brain activity to cause me to look up at him. "I called the cops as soon as I figured out what he was up to. I didn't know he'd try to physically hurt you guys. I'm really sorry."

I shrugged and hung my head again. I guess I knew he was trying to be sincere because I didn't say something cynical in return. Russell's apology was ridiculous, anyway. He didn't do anything. Mike did! There was nothing Russell could have done to stop Mike, and I guess a part of my brain was mulling over my thankfulness for his quick thinking. He had the presence of mind to call the cops and keep Mike talking until they got here. I guess I should be thanking him.

"Let's go inside, Cole," Ellis urged, waving his crutch in the direction of our apartment. When I didn't move, he nudged me.

What else was there to do? Breakfast was out because I certainly didn't feel like eating. I'd been humiliated for my personal choices and it felt abysmal. I numbly followed Russell and Ellis up the steps. Ellis limped. Shouldn't I care?

On some level, I knew people were that cruel, but until now I hadn't experienced it firsthand since high school. I'd been out for a few years. I wore gay pride T-shirts, and I'd walked in pride rallies in nearby towns and stuff. And on one rare occasion, I even joined in an open debate on campus with gay-rights supporters and their opposition! But never had someone acted out in a hateful retaliation of my position or theirs. This campus had been a peaceful combination of both, and I had started to believe I could be gay and live a normal life like everyone else. How naive of me to be so trusting of the human race.

Being the recipient of a hate crime sucked! And this was small in the greater scheme of things. Some people get bashed for their personal choices. Some die. I should be happy all he did was total my car and shove me to the ground, but nothing could make me feel good about it. It was terrible, and the worst part was that I thought he was my friend. My boyfriend's friend totaled my car! What an asshole. I wanted to punch his lights out.

As soon as I walked through the door, I began to cry. I stood there in the middle of the floor, holding myself around the middle with one arm and covering my eyes with my other hand. This was so ridiculous and awful and mind-boggling that I couldn't control my emotions. I felt so alone in my misery. That is, until Ellis touched my shoulder and I jumped away in response.

"Don't touch me!" I screamed, lashing out at his consolation. "This would never have happened if your homophobic, hatemonger friend hadn't taken out his anger for *you* on my car! It's all your fault." I said it and I regretted it immediately, but I wasn't going to retract it. My pride was hurt and it was too easy to take it out on Ellis. I couldn't control myself so I kept yelling. "I should never have gotten involved with you and your friends. I knew this was going to happen! Nothing good ever happens to me. Nothing!"

Ellis didn't say anything. He hobbled over to the couch and sat down, propped up his bad leg, and examined the bruise on his other.

I kept ranting in my sarcasm since he wasn't rebuking me. "It had to happen to me. *You* don't have a car so naturally they would total *mine!* The universe hates me!"

"Are you blaming me?" he asked calmly.

"Yes!"

"Cole, you—" Russell started shouting back.

When he didn't continue what I suspected was a rebuke of my harsh treatment of Ellis, I glanced over at them. Ellis was shaking his head and Russell was holding his hands out to either side, giving him a weird look. "No, Ellis, let him continue," I snapped. "I'd like to hear what he has to say. So Russ, tell me what you think of our relationship? I didn't see you jumping to our defense *yesterday* when Mike was being an ass. So why today?"

Russell looked stung by my words, but to his credit he didn't let me dissuade him from responding. "I'm sorry, Cole. I admit I'm not perfect. I was shocked when I saw you kissing. What can I say? I didn't know Ellis was gay, and it threw me. I've wondered about you for a while, but it's rude to ask a guy personal questions like that. But then Mike.... What Mike did was wrong. He might disagree with your relationship, but nobody should be allowed to destroy your stuff because of it. You're a person, just like me. You have rights. I don't see you interfering in Mike's personal life."

I was listening but a response wouldn't form when I was still too hurt to think.

"If he's mad at me, then why did he take it out on Cole?" Ellis asked.

"I don't know," said Russell, shrugging. "He said it would hurt you emotionally because it was against Cole. And something about you being an idiot for selling your car. He's an asshole."

"True. Can you get me some ice?" Ellis asked calmly.

Russell nodded. "Yeah, sure." He headed into the kitchen.

"Cole! I saw your car," Rob exclaimed frantically as he burst through the door. Sometimes I wondered why we even closed it. "Dude, that seriously sucks. I can't believe Mike would do that! What a douche." He walked over and attempted to put his arm around me. I dodged his sympathy and chose to stew in self-pity by hugging myself with both arms, tightly around my ribs. He apparently noticed my scowl because I heard him say, "I see he's taking this well."

"You got my text," Russell said, walking back in with some ice in a plastic baggie. (He was fast.)

Rob turned away from me and looked over at Russell. "Yeah. I was on my way over anyway when I heard sirens. I'm glad Cole didn't get hurt." He must have noticed the bag of ice because he quickly asked, "What happened to you?"

"Mike kicked me," Ellis explained, holding the ice to his wounded shin.

"What? Why? What changed?" he asked, bewildered. "Why *now* does Mike go psycho?"

"He saw me kissing Cole yesterday. He didn't like it."

"Oh. I see. Still… trashing Cole's car? I knew he had a criminal mind, but this is way too far. I hope he gets what he deserves this time."

Russell pointed to Ellis and then to me and asked, "How long have you known about the two of them, Rob?"

"Officially or unofficially?" Rob asked sheepishly.

I was oddly curious how this conversation would play out. I was feeling sorry for myself, and now I was feeling slightly bad for Rob. He'd been great at accepting our relationship. Would he get criticized for it now? I could only take so much.

Russell narrowed his eyes. "Officially."

I saw Rob's Adam's apple bob. "Um, a week, I guess."

Russell's mouth hung open and he took a step in Rob's direction. "And unofficially?"

Rob whispered, like a mouse, "Maybe… eight."

"Eight weeks!" Russell shrieked, jumping at him. Russell got in Rob's face but didn't grab his lapels like I anticipated he would from his tone. "How could you know about Ellis and not tell me?"

"I wanted to wait until I knew for sure. I was going to tell you. I was!" Rob desperately explained. "I waited because I thought you'd freak about it."

"I…," Russell started but then stopped with his mouth hanging open. (If he kept doing that, flies would take up residence.) He shut it and then plopped down next to Ellis. "Sometimes it frightens me how well he knows me."

"Are you freaked?" Ellis asked.

Russell nodded. Then paused. Then shook his head. "No, I guess not. Not anymore. Seeing you kiss Cole was a shock, and a little gross, but after I saw what Mike did, I felt more defensive of you than anything. You're my friend, Ellis." He held out his fist and Ellis bumped knuckles with it. "What you and Cole do together is your business. I'm not going to disown you because of it."

Witnessing their little reconciliation was sweet, but it left me standing on the sidelines and longing for some attention. *I was the one who was attacked, wasn't I?* "Hey, what about me?" I pouted. "It was *my* car, you know. Mike destroyed *my* property, not his."

Rob responded on cue. "Aww, is someone feeling left out?" Rob made a sad face that made me regret saying anything. He stepped closer. "Does someone need a hug?"

"No," I frowned, stepping backward.

Rob advanced. "I think you do."

"No, I don't," I insisted, but Rob's fervor for compassion kept him coming. I backed up into the wall and had nowhere to go.

"Come here, you big lug." In seconds, he scooped me up into his arms and crushed me to his chest. "You know we love you, Cole. Your gayness makes no difference."

"Nope," Russell agreed, hopping off the couch and then joining Rob in the hug.

"But I've been out for years!" I protested, squirming in their loving embrace. "Ellis! Help! Tell them!" No matter which way I moved, I couldn't break free.

Ellis observed from his seat on the sofa. He coolly commented, "No, I think you've got it all under control."

His smug response from such a comfy position nagged me. "This should be *your* support group, not mine! Get them off me, Ellis! Rob, stop!" I hissed and thrashed, yet their hug only tightened around me. "Ellis!"

An earthquake rumbled in Rob's chest and he finally released me, collapsing on the floor in an uncontrollable guffaw. "You are so easy, Cole." He laughed, rolling around.

"You seriously are!" Russell agreed, laughing through tears, bent over, supporting his body with his hands on his knees.

I stomped over to Ellis and demanded, "Are you gonna to just sit there, or are you going to do something about your friends?" *Again with the damn, bemused expression!*

"They're *your* friends too, Cole," he said matter-of-factly.

"Which is the whole point," Rob added. He made his way off the floor and over to my side, placing an arm across my shoulders.

"What?" I squawked. "Did I miss something here?" Because I felt like I'd missed reading a chapter on my own life. What happened that I didn't know about? I shoved Rob away and collapsed on the couch next to Ellis. They were cracking my defenses, and suddenly, standing across the room alone felt cold. I had to be near Ellis.

Rob and Russell took positions on either end of the coffee table. (Had I been thinking clearly, I would have commented on the maximum load sustainable on four three-by-three wooden legs, but I didn't.)

"Jonathan told me about your lack of friends way back when I moved in." Ellis filled in my question mark, and I gawked at him.

"What? Why?"

He ignored my vexation, which irked me more, and continued to explain. "He and I *also* talked a couple days ago, because he was planning to surprise you over Christmas. He asked if I'd mind. When I said *no*, he asked how you were doing and that prompted an hour-long discussion of you and your background, your dating history, and yes, your lack of real friendships since about the fifth grade."

"What?" I yelped again in a pitch that hurt even my own ears. "He had no right. First Jon pays Stan to find me a roommate—which, by the way, I hope you realize was Stan's freaky way of playing matchmaker—and now this? Why does everyone think I'm a socially inept half-wit?"

No one spoke, for the first time in history. They looked to one another. Russell to Rob, Rob to Ellis, Ellis to me, and back on around. Rob broke the silence with, "Have you met you?"

"Okay, fine. I guess I set myself up for that, but I'm serious. Why do people feel the need to point out I have no friends?" I turned to Ellis and accused, "I told you this is your fault! You come in here with your big blue eyes and flip my world around! I was fine before all this happened; plus, I had a car!" I crossed my arms and looked away. All the personal attention was stirring me up. Either I was going to end up angrier than a nest of hornets, or the floodgates of emotion would pour forth for the third time in twenty minutes. I tried to thrust the anger out there in order to psych myself into thinking crying wasn't necessary. It had to work!

Rob leaned closer and patted my knee. "Easy there, Mini-Me, no need to go postal on the guy with one leg." He looked at the bag of ice sitting on Ellis's good leg and corrected, "*No* legs."

"Why not? Mike was *his* friend!" My rebuke, though valid, was harsher than it needed to be. I felt frost lacing the silence. It was obvious, even to me, that restating Mike's betrayal was just plain wrong. I took a cleansing breath to calm my nerves. "I'm sorry." I looked at Ellis, who seemed contemplative yet calm. "Can I just ask… how does talking to Jonathan have anything to do with accepting *me* for being gay? Shouldn't you guys be smothering Ellis in supportive adoration? He's the one that's out now. Why is Russ all 'We love you, Cole' instead of 'We accept you, Ellis'?"

"You're the one who was attacked," Rob answered. "And you, Cole Reid, are the one who can't fathom the idea of anyone liking you for who you are. Ellis notwithstanding."

"But…." I was shocked into confusion. I pointed to Ellis. "He…."

Russell spoke up. "We have an unspoken understanding with Ellis. He knows we're good."

Without even much eye contact between them, Russell held up a fist and Ellis bumped knuckles with him again. (The gesture was so home-boyish that I should have rolled my eyes in amusement.) These homeboys, however, were all fixated on *me*, for some reason. I didn't like the attention. I wanted my safe house of anonymity back.

Russell went on, saying, "Besides, Rob and I break the best of them. We knew the day we met you, you wouldn't be curmudgulous forever."

I frowned. "That's not even a word."

Russell didn't refute the fact. He shrugged, an amused smirk affixed to his face.

Then I felt Ellis put his fingers on my chin. He tenderly coaxed me to look at him and stroked my goatee, as he was fond of doing. Somehow the room faded away for a few seconds as his beautiful eyes held me still.

"I love you, Cole," he said quietly. Ellis's gentleness pricked a hole in my puffed-up irritation, and I felt his confidence tethering me to safety. I stopped fighting against the emotional torrent and gave myself over to it. Ellis stroked his thumb across my cheek and wiped away my tears. "You… are *my* boyfriend." He spoke slowly and intentionally, as if to avoid any miscommunication. "For *my* friends… to jump to *your* defense… not only proves their loyalty, but their love. For *me*… and for you."

"Basically," Rob said, "I've been trying to convince him of that for weeks." I heard Rob, but nothing really mattered in the moment except Ellis.

Ellis was smiling at me. "You're not alone, L-D. You have friends. Good friends."

"I'm afraid to ask what that stands for."

He winked. "I'll tell you later." Ellis leaned forward, guiding me into a kiss with the hand that cupped my cheek. His lips were soft in their boldness. After a few seconds, I heard Rob pretending to gag.

"Eegack. Grungth. Mlah." His unintelligible, made-up vocabulary almost made me laugh as Ellis kissed me. "Come on, Russ. I can't watch this."

I heard Rob move away as Ellis pulled me closer and held me behind my head, deepening his kiss. He snuck his tongue out to lick and tease me before fully engaging. I admit I was a little embarrassed that he was so bold in front of his friends. While he fingered my hair and stroked my neck with one hand, he squeezed my thigh with the other. Oh, that was daring! (I, on the other hand, had my hands on his cheeks. It was much more dignified in front of people.)

"I don't know, Rob. It's kind of fascinating," Russell replied, still—from the proximity of his voice—sitting on the coffee table in front to us. "I mean, if Cole lost the goatee and grew his hair out, Ellis could be kissing a girl. It's not that hard to visualize."

Ellis withdrew his tongue and slowly turned to face Russell. "Cole. Is not. A girl." He said each part with deliberate conviction. His eyes burned, and I felt his tension in the fingertips that gripped my thigh.

However, his anger was lost on Russell. "Oh, I know." His voice was carefree. "I was just saying that it looks the same. Ellis could be kissing a girl or a guy; there isn't any difference. His lips are still all smashed up against Cole's. It only looks a little weird because of Cole's facial hair. I can't imagine kissing a girl with facial hair. Does it feel weird kissing a guy with facial hair?"

Ellis shook his head at the absurdity of the question. He no longer seemed angry, but amused at his friend. (Our friend.) "No, Russ, it doesn't feel weird." Ellis rubbed my chin and smiled at me. "I really like it."

I looked down, knowing I'd blushed. He had a way of making me giddy.

Russell slapped his thighs and hopped up, apparently done with his educational observance. "Oh hey," he said to Rob across the room, "that must mean that *you* are the only virgin left on campus!"

"Oh gosh! You did not just go there!" I heard Rob groan. Ellis and I both looked in his direction.

Russell pointed and taunted, "Virgin. Virgin."

Rob walked up and got right in his face. "Don't make me wipe that grin off your face!"

Russell wiggled his body, wound up with unspent energy. "What'ya gonna do? Virgin. Make me?" He put up his dukes and danced around Rob.

I had to give Rob credit; he held his cool for three whole seconds before he burst out laughing. "Okay, okay. I'm the last remaining virgin. Unless you're going to film a blockbuster documentary about me, I don't see how it matters. I'll find the right person to kiss eventually; but just so we're clear, I'm saving my body for matrimony."

Russell got suddenly serious and stepped oddly close to him. "You could kiss me."

Rob's eyes bugged out. "What? Are you… no way!"

"Gotcha!" Russell laughed, pointing at Rob and covering his open mouth.

Rob shoved at his chest and pushed past him, heading toward the door. "That's not funny."

"Oh yes, it is," Ellis said.

Rob stopped in the open door. "Cole, I'll be there to testify about your character if need be when Mike goes to trial. Ellis, you have my support and friendship. Cole, you too." He looked across the room and his face lost all mirth. "Russ, I'm hurt and offended that you would poke fun at my relational status. You… are no longer my friend." He pressed his hand to his chest, stood up straight, and very seriously turned his face away. Just before he closed the door behind him I heard a gasp of fake crying echo in the stairwell.

We all burst out laughing.

THE campus police came by to take statements, and the dean assured me that the school would officially handle any hate crimes committed on campus. That made me feel good. I didn't relish the thought of asking my dad to help foot the bill for a lawyer. He would not be happy about my car, so I wanted to wait to tell him.

Mike Foster apparently had all kinds of propaganda in his dorm room. Besides lashing out at me and Ellis for being gay, and Mr. Flannery for marrying interracially, Mike had articles on anti-Judaism, instituting height requirements for employment (I guess he hated short people?), and scrawlings about forcing the aged to live in segregated communities away from the "normal" populace. Mike was a sick puppy! I suppose you never know about a person and what they do in the privacy of their own room. That scared me.

Anyway, Mike was locked up, and it seemed there was sufficient evidence of psychosis to keep him that way. I breathed a little easier because of it.

Chapter 16
Caught In The Act

LIFE with a broken leg could not have been better. Ellis whined in the beginning—who wouldn't? But it didn't take long for him to see the benefits of his *particular* broken leg. For one thing, he broke his *leg,* not his ankle. The orthopedist had said an inch lower and he might never have played soccer again. (At least not competitively.) It was also a lateral break to both tibia and fibula, yet clean enough to patch back together with a plate and eight screws, to the point Ellis could be back to normal in a few months.

Not bad!

Ellis had also gotten some one-on-one attention from his mom, which was rare, and something he'd enjoyed very much. Well, until he'd realized how much he missed a certain someone and then couldn't seem to enjoy anything, even the homemade bread pudding. Ellis liked the attention from his mom regardless of what Rob and Russell might think. He hadn't left home to live on campus to escape her; it was more to see what was out there. The guys didn't quite understand that, and Ellis didn't bother to explain. It didn't matter. He'd sold his car for a chance to find himself and possibly find love.

And his roommate had turned out to be Cole.

Cole. He'd never thought one person could consume his entire reason for being so quickly and so completely until he met him. Deep down, he knew that he'd meet "the one," and he'd fall head over heels. His mom used to tell stories about how it had happened that way for her and his dad, and Ellis secretly wished for the same love-at-first-sight experience. He knew he'd gotten his wish, despite his "freak out" over sex.

Sex… another incredible plus.

Ellis glanced at Cole where he lay next to him in his bed. He was reading—studying—and getting ready for finals week. He looked tired. Ellis was studying too, but he already read the same sentence three times because his mind kept drifting to Cole's bare skin and the sex they'd enjoyed twenty minutes ago.

Ellis had never realized how much he'd think about sex, and want to have sex, until Cole convinced him to go with his instincts and push past the terror he'd felt the first time. Before, back when he was younger and yearning for the day he'd experience it for himself, Ellis hadn't understood what the hype was about. Teachers and parents always warned not to "do stuff" with girls (not that he'd want to), but he didn't quite get why they'd emphasized it so much. Sure, it felt good jerking off sometimes, but why flip out over him having sex? Ellis figured it was because Ben got a girl pregnant. (Ellis surely wasn't going to do that!) But what was the big deal about having sex?

Now he understood.

Pictures on the Internet and touching himself might have been satisfying, but it was nowhere near the level of gratification that made his chest explode. Making love to Cole was *just* that! And he couldn't get enough.

Ellis touched Cole's arm and felt his stomach flutter.

"You're supposed to be studying," Cole said.

"I am studying."

Ellis closed the book and placed it on the nightstand. He maneuvered onto his side and looped his leg over Cole's under the blankets. It was a twin bed; very tight for two people, so he was practically laying on Cole to begin with. He turned his hand over and ran his knuckles down Cole's bicep while he let his eyes wander over Cole's chest. He was thin. And pale. But his flat nipples made Ellis's mouth water every time Cole had his shirt off. Ellis moved his hand and circled his finger around one nub. It hardened and Ellis sighed.

"If I fail this test, I *will* kill you."

Ellis didn't bother to reply. He chuckled and kissed Cole's shoulder. One kiss would not satisfy his needy lips. One kiss against

Cole's skin was never enough. He leaned closer and kissed his collarbone over to his neck, and then behind his ear.

"Some of us have to work hard for our grades."

"Uh-huh. Grades. Got it," Ellis mumbled and slid his arm across Cole's chest and swirled his tongue in circles over Cole's artery. He nipped his skin just before latching on. He heard a textbook hit the floor, and Cole whimpered.

He sucked Cole's neck as he wriggled his body on top of him. He slid his arms under Cole's shoulders and pressed his groin into Cole's. Cole caressed his back and moaned delightfully. Ellis had to admit he was hesitant to believe it could feel so different from the first time, but Cole was right. *Ellis* doing the fucking was what he'd needed. Not that Ellis deemed Cole less manly having *his* dick up his ass; it simply didn't threaten his own self-image. Ellis wanted to be the one burying himself inside of Cole, and Cole's eagerness to capitulate revved his engines.

And Cole's moaning and begging certainly spurred him on.

He reached for the lube and managed to pop the top, one-handed, without looking.

"Oh, Ellis! Yes. That's so good," Cole moaned as Ellis kissed across his neck while prepping him with two lubricated fingers. They were both writhing with eager anticipation, rubbing their legs together and thrusting their pelvises.

"Please. Don't make me wait," Cole begged.

Ellis chuckled and pushed in aggressively, causing Cole to arch his back and release a high-pitched cry of delight. Ellis loved that sound and thrust harder because of it. He knew Cole came unglued when he was rough. Not that he could ever imagine hurting him intentionally, but holding back his passion wasn't necessary. He reached down under Cole and held his ass. He pulled Cole closer as he moved in him, and he gazed into Cole's open eyes as the undulating momentum built between them. Cole's breathing came quicker, and his eyes glazed over in ecstasy as he reached the edge.

Ellis felt the pressure mounting, and just as Cole started crying, "Yes, yes," he felt his own release spread shock waves of electricity throughout his body.

Oh God, there was nothing that compared to an orgasm; but when it happened inside of someone he loved and who gave him purpose, Ellis finally saw that his addiction to Cole was going to get him into trouble if he couldn't control his hunger. And, holy shit, did Cole make him ravenous!

He slowed his thrusting and his breathing came less labored. Ellis held Cole's head in both hands and kissed him slowly, enjoying the aftershock of climax and the heat rolling through his extremities.

He thought he heard a noise in the other room.

"Was that the door?" Cole whispered.

Ellis smoothed Cole's sweaty hair off his forehead and looked into his eyes. "I don't know."

They both turned their heads when they heard a gasp from the open bedroom doorway.

"Oh shit!" Ellis exclaimed, making eye contact with his mother.

She clamped her hand over her mouth and turned away.

"Mom!" he called after her. "Mom, wait." Ellis let go of Cole and struggled to get out of bed without falling on the floor. His leg was still tender and wobbly after having the cast removed and in his need to get to her quickly he got all tangled in the sheets. He snagged his underwear off the floor and ran after her as fast as he could.

She'd told him over Thanksgiving weekend she would visit after the cast came off, just to see how he was doing; but Ellis didn't know it would be today.

Ellis made it to the parking lot and caught up to his mother before she had the chance to get into her car. "Mom! Stop!" When she turned to face him, Ellis continued. "Please don't go. I'm sorry you had to see that. I didn't mean for you to find out this way. Please come back up to the apartment and maybe have some tea." He lifted his eyebrows in hopes it would sway her.

She stared at him. Then, little by little, the hurt and frustration softened and she nodded in response. "Alright."

"Good," Ellis said with a smile. "I have Earl Grey. Remember how you used to make me that when I had a fever and stayed home from school?"

"You remember that?" She seemed shocked.

"Yeah, Mom. I remember lots of things." Ellis offered his elbow and she looped her arm around his and they walked back up to Cole's apartment.

"Can you promise me something?" she asked as they climbed the steps.

"Anything."

"Will you promise not to run after me in your underwear again? It's embarrassing."

Ellis chuckled. If *that* was embarrassing, then what did she call walking in on them having sex? "Yes, Mother, I promise."

ELLIS was really glad that she bounced back so easily. After catching them in bed together—which was the very last thing he'd ever want to happen—he figured he'd have to grovel for forgiveness or something. He made her tea, as promised, and she sat and drank it slowly.

"Do you want me to go?" Cole asked, lingering by the bathroom door.

Ellis wasn't sure what was best. He didn't want to make his mom more uncomfortable, but he also didn't want Cole going *anywhere*. He wanted him here! "No," he answered simply.

Cole held back, but Ellis's mom ended their deliberation. "I don't bite, Cole," his mother said, patting the sofa cushion next to her. "Join us."

Ellis smiled again, appreciative of her inclusive gesture. "You're okay with that?" Asking, because if he assumed it was okay and it really wasn't, then she could come back and blame him. He sat across from her on the coffee table. *I think we really need to buy a chair or two,* Ellis thought.

"Yes. It's fine. I want to get to know the person my son is involved with."

She wasn't cold, but her voice wasn't chirpy-happy either. Ellis felt like he had to take this like a Q & A session for a magazine article and allow her all the information necessary to make things right between them. "Do you want *me* to do the talking, Mom, or would you prefer asking the questions while we answer them?" Her face relaxed more. *Perhaps she likes having the ball in her court?*

"If I ask, will you be truthful?" she asked.

That question hit him wrong. "When have I not been honest?" he asked suspiciously.

She reached across and touched his knee. "You don't need to get defensive, dear. I'm just wondering if this secret you've had is something you are willing to own up to? And if so, how much you'll be willing to share?"

He wasn't sure what that exactly meant, but he figured how much worse could it get? "Just ask, Mom. You've already seen more than I *ever* want to repeat. So now that it's out, I'm ready to deal."

"Okay." She sipped her tea and sat there.

Ellis was itching to divulge everything and he wasn't sure he could contain himself while she took her sweet time sipping tea. "Mom?"

"Yes, dear?"

"Are you going to ask something?" he pressed.

"I will," she answered, all smug and confident of her upper hand.

"Like today?" Cole added.

She lifted an eyebrow in his direction and set her teacup back on the saucer. "Where did you get a teacup as lovely as this, Ellis?" She studied it as she asked.

"Um, it's mine," Cole offered.

She cocked her head. "Really?"

Cole nodded. "Yes. My mom loves tea and over the years I acquired a taste for it. I like English Breakfast, Chamomile, and Lady Grey, Tibetan Tiger, and some others. When I moved on campus, she said I could take a cup or two to drink it *properly*." Cole offered his best British accent and stuck out his pinkie for demonstration. Ellis's mom giggled.

Ellis inwardly sighed. "Would you like some more, Mom?"

"Yes, dear, I would."

After the second cup was in her grasp, Meredith looked directly at her son. "So, how long has this been going on?"

Ellis, who thought he was ready for the questions, suddenly stuttered. "Um, what do you mean? Me being gay, or going out with Cole?"

Cole mused out loud, "Ellis, is it considered dating if we haven't actually *gone* anywhere?"

Ellis glared. "No comments unless they simplify the conversation."

"Which would be easier for you to start with?" asked Meredith.

"Cole, I guess," Ellis answered, feeling less sure of himself now that he was expected to say something. "He's been my boyfriend now for what...." He looked at Cole. "Two weeks?"

"Are you asking me?" said Cole.

"Sort of," Ellis whined. "I'm not really sure what date to count."

She asked, "When did you start having a relationship?"

Ellis scratched his head. "I'm still not sure how to answer that one."

"Ellis," his mother warned. "If you're going to tell me that I walked in on you and… Cole… and that this doesn't mean any—"

"No! Mom! It does. I swear. I love Cole. I'm only having difficulty figuring out what to call 'the beginning' of our relationship."

"What are the choices?" she asked.

"First kiss," Cole offered easily, holding out his open palm with one finger extended.

Ellis asked, "When I kissed you or you kissed me?"

"Oh, I guess when… no wait, you kissed me both times," Cole pointed out.

"Oh, I did, didn't I?"

"Yup. How about first sex?" Cole suggested.

Ellis skeptically pointed out, "First time we did it, or first time I *enjoyed* it?"

"Ouch." Cole cringed.

Meredith held up her hand. "How about when either of you had feelings for the other?"

"Oh, easy." Ellis grinned at his mom.

And just as he opened his mouth to give the answer, Cole piped in and they said in unison, "When I first looked into his eyes."

Ellis snapped his gaze over to Cole. "Really?" He was shocked and surprised to hear it was the same time, and in the same way.

"Yeah," Cole gushed.

Color blushed over Cole's cheeks, and Ellis reached over and touched his knee. Cole grinned and looked away, and Ellis heard his mother clear her throat. He took his hand back. "Sorry, Mom. Is there another question?"

"We're still debating the first one. We've established there is a 'first kiss' confusion, and I don't want to think about first sex, so is there another first? First date, maybe?"

"I already pointed out that we haven't dated. Unless you count breakfast?"

"Oh yeah!" Ellis said. "I guess we could, but we didn't go alone. We were with the guys and we didn't sit together. I didn't even pay."

"Who says you have to pay?"

"Uh, I do," Ellis emphasized.

"I could pay too, you know."

"No." Ellis shook his head. "Not gonna to happen."

"But you don't have any money, Ellis."

"I have money."

"Good thing, since you owe me a ring." Cole pointed it out and then snapped his fingers. "There's a good 'first' to refer to, Ellis asked—"

Ellis raised his hand and tried to interject, but Cole was faster at finishing his thought.

"—me to marry him."

Meredith exclaimed, "He what?"

Ellis winced. His mom's voice actually jumped an octave higher than when she'd walked into the bedroom. *Oops. Maybe that wasn't the worst thing in the world.* "Sorry, Mom. Maybe I should have started with the day I moved in."

"Maybe." She sounded sarcastic.

His mom didn't look good, but he wasn't sure what her expression was. It wasn't sickness, or repulsion, or even anger. She looked strained, and he wasn't sure why, since he was the one in the very awkward situation.

"Mom, are you sure you want to hear all this now? You don't look good."

"No, no, I do. I think I've missed out on way too much, and I'm glad you're willing to talk to me finally. I *want* to know you, Ellis. I don't want this wall between us to get any thicker, so start wherever you like and tell me as much as you want."

Wall? Ellis didn't like the sound of that. "What are you talking about, Mom? You know me. And since when is there a wall between us?"

"Since always. You never talk to me about anything. How am I supposed to know you?"

It pained him how mouselike his mom's voice had become in mere minutes. She was confident when she thought she could ask anything, but now she looked petrified of that very notion. "Mom, I never talk much. I've always been like that."

"Trust me," Cole added. "He's very difficult to drag information out of."

"You mean, you're not shutting me out of your life on purpose?"

"Mom! No, never. Where did you get that from?"

"I just thought…. You don't need me. You only call because Russell bugs you to, and even then you only say three words." She started to cry. "I know you're grown up now, and I'm in the way."

He quickly switched his seat, pivoting around to squeeze between her and Cole. (Cole kindly moved out of the way.) He put his arm around her. "I always need you, Mom. I don't know why you'd think I wouldn't. I'm sorry if I don't open up the way you want, but I don't talk to anybody. I just don't have loads to say."

"You don't?" She sniffled. Cole grabbed the box of tissues from the side table and handed them to her.

"No. I don't. I thought you understood that better than anyone. Russ's mom bugs the shit out of him for every detail of the week; you never did. I thought you understood how glad I was."

"No," she peeped, looking absolutely forlorn and miserable.

"Oh, Mommy, I love you," Ellis assured her, hugging her to him as securely as he could. "I'll always love you. I never meant to make you think I didn't care. I didn't build any walls. I think we have the best relationship ever!"

"You do?"

Ellis pulled back. "Yes, I do!" He caressed her cheek. "Even when Ben was going through all that crap with Rachel, you always had time to help me with homework. Remember?"

"Yes."

"And when Sara told you about Lori, you never told me not to be like her or that it was about time I found someone, like other moms told their kids."

"No, I didn't." Her voice was lightening.

"You were supportive and you let me be the quiet kid I wanted to be. You never pressured me to be something *you* wanted, only the person *I* wanted."

"I *do* want that for you."

"Well, guess what? I *am* the person I want to be. It took me a long time to figure out why I felt different. Why girls really didn't interest me. Why I preferred reading over alcohol. And why, even though I'm a kick-ass soccer player, I'd rather teach English and be poor than travel the world playing for Milan."

Ellis heard Cole chuckling at his embellishment, but he let it go. He knew he'd never make a professional team, but for the sake of explanation, he wasn't about to alter his words.

"So, you think I'm a good mother?"

"Yes. The best. Who's been filling your head with these notions of inadequacy? It's not Dad, is it?"

"No. It was something on a talk show about 'the middle child' and opening lines of communication."

"Can you do me a favor? Don't watch any more of those shows. They don't know shit. I'm just fine, and our communication level is just where I like it. But I do promise to fill in more details just so you don't go through this phase again."

"Okay," she said. She sniffled and wiped her nose again. "So, you asked Cole to marry you?"

Ellis felt warm pride. He looked at Cole affectionately and touched his knee. Cole squeezed his hand and smiled at him. "Yes," Ellis answered, smiling back at Cole. "I did." He felt so sentimental about it he had to kiss him.

Meredith stood up and walked toward the kitchen, and Ellis jumped up and followed her. She started washing out her cup as he reached her side.

"Mom? Are you alright?" Ellis asked tentatively. "Are you really okay with me... being... you know, gay?"

"Why wouldn't I be?" She set the wet cup in the dish drain next to the sink.

"I don't know. You're sort of quiet. And you did walk in on us when we were—"

Her hand came up to silence him. "Can we, maybe, *not* mention that part? I know that my children are all grown up. Ben is a father, Sara's been living with Lori, and now you... I know you're adults. But I don't want to think about you having sex any more than you want to picture me and your father."

Ellis recoiled. "Eww, no!"

"Specifically my point," she admitted. "I want to forget that part. If you want to kiss Cole while I'm in the room, I think I'll be fine with it once the image of you two naked and in bed together fades from my memory. I've never seen anything like that, and frankly, it's a tad unsettling."

Cole murmured from behind them, "A *tad* in space terms is half a million miles."

Meredith looked at him. "That's a quote from *Airplane*. Surely, you're too young to know that movie."

"*Airplane II*, actually. I watch a lot of movies and I memorize dialogue easily. It's a gift." Cole shrugged casually. "And please, don't call me Shirley."

Ellis's mom laughed and held out her hand to Cole. He walked over to her. Ellis watched as she took one of his hands in her left and touched the side of his face with her right. She smiled at him. "So you're the one he loves."

"Yes. I guess so. Although the reason why evades me."

"Cole!" Ellis warned. He knew Cole was cynical about lots of things and self-deprecating at best, but he didn't need to give his mom that as a first impression.

"Let me tell you something, Cole. If my son says he loves you, then you never need to doubt that. He's always been kindhearted, but he's very selective in the friendships he makes."

"I am?" Ellis asked, but she kept talking.

"I think he has a sixth sense of knowing who he can trust in his life."

"That didn't work with Mike," he mumbled.

She looked at him. "Mike Foster? What happened with him?"

"Oh, nothing," Ellis said, trying to avoid the subject for now.

Cole did not pick up on that and said, "Nothing except smashing my car to bits after seeing us kissing on campus. I think Ellis's sexuality was offensive and he took his anger out on me."

She gasped, "Oh dear! Really? How awful. Are you all right? What happened to Mike?"

Ellis shrugged. "He was arrested. Turns out he's some sort of Hitleresque psychopath. When the cops went to his house, they found two pounds of marijuana and crystal meth. His mother is now in rehab, his dad was arrested for possession with the intent to sell, and his sister was taken in by the Davenports. That's something, at least."

"Oh, sweetie," she sighed, reaching up to stroke Cole's cheek again. "I'm so sorry this happened."

Cole tilted his expression Ellis's way and scowled. "You are just like your mom, aren't you?"

Ellis grinned. "I think so… *sweetie*."

Cole groaned and Ellis laughed out loud.

ALL in all it was a good visit. Ellis was glad his sexuality was out in the open, even if he'd have preferred a gentler method. His mom took a shine to Cole, which made him happy, and she even invited him over at Christmas. And he even managed to get some studying in over the weekend before finals. Life was looking pretty sweet, and Ellis could not have been happier.

Chapter 17
Home For The Holidays

HALLELUJAH—finals are over! I normally didn't mind them. I liked studying because I found that challenging myself to get a better grade than the last one was incentive enough to push aside everything else in my life until all my tests were done. This time, good Lord, I couldn't keep my mind on my studies at all.

Ellis's presence was overwhelming and almost unbelievable. *He seriously loves me.* I, Cole Reid, had a boyfriend who loved me. I constantly wanted to pinch myself to make sure I wasn't dreaming. I think I cried a few times in his arms for no reason at all, and instead of making fun of me, Ellis held me and kissed me and whispered, "I love you," over and over which made me cry more. It was ridiculous, but I couldn't seem to stop.

Every time he looked at me, I felt warm and cold and silly and scared, and all the laws of physics and thermodynamics that Newton and Einstein came up with couldn't explain to me why the universe slowed down and time stood still, and why my heart skipped a beat. None of it made sense. Ellis loved me.

And the fucking tears wouldn't shut off!

I couldn't think of anything else while I packed Saturday afternoon. Ellis and I were going home in the morning, and we were avoiding a "talk" about when we'd see each other again. Christmas was next weekend. It's typically my favorite holiday, but this year I'd have to spend it away from the only person I wanted to be with. I know his mom invited me over, but logistically we were still working through the relationship details. He wasn't out yet to most of his family. (Apparently he had a large one. Cousins and aunts, etcetera.) I know the kind of rejection that can occur; I didn't want Ellis to go through that. I told him I'd be patient and we'd see each other whenever it seemed reasonable. I wasn't going to push.

So after cleaning the apartment together this morning, we each decided to pack, separately, in our individual rooms. I shoved my socks into my luggage and felt tears welling again. "Damn, fucking tears!" I dashed them away hastily, ashamed of my emotional display, although no one witnessed it but me. I could not believe what I'd become. It was his fault! Ellis did this to me!

The next thing I heard was a knock at the door.

"Shit!" I rubbed my face with both hands and walked out of my room. I met Ellis on the way out of his and ignored the impulse to dive into his arms. If I missed his embrace this much, and we'd only been out of each other's sight for thirty minutes, then what the hell was I going to do when I went home and Ellis wasn't there?

I suppressed my feelings for now. I had to. I pointed toward the door. "Russ?" I questioned casually, giving a logical explanation to the knock-knock-knocking at our door.

"No. Rob," he replied blandly. His eyes looked tired and maybe pink. Had he been crying? Or was it my hopeful imagination?

"Rob has a key," I pointed out.

Ellis shook his head and disagreed. "Rob walked in on us after the food fight."

"Ah!" I nodded. "I guess if we are going to give out keys, we shouldn't have sex anywhere but in the bedroom with the door closed."

Ellis grinned. "Or we take back the keys." His tired expression brightened a smidgen.

My mischievous mind shot an eyebrow up as I questioned him with my eyes.

Ellis gestured toward the couch with a tilt of his chin. "I've been thinking about fucking you over the back of that sofa."

Butterflies erupted inside of me. I know I had a rule about sex on the couch, and even though we already broke it, I could see that I was somehow willing to break any rule he wanted with a mere mention of sex. Hell, I'd probably blow him in the middle of the dean's office if he asked. I was so over-the-top gone for Ellis it scared me. "After whoever's at the door leaves," I responded with a wink.

It was easier to avoid sappy emotions by fixating on the carnal ones. I didn't want to go home without Ellis, or for him to go home without me, but that was tomorrow. I didn't have to think about tomorrow *until* tomorrow. Right now, there was a person at the door who needed to go away so Ellis could have me however he wanted, wherever he wanted, however long he wanted. "Tomorrow" was not on the to-do list today.

Ellis closed the gap between us hesitantly. "Maybe if we ignore the door, he'll leave?" He was faking *playful*. I could see the slight mirth in his eyes wane. Seriousness hung in the air around us. He planted firm hands on my shoulders and gripped them tightly. I could feel his tension traveling through his fingertips, and I could see the desperation in his eyes. It was more than lust. It was more than desire. Maybe he was feeling the weight of the morning too?

"Ellis?" I tried to ask the question. I pleaded with my eyes. Didn't he know I didn't want to be away from him for a few minutes, let alone a few weeks?

He brought his mouth down hard on mine. He slammed into me. I felt his hands all over me—in my hair, grabbing my ass, up the back of my shirt. I clung to him as he kissed me wildly on my lips, down my neck, across my temple and eyes, and then back again. As soon as he lifted my shirt over my head, there was pounding at the door.

Ellis was maddened. "Fuck!"

"I guess our guest is in a hurry?" I deemed, gasping for air. (That was one heck of a kiss Mr. Knocksalot interrupted.)

Ellis snapped. "I wish people would just leave us alone!" I guess he noticed my shock at his indignation because his expression softened right away. "I'm sorry." He caressed my arm and kissed my temple after I slipped my shirt back on. "I just don't want to deal with anything right now." He smiled a weak smile—faking it again. I'd seen that fakeness in his eyes enough to recognize it. *He* is *thinking about tomorrow.*

I followed him to the door and he opened it. The offending "guest" was Geoff.

"Am I late?" he asked, holding up a six-pack of beer.

"Late for what?" Ellis asked, looking at me.

"The party. Rob said there'd be a party here at four. Seeing how it's five o'clock, and quiet, I thought I missed the whole thing!"

"I don't know what you're talking about," Ellis replied, baffled. "We aren't throwing a party."

"Yes, you are." I heard Rob's voice drift up the steps behind Geoff. He pushed past Geoff, Russell scurrying behind him, carrying beer and other assorted bagged goods.

It was no surprise to me that Rob would show up unannounced and that he'd bring Russell and even some beer. The surprise came when he started moving the furniture! "What's going on?" I asked impatiently.

"It's Christmas, there has to be a party!" he responded.

That was not an acceptable answer. Ellis didn't think so either, as he sternly questioned Russell. "What are you doing? Why are you moving the coffee table? You know Cole likes it exactly where it is."

Russell responded, "Chill, bro. We've got it all under control."

Ellis was about to say something else, except more people poured through the open door, interrupting his train of thought. (I surmised this from his gaping mouth and gesticulating hands.)

Kevin from the soccer team walked in carrying folding chairs. Marcus Something, also from his team, stumbled in with an armload of bags. And several others followed them, toting party hats, beer, and oodles of chips and pretzels.

Ellis stormed over to Rob and grabbed his arm, demanding, "Rob! What is—" Loud music blared from a stereo system that had materialized with all the rest of the party essentials, cutting him off. "Why are all these people here?" he screamed, trying to be heard over the music.

I heard him, but that was only because I was clinging to his arm. I didn't do crowds. (Did I mention that?) I liked quiet and peace, and small gatherings of friends who played canasta. I loathed parties where a mass of intoxicated underachievers gathered to challenge one another onto greater feats of brain-cell-frying action. Pointless, if you asked me!

The mix-master turned down the volume by two hundred decibels and called over, "Better?" Rob gave him a thumbs-up, and he went back to selecting which discordant noise fit the venue best. I'd seen movies that depicted the same type of dude. He was standing there with headphones on, moving to the beat, nodding in time with the beat-box percussion sound… *why* exactly? What was wrong with an iPod set on shuffle? And what were the headphones for? Ear protection? That was my guess, because I would certainly go deaf if this racket kept up much longer.

Geoff stepped in front of Ellis as he attempted to move in the direction of the music coordinator. "So I'm not late?" he yelled—the music still too loud to hold a conversation.

Ellis, again, had no chance to reply because Rob clapped him on the back and answered Geoff for him. "Nope, not late!"

Geoff seemed overly jazzed about that.

Rob continued. "You're right on time, man! I got the skinny on your reputation for procrastination. I knew you'd be late. I told you four so you'd show by five to help set up for the party at five thirty."

I looked at my watch. "Five fifteen!" No, my hysterical screech did *not* give them pause. The conversation carried on as if my shortness of breath didn't matter. I started hyperventilating, and Ellis was the only one who noticed. Even with his soothing hands on me, I could not move past the growing number of people in my apartment and the increasing probability of something getting broken. The likelihood that my once-clean living space would be trashed in less than fifteen minutes was 100 percent. When the ruckus began, how many of my personal effects would fall as collateral damage?

I started shaking and fled to the safety of my room.

"Why? Why would Rob do this?" I asked out loud. Somehow, hearing myself ask it, made the question ten times worse. *Why indeed?* He was *just* in my apartment after Mike attacked me, explaining how he was my friend. Obviously he didn't know what the word meant! Friends didn't throw parties in their friends' apartments without asking!

My door opened and Ellis entered. He closed the door and walked over to me.

"What do you want?" I demanded.

"Do you have room in here for a hedonistic Viking?"

I was not amused. "That isn't funny. None of this is funny! I can't believe your stupid friends would do this to me!" I turned away from him and moved around to the other side of the bed.

"Hey, I don't know what's happening, but I'm sure Rob has a logical explanation."

"I don't care about logic!" The noise vibrating my walls was digging under my skin. It had to stop or I was going to have a nervous breakdown. "I can't do this with all these people here!" I yelled it, but as soon as the words left my mouth, I began crying. *Fucking tears!* I covered my face.

Ellis immediately rushed to my side, soothing me with whispers and shushes and kisses on my cheeks and eyelids. He petted my face and ears and neck. The room began spinning, and all I could visualize was that scene from *Latter Days* after Aaron got back from the hospital and Chris was comforting him. Ellis wrapped me in his arms and held me tight.

"Everything will be okay, Cole. I promise."

I pushed against his embrace. "How? How can things be okay? You *told* me they were my friends. You *told* me I could trust them and just be myself. You *told* me you loved me."

"And I do," he stressed. "I do love you. Whatever's going on, I'll figure it out and I'll fix it. Okay? But you have to give me a chance. I'm not omniscient, and I can't read minds. I have to wait until I can get Rob alone and get him to give me a straight answer. Okay?"

I had no other options—I had to nod.

Ellis hugged me until my nervous shaking subsided. Then he took my hand and led me back out into the commotion.

I was stunned how many bodies could occupy the same space. My apartment looked like a rave dance floor where the people had no room to move and danced by hopping, meshed up against one another. And, evidently, the dollar store had dropped by and vomited Christmas decorations on every square inch of wall, ceiling, and floor, as if to outdo Ellis's slathering of salad dressing in the kitchen. In other words, my apartment had become my version of hell.

An odd calm settled over me then. Knowing I was dead—and in hell—gave me closure. I would endure it, but I wasn't going to watch. I turned in to Ellis and buried my face in his neck.

"Isn't this great?" I heard Rob yell enthusiastically. "What a terrific turnout! There are people on every floor, and the party extends outside onto the lawn. It's awesome!"

Ellis held me tight. I think he knew I'd be upset hearing what Rob found so thrilling. "Can we talk?" he screamed over the noise.

"Yeah, let me get Russ to join us in Cole's room. Okay?" Rob hollered back.

"Okay. We'll meet you in there in a few minutes."

"Okay." Ellis nodded and took me back to the safety of my room.

I guess I should be thankful the partygoers had respected my bedroom. So far, I didn't have strangers having sex on my bed.

"Sit down," Ellis instructed. "Try to stay calm. Rob will be here any minute to explain."

I numbly sat. "Why does it matter?" I asked. "I'm dead, right? If I'm in hell, then I'm doomed to relive this nightmare over and over."

Ellis was taken aback. "What? Cole, you're not dead."

"I have to be. You wanted logic. Death is the only logical explanation."

Ellis shook his head and sat next to me. He touched my face. "If this was hell, would I be here with you?"

"Logically?" I considered what he was suggesting. "I suppose not." Ellis stripped away my secure delusion and left me with ambiguous ignorance. I started crying again.

"Shh, L-D. I gotcha." Rewind and replay—Ellis was holding me again.

I questioned his absurd nickname. "You keep calling me that! What does it mean?"

He smirked. "Little dictator. Or little darlin', but I kind of think it depends on your mood."

"Shut up!" I smacked his chest.

"No, seriously. You're both. And shortening it to L-D keeps you guessing." Ellis smiled, pleased with his teasing at my expense. He easily trapped my swatting hands in his strong grip and forced me to stop moving. I was angry but could not remain so long. He was so devilishly superior that I could not stand my ground. I had to give in, submit, and trust his every word. He carried my soul in his.

I closed my eyes and he kissed me.

Rob and Russell joined us in the room as promised. Although why they had to do so in a timely manner eludes me. The *one time* I wanted Ellis to convince me how wrong I was, and Rob and Russell showed up. My lack of luck kept on coming!

"Hey," Rob said.

"Hey," Ellis said back.

Rob sat on the bed next to Ellis and Russell remained standing, hiding something behind his back.

"Will you please explain what's going on? You know Cole's head is about to implode."

"Eww, that would be so messy," Rob commented. "Reminds me of this episode of *Red Dwarf* where Lister gets a case of space mumps and his head *explodes*, splattering globs of yellow puss all over Rimmer. Classic, man. Truly classic."

"Rob," Ellis insisted.

"Oh, sorry, squirrel moment. Anyway, back to Cole's party."

"It's not my party!"

"Annywaay…." Rob kept a pleasant tone even though I yelled at him. I would never be that patient. Rob continued, "I was thinking about Cole's recent incident of misfortune and came up with a plan. Being the season of giving and all, and wanting to spread the Christmas cheer before we all head home for the holidays, I decided to throw a party… for Cole."

"I hate parties."

Rob's glee obviously did not catch on to the hint of disdain in my glare. He went on to chirp, "Actually, we're throwing a kegger in honor of Mike's incarceration. The cover charge at the door is ten dollars a head to hang out, and twenty-plus to drink. All proceeds benefit the purchase of a new car for Cole." He corrected quickly, "A new used car—college students aren't rich."

Did I hear him correctly?

"Ta-da!" Russell beamed, bringing a giant plastic cheese ball jar from behind his back. Only, it was cheese-ball free. It was filled to the brim with dollar bills. I could see fives and ones and twenties crammed against the sides. "All for you, Cole!"

Rob corrected him before I fainted. "Well, minus a small amount to cover the beer and the cleaning lady I hired to straighten the place up after, but the rest is yours."

My vision suddenly blurred and their faces became elongated. I heard the pounding of the bass rhythm vibrating the walls and my ribcage, but even that got quieter and quieter. Maybe *now* I was dying? I closed my eyes to will away my confusion.

WHEN I opened them again, I had something cold on my head. "What just happened?" I asked, looking into Ellis's concerned expression.

"You fainted," he said as I sat up.

"I had a dream," I said woozily. I looked to Rob and Russell and then to Ellis. "And you, and you, and you were there. Only… I wasn't in Kansas, and Murphy's Law had opposite results."

"Okay, Dorothy, we believe you." Rob said, patting me on my chest. "When you're ready though, I think you should at least *try* to join the party and thank people for coming. It's the polite thing to do." Rob got off the bed and headed to the door. "Besides, after the first twenty guests, I think we violated the fire code. So you should probably make an appearance before campus security instructs everyone to vacate the premises."

Russell grinned as he always did at his friend's inventive way of describing the state of affairs and followed Rob out the door, leaving me alone with Ellis.

"I'm not dreaming?" I asked.

He shook his head. "Nope."

"My friends threw a party for me?" I asked, feeling those dreaded emotions rising again. "To raise money for a car?"

"Yup." Leave it to Ellis to keep his answers short but convey enough sentiment through his tone that my tears rolled like rivers. "When you're ready, I think we should go out and thank them."

My words were stuck in my throat.

I FINALLY managed to go out and mingle, although I can say with great conviction it was my first and last kegger! Way too many people. And noise. And mess! I think when it got down to the last eighteen or so—around two in the morning—I might have started enjoying myself. Maybe it was the quieter volume of the music? Hmm.

Most of the people who remained were from Ellis's soccer team, but I also noticed Stan in the corner, sipping a soda. The weird way he watched everyone creeped me out, but no one else seemed to care. (Either they didn't care, or like he said—he was invisible to them.) Ellis's sister and her girlfriend also showed up. I was glad they'd hung around long enough to chat.

Ellis introduced me. "Cole, this is my sister and her girlfriend Lori."

I tried to shake Sara's hand, but she hugged me instead. "Oh! Wow." I expressed my surprise and she giggled as she clung to me. "I suppose I need to get used to this?"

"Yes, you do," she said with a bright smile that made her eyes glow. They didn't really look like each other, but I could see that same gleam in Sara's eyes that often filled Ellis's. Joy. Pure manifested joy. I could tell I was going to love this family.

The brown-haired girl named Lori smiled at me like she knew me. It was odd. "It's nice to finally meet you."

I looked at Ellis as I shook her hand. "Am I missing something?"

"Lori and I go way back. We talked a little when I was confused about some things. She told me I needed to talk to you."

Somehow that sounded purposely vague. "Oh, okay."

Lori qualified his ambiguity by adding, "I've had experience with relationship issues. My best friend went through loads of counseling, so I used my secondhand knowledge to help Ellis. Basically I told him how important communication is in a relationship. I'm glad he took my advice."

"Then I'm glad you said something. Thanks. Ellis isn't normally bountiful in the sharing department."

Ellis slipped his arm around me. "I'm working on it."

Then he leaned in and kissed me on the lips. His newfound confidence in our established homosexual relationship in front of friends and family pleased me. From what I'd seen, gays coming to terms with their sexuality in relation to the world around them could be tumultuous. (I was.) Comfort and security in our own skin could be a long battle, often with bouts of regret, anxiety, and apprehension. For Ellis to so boldly embrace me and display affection made me believe again that I was dreaming. I'd wanted affection like this for so long; and given the fact that my life never went right, I found this revelation in our relationship hard to believe. Not wishing the sappiness between us to vanish if I blinked, I looped both arms around his waist and leaned my head against his jaw. Ellis squeezed me again and rubbed my arm.

Kevin, Ollie, and Marcus joined our little huddle. Ollie mock punched Ellis in the arm before saying, "Great party, man." He looked at me all snug against Ellis's side. "Sorry about the car, dude. Mike is such a douche. I sold some of the textbooks I didn't need and slipped a hundred in the jar."

"What?" I was shocked. Again, these things *don't* happen to me! And for that kind of generosity to come from a jock—the very same type of person that, in tenth grade, crippled my emotional self-worth at its most vulnerable stage of development—was astonishing.

"You didn't have to do that," Ellis said.

"I know, but he's your guy!" Ollie offered casually.

I felt my emotions trembling again. I *wasn't* going to cry, not in front of everyone. I just wasn't. But Ollie—and the rest of Ellis's friends—made me reconsider how I'd lumped all "jocks" into one group. I guess I saw them as others saw "gays," as a stereotypicalized people group. I'd always wanted to be treated as myself, for the person I am and not how people view I should be or act. Being a recipient of unexpected kindness made me see how I'd been judging Ollie for being a jock, just like others out there judged me—or Ellis—for being gay. I guess the whole world needed to open its eyes to the prejudices in its own backyard.

I think Ellis felt me tremble, because he flexed his fingers and tenderly caressed my ribs as he held me while talking to his soccer friends. "And you're okay with that?" he asked.

Kevin shrugged and answered, "Sure. Why not? We're a team and you're our striker. That makes us family. Right?"

"And you're not surprised to find out I'm gay?" Ellis asked the question, but he wasn't being defensive about it. I got the impression he was simply feeling out their opinion.

"No. We all knew Cole was gay. Marcus saw him at a campus alliance rally when gay-rights supporters were addressing the opposition on equality under the First Amendment."

"You heard that?" I was little surprised and embarrassed because that was the first and only time I spoke out. I hate confrontation, and I was so nervous at that rally.

"Yeah, you were great!" Marcus said as he clapped me on the shoulder in a friendly manner. (And not too hard either, which I appreciated.) "Plus, I thought your T-shirt was funny."

I couldn't remember which one I'd worn, but in my opinion they were all epic!

A few other guys that I remembered from the soccer field walked over to our living room huddle. Kevin continued his explanation as if he spoke for the whole team's feelings on the matter. "You've never had a girlfriend, Ellis. And at the pool party last year, you looked as if you'd barf on that girl if she kissed you. And she was hot! So when you and Cole started hanging out and you said you'd rather stay home and study than kick the ball around, we just figured you two were getting it on."

A guy I didn't know slurred, "No offense if you aren't actually screwing." I seriously hoped he was drunk because that was inappropriate and I know I blushed.

Ellis didn't comment. In fact, I felt him relax, and then he lovingly touched my face with his free hand. I think he was trying to tell me without words to ignore the drunken guy. "I guess I wasn't fooling anyone?"

"Except maybe yourself," said Lori. I realize I hardly knew her, but I appreciated the sympathy in her tone. I liked her. And I also like the way she protectively stood behind Ellis's sister Sara, holding her around the waist; it certainly made me feel less self-conscious about my hold on Ellis.

"I think you had me wondering for a while," I pointed out.

Ellis looked at me. "Unintentionally." He kissed my forehead before looking back at his friends. "I guess I can't thank you all enough for coming and for being so supportive; I'm blown away."

"It's like Cole said at the rally," Marcus explained. "Equal rights should extend to everyone. Homosexuals cannot be excluded because their relationship is unavoidably conspicuous. Same-sex couples are entitled to the same discreet displays of intimacy that heterosexuals entertain. Handholding and kissing are not viewed as vulgar among the masses and should not solely determine acceptance or rejection. People need to be viewed as human, sentient, and feeling creatures in their pursuit to love. Until we acknowledge that, no gay-straight alliance will succeed. Because it's not about being gay *or* straight, it's about being human."

Ellis gawked at me. "You said that?"

Embarrassed, I could barely answer him. "I guess."

"Wow!" Rob commented. "That's...."

"Profound," Lori said, completing his thought for him. Yeah, Lori was cool.

The group looked at each other, and there was a sense of finality to it. Marcus had summed up what Kevin already touched on, and there really wasn't more to say. Plus it was two in the morning! I was glad they didn't make a huge deal about my speech. It was the only time I ever said what I felt about gay rights in front of a crowd. It had made me nauseous to take a stand, and I threw up when I got back home. I could see why public speaking was so high on the list of fears people had; I didn't wish to repeat the experience.

It didn't take long before good-byes were said and we turned out the lights. All in all, the party went well, and the attendees contributed $2,300 to the "Cash for Cole" fund. I was chuffed.

Chapter 18
A Perfect Ending

"WE WERE at breakfast for, like, an hour, how'd they get everything so neat and tidy?" I asked as I ran my razor over my lathered left cheek. I wished to be well groomed for my parents when they picked me up later.

Ellis grabbed a towel after turning the water off. He stood in the tub, drying his hair, as I shaved. "Rob said he hired a cleaning company. Somebody his mom knows," he said. I wiped the steam from the mirror for the fifth time so I could watch his movements. His genitals bounced as he rubbed his legs dry. Even soft, his penis was larger than mine. I sighed. My inadequacies never stopped pointing themselves out.

Ellis, though—he was perfect.

I wanted to walk over and take the towel from his grasp. I could imagine running my fingers over his hairy chest and sucking on his nipples. Being near him was turning me into a sex fiend; we'd already made love twice this morning, what more did I want? "To make love to him again tomorrow," I mumbled my answer as I rinsed my razor under the faucet.

"What?" Ellis asked.

"Oh, nothing." We still hadn't talked about Christmas break. He was leaving in another two hours, and so was I, but we were not planning on driving in the same direction.

Ellis stepped out of the tub and hung up his towel. I grinned. It excited me to see him walking around naked, even if we *were* in the bathroom. He came up behind me and placed his palms on my shoulders, leaning close to kiss my neck. His mouth was so deliciously distracting I nicked my chin.

"Ouch." I winced.

"Careful, little darlin'. I don't want to have to take you to the emergency room for a shaving accident." He rubbed the back of my neck and watched me in the mirror.

"Ha ha." I stuck my tongue out and he smiled. "And I thought you settled on L-D?"

"You like it?" Ellis continued massaging my shoulders. It felt so nice.

"No. But it's kind of nice being mysterious and something just between us."

"Okay. L-D." Ellis smiled, but it wasn't so much mirth as desire. His eyes were very intently watching me as I finished shaving. I wiped off my face, and he turned me around. He went down to his knees and stripped me of the towel I had wrapped around my waist.

I gasped.

It surprised me how fast he had my dick in his mouth. I had to grip the sink behind me because my knees were buckling. I watched, stunned and enraptured. His hand followed his stroking mouth and I could barely breathe. Ellis hadn't done this since that first night. Maybe it was my cutting remark or maybe his lack of confidence had stopped him from trying again until now. Whatever the reason, I didn't care. I was glad he'd found the courage to try. Blowjobs are the number one most incredible feeling on the planet—hands down!

Ellis was way better this time. He had me hard in seconds and the pressure built exponentially with every stroke. Ellis sucked with the exuberant aggression I longed for in my fantasies. *He really is perfect!* "Oh!" I moaned, tilting my head back. I could feel the mirror behind my head, but I could not rest it there long. I wanted to watch!

"I'm gonna... Ellis... I'm gonna come," I said, breathing heavily as I laced my fingers through his hair and tugged as my muscles exploded with electricity. Every part of me was quaking with my release and pulsing with the jets of my come.

Ellis choked and pulled back. "Sorry," he said.

I closed my eyes and took a hold of myself, stroking a few more times as I finished. I felt Ellis lick the tip of my penis, and I looked at him, still on his knees. I think my insides quaked even more from the look in his eyes—staring up at me with come on his lips—than when he was sucking me off. *He's beautiful.*

Ellis picked up my towel and wiped off his face and hands and my groin. He planted a kiss on my cheek and then left the bathroom. "I'm gonna get dressed. Okay?"

It wasn't okay, but I knew we had to get going. "Yeah." I took a deep breath and went to my room. This was depressing. I hated packing. I didn't want to go home. I didn't want Christmas to come. I wanted this semester to drag out several months longer so we could remain in the blissful living conditions we now enjoyed. Together.

I tucked my toothbrush into my shoulder bag and spied the T-shirt Ellis had been wearing the morning he ran suicides. I paused. I thought he had it. Why would he give it back? Was he telling me something? I thought he liked this one.

I took it out and walked to his room.

"Ellis?"

"Huh?" He turned to face me. He had just snapped his suitcase shut.

"Why did you give this back?" I held out my shirt. "I thought you liked this one? Don't you want something to think of me by while we're apart? Don't you want to have something of mine?" Because the thought that he didn't frightened me.

He tilted his head to the side and softly smiled. "Cole, are you upset that I didn't steal your shirt or that you think I'll forget about you?"

Why did he look like he'd read my mind? "Um, I don't know." And why did I suddenly sound pathetically whiny? "Both."

"Come here." He beckoned, and I sank into his open arms. "First of all, I gave that shirt back because I stole a different one.

The shirt that says 'Even My Protons Have Pride' is a little looser and doesn't pinch my armpits."

"Oh." That made me feel better. I didn't mind if he stole a shirt and I knew the "Speed of Dark" one was really tight on him.

"And second, I'm not going to forget you. In fact, I'm not leaving you."

I pulled back in surprise. "You're not?"

Ellis shook his head. "Nope. I talked to my mom this morning. She's fine with us visiting your folks first and then coming back to my house whenever we can. I think she's more confident in our relationship since our talk. She likes you, and I think she's happy that she can get to know you over the break."

"So, you're not hitching a ride with Rob?" I couldn't believe it.

"No. But he hasn't texted me back, so I'm not sure he got my message."

We both heard the apartment door close.

"Hey, El? You here?" Rob's voice made us look at one another and laugh.

"In here," Ellis called.

We let go of each other as Rob walked in. "I'm not interrupting anything, am I?"

"Nope," Ellis said as he lifted his suitcase and carried it to the door.

Rob and I walked out of the bedroom too, and I turned the light off and closed the door behind me.

"I got your text, but I wanted to come by and say Merry Christmas." Rob handed Ellis a round, wrapped object.

"Gee, I wonder what that is?"

Rob pointed his finger at me. "Hey, no comments from the peanut gallery. You know how hard it is to disguise the shape?"

"Did you try a box?"

Ellis smiled and ignored me. He ripped the paper off his present and immediately bounced the new soccer ball on his knee. "Thanks, Rob. It's just the right size!"

"Yeah, I know it's lame, but I gave all my money to Cole's car fund."

"Hey, don't try to make me feel guilty for being needy."

"I'm not. I want you to have it. Plus, I got you this." Rob handed me a gift bag.

I think Rob is one of the most loyal people I've met. He's genuine and caring and doesn't pretend to be anything other than he is. I like his honesty, and I was touched by his generosity. "Thanks. But I didn't get you anything."

"That's okay. I'm happy that you finally admitted we're friends."

I picked through the tissue paper and pulled out a blue T-shirt. I read the front out loud: "'I'm not lazy; I'm overflowing with potential energy.' Hah! Thanks, Rob. That's great. I like it." Then I looked at Ellis and said, "It reminds me of *you*."

"I'm not lazy," he refuted.

"Rob, do they make a T-shirt that reads 'I'm not messy; I'm demonstrating chaos theory'?"

Rob laughed. "I wish!"

"Thanks, Cole." Ellis grinned. "Way to support me." I could tell he wasn't mad. He turned to Rob and said, "This is really nice of you." Ellis patted his back. "You're such a great friend."

"Yeah, well, don't get too emotional about it. I'm still trying to understand the whole gay thing. I don't want to cause too much sentiment and have you both hugging all over me."

Ellis and I looked at each other. I think we both knew that was exactly what Rob was not so discreetly hinting at. "Does someone need a hug?" Ellis asked facetiously.

"No," Rob answered simply.

"I think someone does," I said, following along with Ellis's unspoken intent. Simultaneously, we lunged at Rob from both sides, wrapping him in a group hug. But unlike when he and Russell did it to me, Rob wasn't trying to get away. He loved it.

"Hey, what'd I miss?" Russell asked as he entered unexpectedly.

"Group hug," Ellis explained.

Russell joined in and we stood like that—clinging—for a full five minutes. I think going home for the holiday break, and away from each other, was something all of us weren't ready to do. But we did.

My FOLKS were better than I thought. My dad was quiet, but he did give Ellis a "garden tour." That made me happy. We spent five days with my family and then headed to Ellis's house with the intent of being there until after New Year's Day. (We promised to visit my family a half day on Christmas Day just to be fair.)

I loved Ellis's family right away. They were so very different from mine. Very touchy, very affectionate, and everything I'd ever wanted growing up.

I was a realist by nature. I'd grown up thinking that everything I witnessed made sense. The universe by design made sense. And my lot in life somehow made sense. I was doomed to live with a black cloud over my head and exist in a world were nothing good went my way. But what I'd learned this semester in college was that the realistic nature of life was predictably unpredictable. You'd never know what lay ahead; even if you'd scientifically calculated the probability of coming events by analyzing any given data from your past. History didn't always predict the future. You had to live it one day at a time to find out what happened next.

Right now, my every moment was Ellis.

Christmas night, when the stars were bright, and everyone else was in bed sleeping, we snuck out of the house and sat on the bench swing his dad had built in the garden next to the house. We snuggled there, swinging quietly, for a long time in silence. It was cold, so Ellis wrapped us both up in a blanket. I had my head on his shoulder and a placid smile permanently glued to my face. I guess it shouldn't have surprised me when he took out a little box and handed it to me, but it did. I immediately grabbed the box and clutched it to my chest.

"Merry Christmas," Ellis said, as he watched me open it.

I pushed the ribbon off and ripped the paper. Inside a fuzzy velvet box was a platinum band etched with two parallel lines and inlaid with three small diamonds between them.

"Oh, Ellis!" I cried.

"I didn't forget I owed you a ring. Are you still sure you want to marry me? I wouldn't blame you for changing your mind. It *was* kind of early to ask you something so serious. I do things without thinking sometimes. I know people might ridicule us for—"

I thrust my hand out and covered his mouth. "Oh no! You did not just dis the romance!" I exclaimed. "You're the guy I've been dreaming of all my life. Too early? Fuck early! I *want* to marry you." I wrapped my arms around his neck and smothered his face in kisses. *Yes,* apparently I am very sappy and sentimental—a fact I was happy to discover. "You're mine, Ellis Montgomery." *Kiss, kiss, kiss.* "All mine. I don't care what other people think; I'm not waiting for the sake of popular opinion."

Ellis rode out my efficacious refutation and lovingly stroked my face. (I know I've mentioned how wonderful his hands feel on my face a hundred times, so what's once more?) I loved his hands on my face! Ellis said softly, "Okay. You win. I guess I got all caught up in the fact that my dad asked my mom after only eight months. I didn't even want to wait that long. I love you."

I know my expression glowed bright enough to outdo the moon. Ellis really knew how to woo a guy. "I love you too. Can I put it on?" I asked.

"Of course." Ellis took the ring out of the box and slipped it on my finger.

I frowned.

"What? Don't you like it?" he asked, thoroughly bewildered as to *why* I was not pleased as punch with the ring of his choosing.

I lifted my elbow up, and my hand down. The ring promptly slid off into his lap.

He caught it before it got lost in the folds of the blanket. "Oh no! I'm sorry. I guessed your size based on mine. I didn't know."

I scowled. "It figures. The happiest day of my life and the ring is so huge it will never stay on!"

"We can get it sized. Tomorrow! I promise. Give it here."

I crossed my arms and sulked. It was even more disappointing to *have* a ring that didn't fit than to not receive one at all.

He put it back in the box and pocketed it. "We'll take care of it tomorrow."

"But tomorrow we're meeting Jonathan and Cathy for lunch."

"Then we'll go after."

"What if the store is closed?" I could always find one more negative to support Murphy's Law.

"It won't be."

"You know the universe hates me, right?" Because that was exactly how I saw it. Doomed. I was destined to fail.

Ellis, of course, being the glass-half-full kind of guy he was, countered my negativity by responding, "Then I guess it's a good thing that the *God* of the universe likes me."

I turned my frown upside down and gazed into the most beautiful blue eyes I've ever seen. "Yeah, I guess it's a good thing. But are you sure yo—"

Ellis put his finger to my lips. "Cole. Don't start." Ellis gave me a look of finality. I was not to challenge him with another question. I got it. "Now hush up and watch the stars with me." He took his silencing finger away and kissed me. Then he pulled me close and held me securely against his chest. "I love you, Cole. You never need to question that."

As we sat there Christmas night, listening to our hearts beating together in the stillness, I mused over giving optimism another chance. Yeah, maybe I could try it… if the world didn't end first.

WADE KELLY lives and writes in conservative, small-town America where it is not easy to live free and open in one's beliefs. Wade writes passionately about the controversial issues witnessed in real life and strives to make a difference by making people think. Wade does not have a background in writing or philosophy but still draws from personal experience to ponder contentious subjects on paper. When not writing, Wade is thinking about writing and more than likely scribbling notes on old napkins in the car.

Visit Wade Kelly at http://wadekelly.weebly.com/index.html. You can contact Wade at writerwadekelly@gmail.com.

Also from WADE KELLY

http://www.dreamspinnerpress.com

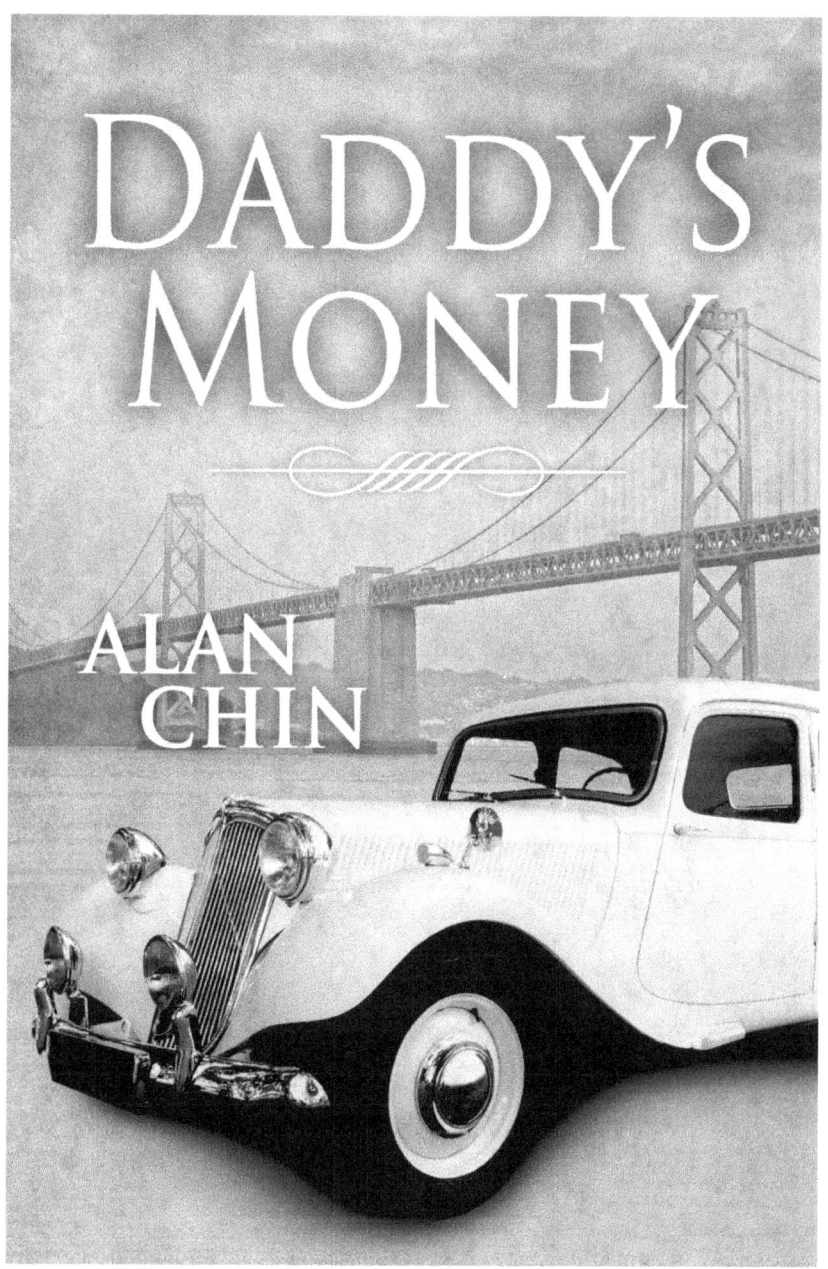

DADDY'S
MONEY

ALAN
CHIN

Also from DREAMSPINNER PRESS

http://www.dreamspinnerpress.com

Romance from DREAMSPINNER PRESS

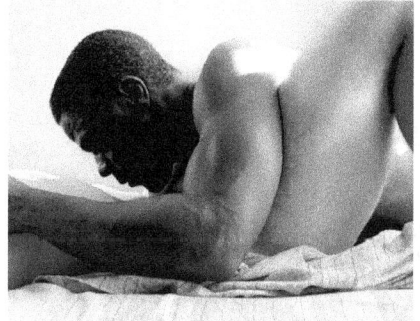

FROM THIS DAY
J.R. Patrick
Jambrea Jo Jones

Fall Into You
Posy Roberts

DAY OF THE DEAD
A Romance
ERIK ORRANTIA

THE NOTHINGNESS OF BEN
BRAD BONEY

www.ingramcontent.com/pod-product-compliance
Lightning Source LLC
Chambersburg PA
CBHW051630260626

47170CB00004B/1119